wildest DREAMS

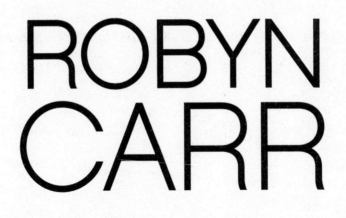

ROBYN CARR

wildest DREAMS

MIRA

MIRA

ISBN-13: 978-0-7783-1827-9

Wildest Dreams

For questions and comments about the quality of this book, please contact us at CustomerService@Harlequin.com.

www.MIRABooks.com

Printed in U.S.A.

First printing: September 2015
10 9 8 7 6 5 4 3 2 1

wildest
DREAMS

To Vivienne Leung, with gratitude and affection.

ONE

Not much that happened on the beach got by Charlie Simmons. He was fourteen and his mother was the nurse who tended Winnie Banks, a lady with ALS who lived on the hill overlooking the beach. Charlie came to work with his mother every day. He hung out around the house, the town, the beach. He was, more than anything, a practiced observer. More observer than participant, something he'd change if possible.

It was the third week of August, the house next to Winnie's was complete inside and out, and a moving truck had finally backed up to the garage. Charlie had seen the new owner back when he'd first looked at the house. He'd ridden across the beach road on a bicycle—a very expensive-looking road bike. He'd visited with Cooper on the deck that faced the bay. They went into the house together and didn't come back out, at least on the beach side. Cooper had later reported the guy with the bicycle was interested and made an offer.

When the moving truck pulled up and began to unload, Charlie went out front to have a look. All the houses along this ridge backed up to the Pacific, with the perfect view from their decks and living rooms, but their front doors and garages faced the road at the top of the hill. Charlie saw Cooper talking to the movers so he waited patiently until he was finished.

"Just be sure that gym equipment goes downstairs—it's heavy. He's making the game room on the lower level his workout room. Living quarters on this level. You should be able to identify the master bedroom, kitchen, living room, bath, on this floor for everything else. I'll be down at the bar when you're ready for me to sign off on delivery."

When Cooper was walking back to the bar that he owned, he passed right by Charlie. "Who's moving in, Cooper? The guy with the million-dollar bike?"

Cooper grinned. "The same. He's out of town right now."

"In a race?" Charlie asked.

"Big triathlon in Australia."

"Holy smokes," Charlie said. "He's an Ironman?"

Cooper laughed. "He is."

"What's his name?" Charlie asked.

"Blake Smiley. You going to look him up?"

"It's what I do, Cooper. You want me to fill you in?"

"I think I have enough information, but thanks."

"You ever want to compete in a triathlon, Cooper?"

"Absolutely never," he said, clearly amused. "Not that I don't admire the folks that can do that…"

"When's he going to be here?"

"I'm not sure. Any day now, I guess."

"I'm going to track the race. Do you know where in Australia?"

"No, I don't know where. Can there be a lot of them?" Cooper asked.

Charlie was on it. He got out his laptop and looked the guy

up. This was what Charlie had been doing for a long time—finding information and learning on his laptop because he didn't have a lot of friends and couldn't run and play like the other kids. Charlie had suffered from some serious allergies and asthma as a little kid and was therefore confined to a quieter life. He believed it was his frequent bouts of bronchitis and pneumonia when he was younger that resulted in him being a little undersized for his age. Either that or his Vietnamese roots through his mother's side of the family. But then one day someone passed on an old laptop, showed him how to use it and all those indoor days had resulted in a smarter than average fourteen-year-old.

Charlie's mother, Lin Su, was Amerasian. Since Charlie's biological father was white American he supposed that made him Amer-amerasian. He could see Vietnam in his black hair and dark eyes.

He looked up Blake Smiley. The man had been racing for fifteen years. He went to college on a scholarship and was thirty-seven years old. Smiley was a triathlon champion many times over having scored his first win in Oahu; he held a couple of records, had a degree in biology and physiology and was sponsored by a few corporations and even made a commercial for a fancy juice mixer. *A juice mixer?* Charlie wondered. Smiley was also a coach, consultant and sometime motivational speaker. Charlie was in love with TED Talks; he'd love to be smart enough or experienced enough to teach or inspire people with his accomplishments. "He's a god," Charlie muttered to himself. And then there was his size. He was five-ten and one hundred and fifty pounds. Not huge. Charlie found that encouraging.

He'd seen the guy. He looked so strong. So ripped. He saw him ride his bike down the beach road, pick it up and jog up

two flights of stairs to meet Cooper on the deck of that house
he bought. But as pro athletes go, he was small.

The second thing to intrigue him—Smiley had to teach
himself to swim. He gave speeches about how he built his athletic career on survival instincts and practice.

Charlie couldn't swim. His mother freaked out if he even ran
and he sure hadn't had a pool in the backyard. He wanted to
swim. He'd spent the summer hanging out here on the beach
watching the older kids paddleboarding and, lately, windsurf-
ing. He'd had a ride on a paddleboard with someone else pad-
dling. And he'd been wearing a life vest...

Charlie closed the laptop and went to Winnie's bedroom.
He knocked lightly on the door. There was no telling what
was going on in there. It could be bathing, primping, reading
or maybe Winnie was sleeping. "Come in," his mother said.

He pushed open the door and saw that his mother had been
giving Winnie a manicure. Winnie loved manicures. Winnie
had become a good friend; they spent a lot of time on their
laptops together, talking, figuring things out.

"You are never going to believe this," he said, pushing his
glasses up on his nose. "The new guy next door? He's an Ironman!"

Blake arrived from Australia late at night. He'd slept on the
plane so he was up for a few hours knowing that in the next
couple of days jet lag would kick his ass. Then it would pass.

He was creaky and stiff. His body had become a little less
responsive in the past few years. Things like prerace training
and international travel were beginning to take their toll. And
it was odd going home to his own house. It was his first. People wouldn't guess that. He was almost forty and had never
owned a home. Not even a condo or town house. He'd given

the location a great deal of thought. He wanted to be near the ocean; he liked the cold of the Pacific. As a workout it was more taxing than warm water; the unforgiving nature of the ocean was more realistic than a lake or pool for training. He needed altitude training and he had that in Oregon. Everywhere he looked…mountains. He had seriously considered Boulder or Truckee but at the end of the day he liked this little spot. When he wasn't racing he was training and when he wasn't training, he was living. He could get his training done here. And while he might keep up with the training for life, he wasn't going to race professionally forever. For living he wanted a quiet place that wasn't overrun by professional athletes and Olympians. Shake a tree in Boulder or Truckee and ten Olympic contenders fell out.

He spent his first day unpacking, arranging his gym and doing a short workout to keep from stiffening up after a seventeen-hour plane ride. Then he drove into a larger town to the grocery store, rounding up his food. He stuck mostly to organic vegetables, legumes and grains, including quinoa. He ordered his supplements online. He wasn't a vegetarian. For his purposes he found it served him best if he cooked up a little poultry or beef to add to his vegetables and grains. Cooper had suggested that if he got friendly with Cliff, who owned the seafood restaurant at the marina, he could get fresh fish, crab and other shellfish.

When he was training, which was almost year-round, he avoided or at least limited his favorite things—cheese, simple starchy carbs, the most flavorful fats like butter and cream. He limited his alcohol to the occasional beer. But when he was off-season and his training was moderate, when he was relaxing for a little while, he indulged. Not too much, of course, because no one was more disciplined. But a good, greasy pizza was the best thing in the world as far as he was concerned. And yes, he could make his own vegetarian with a gluten-free crust, but if he was indulging that wouldn't do it. The way he grew up, he still longed for those things he couldn't have and pizza and beer were a couple of those things.

His second day home he woke up too early, blended up one of his protein drinks, stretched out, dragged on a wet suit and hit the bay. It was eight-thirty but the sun wasn't quite up, given all that sea fog, and the water felt icy. He didn't know the exact distance across the bay but after a fifty-minute swim he'd have an idea. He had already measured a couple of cycling and running routes before making an offer on the house.

He loved the house. He'd looked at a hundred of them, at least, in a lot of places, including Hawaii. Hawaii was tempting; the lifestyle was alluring. But he thought most of his future work would be in the US, and while he didn't mind travel, he'd like to be able to have a base less than ten hours away. If work took him to Chicago or New York or Los Angeles he could get home to Thunder Point in six hours or less. Boulder, being in the center of the country, was practical but wasn't as tempting as this unpretentious little fishing village on the ocean. There was a house on Cape Cod he liked but the East Coast beyond the cape wasn't as peaceful or traffic friendly as Oregon. He remembered asking Cooper, *Doesn't anyone know about this place yet?* The freeways weren't clogged, the air was clean, there were some wide-open spaces… When he was ten years old, the idea that he could live wherever he wished had never occurred to him. But then, when he was ten his most urgent concern was eating and staying warm.

He set the timer on his watch, walked into the water, dove, swam out past the haystack rocks and began swimming from end to end across the bay. When the timer went off he'd made seven trips across the bay—he judged the distance across the beach as slightly more than a quarter of a mile. Maybe four-tenths of a mile. He had a laser measuring tool and later he'd check to see how close he'd been, but even those devices weren't perfect. By the time he exited the water, the sun was shining. He'd ride for a few hours today; tomorrow he'd go for a run. He'd do one test triathlon before the next competition, only one.

There was a kid sitting on the beach stairs to the house next door to his. He had a laptop balanced on his knees and wore black-framed glasses. Blake shook off the excess water and pulled off his hood and goggles. He walked up to the kid. "Hey," he said, a little breathless.

"Hey," the kid said. "You came in second in Sydney."

Blake smiled. "I had a good race."

"Your times were good but McGill beat you. He beats you pretty regular."

"You stalking me, kid?"

"Nah, just looked you up. So, what made it a good race?"

"First, what's your name?"

"I'm Charlie," he said, sticking out a hand. And with one finger on the other hand he pushed his glasses up on his nose.

"Nice to meet you, Charlie. I guess you know me already."

"I asked Cooper who you were and he said you were racing in Australia and I looked you up." He shrugged. "You have a pretty good record."

"Thanks," Blake said, raising a brow in question. In fact, he had a great record. "What else did you find out about me?"

"Well…you had to teach yourself to swim."

"That's right."

"How'd you do that?"

"The   same   way   I   learned   almost   everything—

survival. I fell in a pool. Or maybe I got pushed in, I can't remember. And I couldn't swim. Went down like a rock."

"Did you have to get rescued?"

"Nope. It was in college and I was at a pool party. I don't think anyone was paying attention. I held my breath and walked out. My lungs just about exploded."

"You *walked* out?" Charlie asked, astonished.

"That was my only option at the time. I was an expert on depth because I couldn't swim. Every time I was near a pool I made sure I knew where the shallow and deep ends where. I fell in the middle, eyeballed the shallow end and walked. It was slow. Nobody knows the depth and contour of a pool like a kid who can't swim. Then I taught myself to swim because walking out in water over your head isn't a good experience. I read about swimming, practiced it. I watched some video of little kids taking lessons."

"That pool you walked out of wasn't that big, I guess."

"Any pool when you're in over your head is big. After that I learned to tread water and then, since I knew nothing, teaching me to swim was kind of easy—there were no bad habits to unlearn."

"They start you out with a life jacket?" Charlie asked.

"Nah, that's not the best way to learn to swim. Best way to stay alive if you have an accident, though. Even experienced swimmers will wear flotation jackets under certain circumstances. The best way is to learn to respect the water, learn the moves, breathe right, understand buoyancy. They teach babies, you know. They don't use any flotation devices. They teach them to hold their breath, fan the water, to kick, to roll over on their backs to breathe, to... Hey, you swim, right?"

Charlie shook his head.

"You live on a beach and don't swim?"

He shook his head again. "I don't live here. My mom works for Mrs. Banks. Since I come with her to work every day, I'm going to go to school here in town but we live... We live a few miles away."

"And you don't swim," Blake said again.

Charlie shook his head. "That never came up before."

Blake laughed. He understood that completely. "So, what's up with Mrs. Banks?"

"ALS. She's doing good. She's not end stage," Charlie said, as if he understood such things. "She still walks a little bit but never alone and my mom is optimistic. But she needs a nurse and it's not my mom's first ALS patient. I'm really sorry she has ALS but I think I'm going to like the school... Well, for as long as my mom works for Mrs. Banks."

"Hopefully a long time," Blake said.

"Yeah, for her sake, for sure. So what made it a good race? You got beat."

"Gimme a break, will you? I came in second—that's a damn good show. Like you said, McGill beats me regularly. This time, though, he announced his retirement." Blake made a face. "Gonna really miss that guy." Then he laughed. "Seriously, I had good times. I was close to my personal-best swimming and, in case you haven't figured it out, that's not my easiest sport. But I run like the wind."

Charlie just grinned at him.

"I guess I better come next door and introduce myself to Mrs. Banks, huh? After I clean up, of course. What's her schedule like?"

"After her nap, right before dinner, everyone is usually around. And she's downright perky."

"Everyone?" Blake asked.

"Well, Mrs. Banks's daughter, Grace, and her husband, Troy,

are there. And there's Mikhail. He's been hanging around ever since he found out Winnie has ALS. Mikhail used to be Grace's coach. For, like, years. She's a champion athlete, too. So you're not the only one."

"Is that so?" Blake asked, crossing his arms over his chest.

"Figure-skating gold medalist," Charlie said. "A while ago, though. She retired."

Blake frowned. The name "Grace" didn't sound familiar at all.

"I guess she used to be called Izzy when she was skating."

"Oh, Jesus, Izzy Banks?" he asked. "You're kidding, right?"

"And her mother—Winnie Banks," Charlie said. "Grace is like a second-generation champion."

Now, what were the odds? Blake asked himself. Winnie and Izzy were famous mother/daughter skating icons. Winnie Banks had quit skating to marry her coach and they'd produced one of the best known women's figure-skating champions in the world. "Unreal. What's she doing now?"

"Well, she owns the flower shop and she's having a baby," Charlie said. "Troy is a high school teacher. And in that house there," he said, pointing to the house between Winnie's and Cooper's, "Spencer and Devon live there. Spencer and Cooper have a son together."

Blake's eyebrows shot up. "Is that so? Two men?"

Charlie laughed. "Not like that. One of them is the dad and one is the stepdad or something like that. I can't figure out which is which, but Austin's mom died a couple of years ago. Now Spencer is married to Devon, and Cooper is married to Sarah. And Austin has two bedrooms."

After all the house and community shopping Blake had done he'd managed to somehow land in a neighborhood where kids had moms, stepmoms, dads and stepdads, missing moms and so on. Where he grew up in Baltimore it was like that, but usually someone in the family was in jail and there sure weren't any three-story houses on the beach or champion athletes hanging around. Just gang members, drug dealers, prostitutes and pimps. There were missing parents, dead parents and foster parents, kids raised by aunts, grandmothers and neighbors. Families of every creative invention, now that he thought of it. Back when he was a kid, you practically needed a chart to figure out who belonged with whom. He was always a little surprised when folks who could pay the rent had similar family trees.

No beach houses where he grew up, no, sir. He was raised to the age of thirteen in an urban tenement slum in a city that got so freaking cold in the winter he hung out with vagrants who built fires in trash cans under the tracks and bridges. From thirteen to sixteen he bounced around a lot while his mother tried to get her life together, but at least he went to school regularly. That turned out to be critical. An education was the thing that ultimately got him out of a neighborhood where a lot of young men and women lost track of their lives.

"What do you do on that computer besides research your neighbors?" Blake asked Charlie.

"I look up everything. Anything I can get for you?" he asked. And then he grinned the cutest grin.

Blake had a real soft spot for kids. All kids. But he didn't worry too much about this type, the kind of kid who grew up in places like brand-new, pricey, three-story beach houses with famous retired athletes. He was more concerned about the kids who had tough, deprived childhoods. He'd been working on a project for the past several years meant to serve kids in need and he was nearly ready to unveil it as soon as he had a couple more corporate sponsors on board.

He liked Charlie right away. He felt privileged that he'd be seeing him around. "There is something you can do for me. I have to get on the bike and do at least fifty miles. Then home and clean up." He looked at his watch. "Any time after one o'clock that your mother thinks is okay to come over and meet my neighbors, could you let me know?"

"Could be closer to dinnertime if you want to meet them all. Troy has been helping Grace at the shop."

"I don't want to impose on dinner—just a quick hello. I'm home the rest of the day," Blake assured him.

It was not strictly required that Lin Su wear some kind of nurse's uniform, but she wore clean scrubs every day just the same. For one thing, they were easy to move around in and her job sometimes found her on her hands and knees digging around beneath the bathroom sink or wiping up a kitchen floor. For another thing, scrubs were easily maintained and, if need be, replaced. And importantly, they identified her— even the UPS man at the door knew she was either on the job as a medic or worked somewhere nearby as medical personnel and was dressed in her work clothes.

As a home health care nurse, she could wear civilian clothes while tending patients like Winnie Banks, those who needed assistance and yet were not desperately ill. But when she tended patients in the end stages of diseases, which tended to be incredibly messy, her civilian clothes needed to be spared. After all, they were few and carefully chosen.

So it was all logical, her use of scrubs on the job. And when she opened the door to a very attractive man, they proved effective.

"So, you're the nurse," the man said. "Charlie said I could brave a visit, just to introduce myself and say hello. I'm Blake Smiley. Your neighbor."

"Hello," she said, more wide-eyed than she liked. He was just so damn handsome, it threw her. She'd caught glimpses of him when he was on the beach or on his deck next door, but up close he was shockingly beautiful. She was speechless.

"You are Lin Su. I asked Charlie, you see."

"Ah! Yes, I'm Lin Su Simmons. Please. Come in."

"Is it a convenient time to say hello to Mrs. Banks?"

"Come in! Come in!" Winnie called from the dining room table.

Lin Su stepped aside so that Blake could enter.

Winnie was sitting with Charlie at the dining table, both of them with their laptops open. Winnie closed hers and held out a hand toward him. "And how do you do, Mr. Smiley! Charlie told me you might be stopping by."

"It's a pleasure, Mrs. Banks," he said, taking her hand.

"Will you sit for a moment?" she asked. "And now that the formal introductions are dispensed with, can we proceed as Winnie and Blake?"

"Nothing would please me more."

"Charlie," she said. "Fetch Mikhail from the deck." Then she turned to Blake. "Very nice of you to make the effort to visit. It's not easy for me to get around, as I'm sure Charlie told you."

"He told me," Blake said. "I'm so sorry to hear it. Lou Gehrig's disease, how bloody awful for you. You look positively wonderful. How are you feeling?"

"Until I try to pick up a glass or stand, I feel just fine," she said, adding a small head shake. "Speaking of glass, what can we get you?"

"Nothing at all, Mrs.... Winnie. I just wanted to meet you. I was shocked to hear two famous athletes were living next door."

"Yes, but we're not competing anymore," Winnie said. "What in the world are you doing here in Thunder Point?"

"I'm still training, but I fell in love with the quiet of the place." He glanced around. "If you can find a way to move this house to Boulder you can get three million for it."

"I can't believe the price was what attracted you," she said.

"The town did, as a matter of fact. The size, the simplicity, the building around the bay. That's a great place for me to swim. The hills and lowlands are great bike and running trails. The air is perfect."

"What's your next event?" Winnie asked.

"Tahoe," Charlie answered for him, sitting down again.

"He seems to know as much about me as I do," Blake said. He stood and extended a hand toward the short Russian coach who had come in from the deck. "How do you do, sir. I'm your neighbor, Blake."

"An honor," Mikhail said.

When everyone sat down to visit, Lin Su drifted off to the master bedroom. This was the time of day she put it right for later when Winnie would settle in for the night.

After a nap and a little refreshing, Winnie would spend some time in the living room or on the deck, have dinner with whoever happened to be around—sometimes the entire family, sometimes just Lin Su, Charlie and Mikhail. If Winnie's daughter, Grace, wanted to help her settle in for the evening, Lin Su and Charlie would go home. Most nights Lin Su would stay for the evening ritual and then take herself and her son home.

Her present home wasn't exactly a welcoming place. Lin Su and Charlie were renting a small fifth wheel that had been left behind at a rather scurvy trailer park, but it was completely adequate and she had gotten it antiseptic clean. This job with

Winnie, while demanding, was also accommodating and paid well. Lin Su was working on a solution to that fifth wheel, but it had been all she could afford at the time—she'd been laid off from the hospital and bills had accrued while she was between jobs. There were also old loans like tuition, moving, some medical expenses that hadn't been covered by employers. She finally had some savings but she didn't dare touch it. She was very cautious and the most important thing in the world to her was that Charlie get a good education.

It was all working out, for now. It was Winnie, in fact, who had suggested Charlie come to work with her every day and therefore attend school in Thunder Point. Winnie's son-in-law, Troy Headly, taught history there and Winnie's next-door neighbor, Spencer Lawson, was the athletic director and football coach. She wouldn't have to worry about Charlie being picked on by bigger, tougher kids, and for that she was so grateful.

She drew back the comforter and smoothed out the sheets—six hundred thread count—fluffed the pillows and made it inviting. She shook out and refolded the throw that Mikhail used when he slept in the big leather chair at Winnie's bedside. He thought no one knew. That made her smile. Mikhail was so devoted, but he disappeared before Lin Su arrived in the morning so no one would know he was that protective. Lin Su dusted the room, removing the water glass from the bedside table, tidied the books and magazines Winnie kept nearby. The bathroom just needed a lick and a promise plus fresh towels and facecloths. Tomorrow she would change the sheets and wash some linens. She would love to sleep in such fine bedding but she wouldn't trade places with Winnie for the moon.

By the time she returned to the kitchen and dining room, Grace and Troy had come home and there was a great deal of chatter. They had brought dinner from Carrie's deli and Grace was putting out place mats.

"Please, won't you stay?" Grace asked Blake. "I can assure you it's healthy and nutritious. Carrie is very particular."

But to the disappointment of all, Blake declined the invitation, heading home for some concoction of kale, squash, beef, chicken, quinoa, oil and… Lin Su might not have caught all the ingredients, but he was in training—there was another race in a month.

"Sounds delicious," Grace said doubtfully.

"Sounds excruciating," Winnie said, making everyone laugh.

Blake laughed with them. "After the next two races I'll have a little downtime. I'll exercise and eat well but the strict training and diet regimen is relaxed a little bit. I'll eat and drink like a regular person," he said with a grin.

"Well, when you're done with the next race, I'm buying," Troy said, lifting his beer in Blake's direction.

TWO

The size of the Banks household had grown, if only slightly. Now there was a cleaning crew headed by a woman named Shauna Price. There were three women who swooped in twice a week and applied a devoted two hours to cleaning the house, top to bottom. They were friendly without having much to say, charged a lot, carried their own supplies with them and vanished without saying goodbye. Once a week Shauna dutifully asked Lin Su if everything was all right. She didn't ask Winnie; Lin Su believed Winnie terrified her.

Three mornings a week from 10:00 to 10:45 a.m. Curtis Rhinehold appeared—the physical therapist. He put Winnie through a series of exercises meant to keep up her strength and balance, though whether it did any good was questionable. In his absence, Lin Su continued the exercises because it couldn't hurt anything and maybe it would give her a little more time and function. Winnie grumbled and complained, though Lin Su was confident if she weren't getting this attention her complaining might be worse.

The end of summer was pleasant; the weather was warm and dry. Lin Su was warned it was leading into a cold and wet and often windy winter on the bay. Charlie enjoyed his new Thunder Point friends and anticipated the start of school very hopefully. His buddy Frank Downy, an MIT sophomore who shared Charlie's passion for online research, had headed back east to college in mid-August. Cooper's young brother-in-law, Landon, had gone back to the University of Oregon to begin football practice at about the same time. With Thunder Point High School starting a new year, Spencer was knee-deep into his own football practice with his team, moaning and groaning about those young men taking a toll on his back and knees. Troy was busy preparing for classes when he wasn't helping Grace in the flower shop or helping around the house. Charlie wasn't bored for a second. He had Winnie and Mikhail and was very independent.

And now he had a new friend—the triathlete next door. Charlie saw Blake every day, sometimes just talking on the beach, sometimes hitting the volleyball around or working on his bicycle. One afternoon Lin Su saw Charlie hosing Blake's deck while Blake scrubbed it with the bristle broom. On another warm and sunny afternoon Charlie took Blake for a hike along the ridge to show him the lookout where he'd see the migrating whales in another month or so.

Lin Su was happy Charlie had a friend, and a good male role model never hurt, but she'd rather Charlie be enamored of Troy or Spencer or even Cooper—nice, stable, married men. It would be a mistake for Charlie to think a man like Blake would take a place of permanence in his life. He was a little too free and easy for Lin Su's tastes. And their situation—the job and the location—was temporary. With any luck it would stick for a while, but eventually they would have to move on.

They always had to move on.

For now, the job caring for Winnie Banks was ideal. Lin Su put in a lot of hours, but had long breaks during the day while Winnie napped or didn't need her. And while she would try to play the role of employee and caregiver, always available but at a polite distance and not a member of the family or town, the family and town wouldn't allow it. She'd been with Winnie since June and they were growing close. Winnie was even closer to Charlie; they'd become thicker than thieves. Lin Su and Charlie were drawn in and embraced; they dined together, visited, gossiped, even played games together.

Lin Su was trying to remember her place.

"I don't want an agency nurse's aide," Winnie said. "Think about this. You take care of my bedding, help me bathe, escort me to the bathroom, help me dress—we are intimate, you and me. If you couldn't fit in with this odd crew I now call family—a daughter, a teacher, an old coach—I would have to look for someone else. I'm afraid you're stuck with us."

Three women Lin Su's approximate age who were good friends and bonded in many ways were also all showing very nice baby bumps by mid-August. Grace, Iris and Peyton. Iris Sileski was the high school guidance counselor and had sold Grace the flower shop—they'd been friends since the day Grace arrived in Thunder Point a couple of years before. Peyton Grant, the town physician's assistant who had conveniently wed the physician, made regular visits to check on Winnie's health as did her husband, Scott. It was only natural, then, that there would be small and regular gatherings of those three—sometimes at the end of the day, sometimes for lunch, sometimes morning coffee, sometimes dinner. They were all due to give birth just before Christmas.

When they gathered in or near Winnie's house, if Lin Su

wasn't busy, they pressed her to join them. Winnie very much enjoyed having them around, and with Lin Su's or Grace's help, Winnie could even join them if they met at Cooper's bar or in town at the restaurant. Winnie even enjoyed brief trips to the diner, something that made her daughter howl with laughter, accusing that it must have been Winnie's first diner experience ever.

"True, if it were my diner, it would be decorated far differently and would look more like a salon, but this is fine for me," she said, lifting her perfect nose slightly. "For now."

Lin Su knew it wasn't the diner that drew Winnie and definitely not the decor—it was the women closer to her own age who tended to meet there from time to time. There was Carrie from the deli whose daughter, Gina, managed the diner on the day shift. Carrie's best friends, Lou, a teacher, and Ray Anne, a local Realtor, were known to meet there, as well. Winnie never asked to be taken to the diner on a whim but if one of the women called or stopped by to say they were meeting for coffee and pie Winnie might ask to go. Better still, if they were meeting at Cliffhanger's for a glass of wine, she was sure to make the effort, even if she had to impose on Troy or Mikhail to take her, even if she had to rely on her wheelchair for the outing.

"I've never had girlfriends before," Winnie whispered to Lin Su. "You have no idea what a different experience this is for me."

But Lin Su did know. Her own mother, Marilyn Simmons, would never hang out with a gaggle of women in a small-town diner. Marilyn was her adoptive mother. Her biological mother hadn't survived long after her exodus from Vietnam, thus Lin Su's adoption by an affluent white American couple from Boston at the age of three. They liked to refer to it as a compassionate adoption. Marilyn, wife of Gordon Simmons, a well-known attorney, fancied herself something of a socialite. Her biological daughters attended the best boarding schools and universities while she served on charity boards, played bridge, golf, attended prestigious events, supported political campaigns and shopped. No, she had never been seen in a diner with ordinary women.

That was yet another thing about Thunder Point that Lin Su immediately appreciated—people gathered without deference to class or status or income. She knew that Winnie was financially comfortable; most of her home health care patients had been. If they could afford to pay a salary and benefits to a private nurse, they had planned well. And Winnie did look fancier than the town women she'd meet for a coffee or a drink, but the women didn't treat one another differently.

Lin Su would be lying if she said she wasn't tempted to fall into familiarity and camaraderie with all of these women— the younger pregnant ones, the older ones she found to be settled and sage. But she was trying to maintain that professional distance that would ensure her job was safe and keep her from being disappointed when the day came that someone reminded her she was a servant. A well-educated and highly trained servant, but still...

Her biggest challenge of all was the triathlete next door. He frightened and intrigued her. He didn't frighten her because there was anything wrong with him. Indeed, everything seemed too right. He reminded her of the young man she'd loved when she was in high school. The young man who had played rugby, graduated with honors, had a fancy family name and dated Lin Su for months. His parents were friendly with hers; Marilyn Simmons greatly admired the boy's mother and was thrilled that they were dating. She whispered that it spoke well of them that they could accept an Asian girl as their son's choice.

But when she had told him she was pregnant, he had said, "Sorry, baby, but I'm going to Princeton."

She was standing on the deck with Winnie when she heard talking and laughter coming from the house next door, but there was no one on the deck. Winnie was sitting at the outdoor table enjoying the sunshine while she played solitaire to try to keep her fingers nimble. Lin Su looked over the deck rail and saw that Charlie was balanced atop one of Blake's bikes while Blake appeared to be tightening something on the wheel. Then Blake stood up and Charlie took off down the beach road.

Like a bat out of hell.

Lin Su gasped. Her son flew on that bike. Flew as though he was racing!

"Winnie, will you be all right for a moment? I should talk to Mr. Smiley about Charlie riding."

"I'll be fine," she said. "I'm not going anyplace."

"I'll be right back," Lin Su said, heading for the stairs to the beach. By the time she got to where Blake stood on the road, Charlie was out of sight across the beach.

"Mr. Smiley, it's so nice of you to let Charlie have a turn on your bicycle. But maybe that's not such a good idea."

"It's Blake. And why is that, Lin Su?"

"For one thing, it's a very expensive bicycle. At least, that's what Charlie tells me."

"It is. It's not my primary bike." He tossed a tool in his open toolbox. "He's safe. He's wearing a helmet. We talked about the rules of the road and he understands."

"Did Charlie happen to mention—he has asthma?"

"No. Is he on medication?"

"Yes."

"Does he have an inhaler?"

"He's supposed to have it with him at all times. And sometimes exertion brings on his asthma."

Blake gave a little shrug. "Then if he gets winded, I guess he'll stop."

"Where is he going?"

"I have no idea, Lin Su. I told him not to be gone long. He really likes that bike. He'll probably ride around awhile."

"He could get too far away!" she said.

Blake wiped his hands on a rag and contemplated her. "He's a big boy. He knows how to manage his asthma, doesn't he?"

"Sometimes he's not as careful as he should be!" she said emphatically.

Blake dropped a casual arm over her shoulders and turned her in the direction of the town across the bay. He pointed. "See that building over there?"

"Which building?" she asked.

"The one that says Clinic on the sign. If he has an asthma attack, this is a good place to have one. But I bet he doesn't. You know why? Because I bet he doesn't like asthma much and he's fourteen—it probably embarrasses him. Don't worry. In a few minutes he'll either come riding across the beach at breakneck speed or he'll be flushed and walking the bike."

"You're a little too casual about this for my tastes, Mr. Smiley. You don't seem to understand how difficult something like this can be. And I'm the parent here—I'm a nurse, a mother and very well acquainted with Charlie's condition."

He took a deep breath and frowned. "Lin Su, my name is Blake not Mr. Smiley. As far as I know there is no Mr. Smiley. And I take things like this very seriously. At the end of the day it could be more beneficial to Charlie to have respect for the asthma, work with it, refuse to let it stop him and get to know his body if he doesn't already. Being overprotective isn't going to help. Knowledge helps. Fear doesn't."

Lin Su felt her hackles rise. She wanted to take him down. She pursed her lips and narrowed her eyes. "Fantastic little lecture, Mr. Smiley. You should do a TED Talk someday. You have no idea what it was like sitting up through the night when he was three years old, doing breathing treatments every couple of hours, holding him while he strained to get a breath, watching him get that blue tinge, putting him in the ambulance. He has to be cautious!"

She saw what clearly looked like sympathy come into his gaze. "You must have been terrified," he said. "The good news is, he isn't three anymore."

Lin Su's anger grew even though Blake's voice was gentle.

"Ah, there he is," Blake said. "He's really moving."

Charlie was speeding, head down, peddling madly. He slowed as he came upon them, his grin wide as the sky. He had his mother's perfect, straight white teeth.

"That was awesome," he said to Blake. He was huffing and puffing a little. "Mom, what are you doing here? Winnie all right?"

"She's fine. Are you having trouble catching your breath?" Lin Su asked.

"I'm winded," he said. "I rode hard. Not long, though. I'll be fine in a second."

"Do you need your inhaler?"

"Mom," he said. "I'm fine." But then he coughed.

"Charlie, I don't want you…"

"Charlie, do you have any major plans for that laptop of yours for tonight?" Blake asked, cutting her off.

Charlie shrugged. "No, why?"

"I think you should research famous athletes with asthma," Blake said. "You'll run across some familiar names and get some good ideas."

Charlie coughed on and off through the rest of the afternoon and because of that Grace offered to settle her mother in for the night so Lin Su could take her son home. On the way home she lightly berated him. "You shouldn't have taken the hard ride. A long walk or a ride on a paddleboard is one thing—a burst of exercise could haunt you."

"It's not an asthma attack. Trust me, I'd know." He coughed again. "It'll pass."

"We'll do a breathing treatment," she said.

"I'll do it," Charlie said. "I just wish you liked him. Because he's a good guy."

"Mr. Smiley?" she asked, though of course she knew. "I like him fine. He was being very neighborly, loaning you the bike for a ride. But he didn't know about the asthma. That's your responsibility, Charlie."

"Then let me have it," he said tersely.

Mr. Smiley, she found herself thinking, *is going to be a problem.* He was encouraging this free thinking, letting Charlie learn from his consequences, and he didn't understand that in Charlie's case the consequences could be fatal.

Well, probably not, she relented. Worst case, a manageable asthma attack, relieved by a nebulizer and maybe some oxygen. But she was suddenly desperate that Charlie listen first to *her*.

"It's not going to kill me, you know," Charlie said as if reading her mind. "Sometimes I have a little breathing thing, not very often. I haven't had one of these in a long time."

"May," she said. "When everything was in bloom. And it got a little dicey."

"Because it turned into a cold. This could be just a cold, you know. I felt a little stuffy before I took the bike out."

Lin Su said nothing as she drove. But she counted his coughs, which had become deep and gravelly. He wasn't wheezing. Yet. They were almost home when she said, "I don't appreciate your attitude toward me, as if I'm somehow punishing you. I'm going to make you some soup while you take a hot shower with lots of steam. Then you come out, eat soup and give the water heater time to heat up again and get back in the steam. After that we'll do a breathing treatment. How many times have you used the inhaler?"

"Just twice."

"Let's see if we can nip this in the bud, okay, Charlie?"

He nodded. "Sorry, Mom. The bike was so awesome."

"I know, honey." She wanted to carry on about the use of some discretion to keep this asthma in check but she knew he'd heard enough. And maybe Mr. Smiley was partially right—he might learn more this way, from the consequences, than from her harping. He'd heard it all before. But damned if she'd ever admit that.

They carried out the plan—shower, soup, shower, treatment. After all that, he started to sniff a little and she hoped it was a little cold rather than an attack, even though that presented a different set of problems. If these symptoms persisted it would be wrong to take him back to Winnie's. She shouldn't be exposed to germs if it could be avoided. With all the people in and through Winnie's house it was risky enough—her nurse couldn't bring a known virus into the patient's home.

Then she had a slightly evil thought. It would serve him right to have to spend a day at home as a result of his less than responsible actions, even though she knew it wasn't possible for a bike ride to bring on a cold. He should learn to listen to her. *So you want it to be a cold, Charlie, and not your overtaxed weak lungs—a cold, it is. And you have to stay home. Away from your playmates for a day.*

Lin Su heard every cough through the night. It wasn't too bad—it wasn't getting worse, he had no fever, it was a productive cough and he wasn't wheezing. She gave him another breathing treatment first thing in the morning, checked his temperature, then double-checked with her lips on his forehead. "I think you're going to be fine. But it's the responsible thing to leave you home today. I don't want Winnie and the rest of the family to hear that coughing and get anxious about germs. You understand."

"Yeah, okay. But will you please tell everyone I'm fine? That I'm not having any kind of attack or anything?"

"Of course. I'll explain it's just a precaution for Winnie's health in case you're coming down with a cold. Will that do?"

"Yeah. It's just that... If Blake thinks the bike did it, he'll never let me try it out again."

Lin Su doubted that. Actually, she feared that. Blake was coming across as a challenge, as the guy who wanted to let Charlie be a man about it. Her poor little bubble boy—she wouldn't want to have to live like that, either. But God, what if something terrible happened? And it could—his fragile lungs, his intense allergies, his stressed immune system... "Of course we'll play the cold card here. And if you get another chance on that bike or any bike, let's decide here and now that you're not going to check it for maximum speed. Can we agree to that?"

"That bike is so slick, Mom. No wonder it cost a billion dollars!"

Lin Su sat on the edge of his bed. "Charlie, your health has been good lately. Keep it so. Build up some stamina, get strong, live long. Use that remarkable brain of yours to get ahead and buy a dozen billion-dollar bicycles when you've overcome the worst of this. But go slow."

He grinned. "You just want me to live a long time so you have some rich guy to take care of you in your old age."

"I'm counting on it," she said. "I'll text and call. Try to take it easy today. I'm sure by tomorrow you'll be fine."

This was the lot of a single mother—making a choice between her job, which was vital, and her sick child, the core of her being. If he were younger than fourteen she might have asked one of the elderly neighbors to watch him or at least check on him, but at fourteen Charlie would be offended. Hell, at eleven he was offended! He knew the rules, he was responsible. Still...she wanted to be near...

Blake suited up for his swim, grateful that the sun was shining brightly on the bay even though it was early, mindful of the fact that the water was still going to be freezing cold. He put in his hour and was surprised Charlie wasn't waiting on the steps for him to get out of the water. It briefly crossed his mind that his mother was keeping him away from Blake, the troublemaker with the tempting bike.

He had planned a long run for today but he switched out his plan—he took the bike on a long ride instead. The riding speed was going to be crucial in the upcoming race. When he got back, there was still no sign of Charlie and there was no one out on the deck at Winnie's house. Not even Winnie and her nurse.

Lin Su. The first time he saw her he had actually felt his breath catch. All he could see of her was that she was small, wore scrubs and had black hair twisted into some kind of bun. She had laughed with Winnie and Grace, and even though it was at some distance he could see she was beautiful.

Lin Su was intriguing and now, unfortunately, she appeared to be a little angry with him. He wouldn't necessarily do things differently with Charlie and the bike. He might've asked him if it would be all right with his mother or, had he known about the asthma, he might've suggested he go easy. Then again, he might not. Blake was no expert, but boys that age needed to find their own limits.

Charlie was nowhere in sight.

By the time Blake had showered and put on clean clothes, there were people on Winnie's deck. Troy and Mikhail and Winnie were sitting at the outside table. He went downstairs inside his own house, out through the patio doors of his lower level and next door to walk up the outside stairs to Winnie's deck.

"Incoming," he hollered, walking up the last few steps.

"Hey, man," Troy said, standing. "Come on up. How's it going?"

"Good. I hope I'm not interrupting anything important."

"We're just getting ready to wax Winnie in bridge," Troy said. "Bridge because she won't play poker."

"You're not at school today?" Blake asked Troy.

"I was there this morning and will help Grace at the shop this afternoon. Not much more summer left. You play bridge?"

"Sorry," he said, grinning. "I was wondering about Charlie. I think this is the first day since I moved in that I haven't seen him hanging around."

At that moment Lin Su came onto the deck with a tray of drinks—two cups of tea and two tall glasses of something. One of the cups had a straw in it for Winnie. "He stayed home today," she said in answer to the question. "He might be coming down with a cold and we're diligent about keeping germs out of here when we can for Winnie's sake."

"It took a lot more than a cold to take me down," Winnie said.

"A cold wouldn't help you, however. Can I get you something to drink, Blake?" she asked.

He was ridiculously pleased that she used his first name. He could feel his smile grow to an almost silly width. "No, thank you. I just finished a ride. I hope that cold wasn't because… you know…"

She put the tray on the table. "He's had a good summer. An asthma episode can't bring on a cold but a cold can weaken his resistance to asthma. He seems to be fine—just some congestion and a cough." She pulled up a chair for Blake and then took one herself, passing out the drinks. "Exercise-induced asthma is probably to be expected since he has a history, but I'll tell you what's frightening—when a big attack comes on for no apparent reason. That hasn't happened in a long time." She took a sip of her tea. "I'll leave him home till he's completely over it."

"I apologize if the bike brought it on. I had no idea…"

"Of course you didn't," Winnie said. "Charlie should have mentioned it. I suspect he wanted to get on that bike so badly he wouldn't dare risk it. He's been lusting after your bike since he first laid eyes on it."

"That's the worst thing about being fourteen," Blake said. "Doing all the things you're supposed to do."

"I'll be happy if he learned something. He can have a completely normal life as long as he's careful."

And listens to his mother, Blake thought. There were some teenage boys to whom that was a luxury. They couldn't always be careful.

"Will you promise to stay if we deal?" Winnie asked Blake.

"If I'm not imposing," he said.

"Not at all. I enjoy having you drop by. By the way, when is the next big race?"

"Three weeks, in Tahoe. I'll go a week early to train in the mountains there, to get acclimated. My trainer will come here first. We'll do a trial run, then go to Tahoe together to get ready."

"Where is your trainer now?" Troy asked.

"She's in Boulder, her home base. She's an exercise physiologist. Well, she's a PhD in physiology, not an ordinary trainer. She's a partner in an athletic training facility and I'm not the only client by a long shot. Sometimes she'll send a colleague. Babysitter, that's all—I have my own degree and have been doing this for a long time. But there's no substitute for a trainer who challenges the protocol, pushes at the edges of the envelope and generally provides data on the competition that can be useful. She's a little bit like a manager—sending me daily reports on the results of events from all over the world and making recommendations based on training studies."

It was quiet around the bridge table. "Sounds a lot more complicated than I thought," Lin Su said.

"Is complicated," Mikhail said. "Grace was my full-time job for nine years. You have this trainer part-time?" he asked Blake.

"Yeah," he laughed. "I admit a trainer is beneficial and even necessary, but I'm pigheaded and don't like a lot of interference. I also don't like to be too crowded. So, who's the bridge favorite at this table?"

"Once it was me," Winnie said. "Then I hired a nurse from Boston. On top of that, I might drop my cards at any moment."

"My adoptive mother played a lot of bridge. I learned young so I could sit in if they needed a fourth. I shouldn't play so well—I think my job is at risk," Lin Su said.

"Is a competitive table," Mikhail said. "It will anger Winnie if you win. It will anger her if you don't play well. You are doomed."

The cards were dealt, but before anyone could pick them up, Lin Su's phone chimed in her pocket. "Excuse me please, Charlie is checking in."

Surprise immediately came over her features and she stiffened into a posture of fear. "Your EpiPen? How could you...? Okay, don't talk too much... The oxygen? Did you call 9-1-1?... Okay, stay on the line, I'll get them." She looked at Winnie for just a second. "Charlie can't breathe. I'm going. Will you be all right?"

"Mikhail and Troy will be here," she said. "Just go."

"I'll go with you," Blake said.

"I've got this," Lin Su said, turning and running into the house. She pulled her purse out of the kitchen pantry and was on the move.

Blake stayed with her. When she got to the garage and was heading down the drive to her car he caught her. "I'll drive you," he said. "You can deal with your phone while I drive. I'm calmer and faster."

She gave it about one second of thought. "Do you have your phone?"

He pulled it out of his pocket and traded his phone for her keys and they got in. She gave him the beginning of the directions, out of Thunder Point, headed toward south Bandon and Coquille, then she told Charlie to stay calm, stay on the line; she was on her way. She placed the 9-1-1 call and said she needed medical assistance immediately. She explained her son's condition and even recommended drugs that had been effective before—epinephrine, corticosteroids and magnesium sulfate. She said something very soft to Charlie, then went back to the 9-1-1 operator.

"I don't know what happened. He was fine this morning—
no wheezing, no symptoms—and now he can't explain because he can't talk… I'm a nurse. I'm on my way, I might beat
you there… Yes, he had an EpiPen and when I asked about it
he just said 'lost.' That isn't like Charlie… Yes, I'm coming,
Charlie…"

She had a phone to each ear, would stop briefly and say
"next left" or "right at the light."

Blake was cautious but fast. He wouldn't mind if he picked
up a cop who pursued them. In ten minutes' time he was in
a very different part of town—it looked like an industrial
area full of storage units and fenced-off areas where big road
maintenance and construction equipment were parked. They
passed a poor excuse for a strip mall—a convenience store,
bar, motel. They drove a little farther, past some run-down
apartment buildings and trashy neighborhoods. The sight of
rough-looking people—teenagers and adults—just hanging
out brought a flood of memories back to Blake.

Lin Su spoke to the 9-1-1 operator in a normal voice but
alternately murmured to Charlie, instructing him to remain
calm, take even breaths. Her foot on the floorboard of the car
tapped wildly but her hands were steady.

"This is it," Lin Su said. "Right turn, sixth trailer in. Oh,
God, they're there! I never heard sirens!"

Paramedics had just arrived. Blake was pulling up as one of
them used a crowbar on the trailer door. It popped open like
an old tin can. He parked Lin Su's car at the front of the trailer
so the paramedics would have an unrestricted exit if they took
Charlie to the hospital. Lin Su was out of the car and running
to her trailer before the car was entirely stopped.

It was then that Blake looked around. There was an old man
with a rake in his hand standing between a fairly decent trailer

and Lin Su's extremely small fifth wheel. He held the rake, though there didn't appear to be anything to rake; it could have been his idea of a weapon. Across from his trailer there were three young men—boys—standing around the back of a truck that was up on blocks. They looked scary, wearing their pants very low on their hips, sporting tattoos and chains, hair scraggly and unkempt, torn T-shirts. He didn't see any gang colors but they weren't Sunday school escapees. There were mobile homes and trailers of every variety, all parked within a perimeter of trees on a dirt patch, no grass. There was one small building—a brick structure that could be a public bathroom or laundry facility—and it was covered with graffiti.

A police car entered the park slowly and stopped near the fire rig, and closely following the police car was an ambulance. Two EMTs got out and pulled out a gurney, moving to the trailer. They stayed outside as if waiting for instructions to transport, so Blake did three things. First, he gave the three thugs the stink eye. Then he went to the officer's car and asked where he might find the hardware to close up and lock that trailer. It was that action that finally seemed to persuade the thugs to wander off. He was given directions to the nearest store. Finally he went to the doorway of the trailer and looked inside.

Lin Su was kneeling on one side of Charlie while two paramedics administered oxygen and managed an IV bag on the other. Charlie was between his mother and the paramedics, eyes closed, fingers twitching a little bit. He looked gray.

Blake tried to stay out of the way for the time being. It was about twenty minutes before the gurney went into the small trailer and came out again with Charlie on it. He appeared to be sleeping; perhaps he'd been sedated. Lin Su followed the gurney outside.

"Is he going to be all right?" Blake asked.

"I think so," she said. "They're going to take him to the hospital in Bandon, and if he doesn't improve right away, they'll move him to Pacific Hospital, closer to North Bend."

"Go with him," Blake said. "I'm going to see if I can close up your trailer. I'll bring your car and meet you there. Let me see the phones, please?" She dug around in her purse and handed them over. He quickly punched his number into hers and handed it to her. "If his condition or location changes, give me a call, will you? I'll see you at the hospital as soon as I can get some kind of a lock on this door."

She looked at him in complete gratitude. Her eyes welled with tears. "Thank you," she said so softly he barely heard her.

"No crying now," he said. "It's going to be all right. Just stay with Charlie."

THREE

Closing up that little trailer turned out to be far less complicated than Blake had expected. The elderly man with the rake
informed Blake that he had tools he could loan and together
they fixed a padlock onto the mangled door. During that exercise Blake had seen a little bit of the inside of the trailer. It
was cozy and compact—a bed that folded out when a table was
lifted up, a galley kitchen, a bedroom with a small double bed
that took up almost the whole room, a little bath with shower.

Right in the middle of what would serve as kitchen/living
room/bedroom, right where he supposed Charlie had collapsed and paramedics tended him, things were messy and
awry. The table was pushed up, the bed/bench shoved back,
tracks of dirt on the floor, clutter left behind from opening
packages of gloves, wipes and syringes. Everything else was
shining clean, tidy and spare.

It wasn't much of a house for a woman and teenage boy.
It was so small, leaving little room for belongings. He spied
Charlie's backpack with his laptop in it and scooped it up to

take to the hospital with him just in case Charlie didn't come home that night. It was a mean little shelter in a crappy trailer park and it stung Blake. He didn't like thinking of Lin Su and Charlie living here when "here" was actually so much better than how Blake and his mother had lived. They'd lived with rats, for God's sake. Rats and gang members and drug dealers.

He took the backpack and closed up the trailer. By the time he got to the hospital it was growing dark. He walked into the emergency room and asked about Charlie Simmons, and who should walk out of the exam area but Scott Grant, Thunder Point's doctor.

"Well, hey there," Scott said, sticking out a hand. "Lin Su said you'd be bringing her car over."

"And I spotted this," Blake said, slipping one arm through the backpack strap and presenting his hand for a shake. "How is he?"

"He's going to be fine but I'm keeping him overnight just to be safe. Besides, he's weak—an asthma attack takes a lot out of a person. And he was sedated, as well."

"What happened?" Blake asked. "He was good the last time Lin Su checked with him."

Scott leaned a hip on the counter. "I haven't heard the whole story yet, but I think he got chased by some bigger kids from the neighborhood. He said he went to the drugstore to get a refill on his meds. They know him there. But he ran into a problem and got chased all over hell and gone—at least a mile—and he was already struggling a little bit, thus the rea-son for the refill. Shit like that used to happen to me—I was a little kid in glasses. But I didn't have asthma. I think going to school in Thunder Point will be easier on him—lot of people to look out for him there. Like Troy. Spencer."

"Right," Blake said. "Except they're not just big kids from

the neighborhood. I saw a few of them hanging around, waiting to see what the cops and paramedics did. They're not your
run-of-the-mill bullies. I didn't see gang colors but I talked
to the cop—they're local hoods, all tatted up, using, holding,
selling. The look of longing on their faces might've been for
the drugs in the paramedics bags. If they chased him I bet they
thought he had money in his pocket."

Scott's expression darkened. "Is that right?"

Blake lowered his voice and leaned closer to Scott. "It's a
rough neighborhood," he said quietly. "I grew up around guys
like them."

"You think Charlie was in real danger?"

Blake raised a brow. "He's in the hospital."

"Yeah, there's that. Think they might've beat him up or
something if they'd caught up with him?"

"No telling. Maybe. Or they might've turned him upside
down and shook the money out of his pockets. The paramedics
used a crowbar on the trailer door so a neighbor and I bolted a
padlock to it but… Listen, I've got a couple of spare rooms not
in use and I'm leaving town in a couple of weeks for a race. I
know the price is right on that trailer, but you think it's possible there's something around Thunder Point that might fit
Lin Su's budget that we could…"

"We'll be fine," Lin Su said, sneaking up on them and cut-
ting him off. "I've been looking. I just haven't had much time.
If Winnie is stable and Charlie is going to school in Thunder
Point, I mean to find something closer."

"Good idea," Scott said. "If for no other reason than you're
too far away if Charlie needs you. If you wouldn't take offense,
we can get our friends looking."

"Can we talk more about this later?"

"Absolutely," Scott said. "But…"

"Until something pops up, we can manage," she insisted.

"Are you going to spend the night here with Charlie?" Blake asked. "Or would you prefer a guest room? I'm sure Winnie has one but so do I—my trainer doesn't arrive for another week."

"I'll be staying here tonight. He's being admitted," Lin Su said. "I'll find a corner to tuck into in case he needs me. Once Charlie is settled in his room I'll drive you home."

"I'll take him," Scott said. "I'll be leaving in another half hour, provided no emergencies come in. Charlie's stable. I just want to do some charting and look in on him one more time, but with you sitting watch I'm not concerned."

"I'll call Grace and let her know that Charlie's going to be fine and they should call the home health care registry to get a substitute for me for tomorrow."

"I'll be ready to go in a little while, Blake," Scott said. Then he went back behind the counter and got on the computer to write his patient notes.

"Can I have a word with you, please?" Blake asked Lin Su.

"Of course," she said. "What's on your mind?"

"Can we step outside for just a moment?" he asked. He swung an arm for her to precede him, leaving no room for discussion.

Right outside and a bit to the left of the emergency room entrance was a small courtyard with concrete benches and some potted plants. There were a couple of trash cans and a perimeter of trees. And, fortuitously, no people at the moment.

He faced her. "Your neighbor and I put a padlock on the door of the trailer. I have the key here with your car keys," he said. "But you're going to have a problem locking it from the inside, Lin Su. For that matter, that little padlock isn't going to keep your possessions safe from some of your neighbors if they..."

"It's not a fancy neighborhood, Mr. Smiley, but we know our neighbors and keep an eye on one another. Regardless of how it looks, they're not all bad."

"Mr. Smiley? We're back to that, are we? Listen to me—for the most part, the folks in that park are decent and neighborly. Your neighbor helped me secure the trailer. He made a point of telling me he looks out for you and Charlie."

"We're completely safe," she said. "Mr. Chester…"

"Is eighty-four and his weapon is a rake. I'm sure you're on a budget—raising a teenage son can be a strain on the pocketbook. But there will be rentals in Thunder Point that fit your needs. Given the circumstances, stay at my house for a week or so while you look at available property and…"

"Try not to be offensive, Mr. Smiley. I know we don't live as well as you but we don't need charity."

"For God's sake, Lin Su, I know more about being poor than you'll ever learn and I've been cursed with more pride than even you. Winnie depends on you and doesn't want another caregiver. Charlie is going to school in town—it starts in less than a week. I like the kid—he's amazing, so clearly you are a good mother in every way. Now here are the facts—I have five empty bedrooms next door to your patient. Until you can find your own place, you should take advantage of the invitation for a number of practical reasons. The most important reason is that I saw those thugs who shook Charlie down for the money in his pocket and that could happen again."

The startled expression on her face made him smile.

"I knew it," he said. "He was alone, headed for the store. They marked him."

"Mr. Smiley, I hope you understand that I find this inquisition very embarrassing and have concerns about how my employer might regard me after hearing all this."

"Then we won't mention it, and if you want to, you can pay rent. But what would be better for me is if you'd just move some things into the loft—a room for you and one for Charlie, your own bathroom. And cook your own food—I'm on a training diet. Ask your friends and neighbors to keep an ear to the ground for available space. No one cares if you live frugally—it's a virtue. Hell, I haven't had my own house in my entire life till a few weeks ago—I'm an expert at cutting out the fat and saving money. But after your kid gets hurt because he's not safe alone there, you have to go to plan B. I'm offering you plan B. Because I like Charlie. You? You get on my nerves. So don't play the stereo loud."

She made a small smile. "You don't like me?" she asked.

"Not that much," he said. "I like the kid—he's smart. I like him even more now that I know he's fighting asthma and an overprotective mother."

"I should probably question this interest you have in my son," she said.

"Question your son. He's an open book, says exactly what's on his mind. And I knew you for five minutes when I believed you'd covered every subject imaginable with your son—warning him off creeps and predators. Since he was three, I bet."

He stopped talking for a moment, put his hands in his pockets and looked down. He quietly added, "I work with a lot of kids. Sports training, encouragement, that sort of thing. It's a well-known fact. It's very well documented. I didn't have any of that when I was a kid and I don't have kids so..." He shrugged.

"So, we about ready to go?" Scott Grant asked, briskly walking out to the courtyard from the hospital. "Lin Su, Charlie is going to his room in about ten minutes. He has responded to medication. I'll check him in the morning...probably early since I have clinic in town tomorrow. I'll discharge him then. So? Ready, Blake?"

"Yeah," he said.

"Mr. Smiley? My keys? The backpack?" Lin Su asked.

"Oh. Sure. I'll talk to you tomorrow sometime. I hope you have a good night."

"I know the staff here," she said. "I've worked with a lot of them. They'll fix me up with something."

On the drive back to Thunder Point Blake asked Scott how well he knew Lin Su.

"Very well. I've worked with her for a couple of years. She specializes in home health care, and in the past two years she's had three patients in end stage cancer and was assisted by an excellent hospice team. When she didn't have full-time patients she worked at any one of the local hospitals. She's an outstanding nurse and her ethics are unimpeachable. I know that she moved from the East Coast to Oregon for Charlie's health—this is a better area for asthma—and attended nursing college in Oregon when Charlie was small. I think she's been a licensed RN for about ten years."

"What about her personal life, home life. Does she date? Have family?"

"Why? Are you interested in Lin Su?"

In fact, he could be, but that wasn't why he had asked. "I'm concerned about Charlie running into trouble again. Both of them, for that matter. Her neighborhood is overrun by thugs. It seems to be a combination of elderly and real rough characters."

"She lives in a mobile-home park, do I have that right?" Scott asked.

"Let me ask you something—do you consider yourself her friend?"

"We don't exactly socialize, if that's what you mean. But she's friendly with the Bandon hospital staff and since she's been in Thunder Point some of the other women, including my wife, have gotten to know her a little more on the social side. I trust her. Yes, I would consider her a friend. What are you getting at?"

"'Mobile-home park' is putting a dress on a pig—it's a dump. It's not that it's poor, though it is. It's the whole landscape— down the street from a bar, a no-tell motel and a convenience store that seems to be a clubhouse for hoods. I've offered her a couple of bedrooms while she looks for something closer but she's very suspicious of me."

"Why would she be?" Scott asked.

"My own damn fault. I befriended her son and I'm pretty sure I came across as critical of her overprotectiveness. Do you think you can come up with something in Thunder Point that's cheap but decent? Obviously she's very proud."

"We have a sketchy neighborhood or two," Scott said. "For that matter, we've had some pretty severe bullying issues the past couple of years. The school personnel and sheriff's department are all over it, but I'm just saying—changing neighborhoods doesn't solve all the problems."

"It can reduce them by half," Blake said. "Trust me."

"So, what is it you think I can do?" Scott asked.

"I think you, given your familiarity with the town and your influence with friends and neighbors, can find her something without shaming her in the process. I'd be willing to try but I already offered her space and she didn't go for it."

"And I offered to enlist the help of friends in looking around for her and she put me off," Scott said.

Blake leveled a stare on him. "Do it, anyway."

★ ★ ★

Charlie rested comfortably but Lin Su didn't. Her heart was heavy and her mind troubled. She had devised the plan to keep him home from Winnie's and the beach as a punishment for not following her rules. She could justify it, of course—he was coughing and he shouldn't be around Winnie. But she knew it was manageable, not likely to be a virus and she thought it might cause him to be more careful in the future.

What had Blake meant when he said he knew more about being poor than she would ever learn? Did he have some twisted hope of comforting her by admitting he had come from modest roots? All that statement really meant to her was that he had taken note of their impoverished living conditions. He must certainly wonder—nurses, especially home health care nurses, were well paid. The problem was that Lin Su wasn't able to work twelve months a year. When she was finished with one patient it might be weeks or months until she had another full-time charge. And in those periods in between, the hospitals weren't always hiring.

At the end of the day she still did better in home health care than in a clinic or hospital, but it wasn't enough to pay all the bills and create a family home for herself and Charlie. Charlie had stopped having daytime babysitters only three years ago; babysitting and day care were mighty expensive. She was nearly finished with her college loans and the five-year-old car would be paid for in another year—those two items would add significant cash flow. And the fact that Winnie was providing her a premium health care package worth eight hundred dollars a month was a godsend. Otherwise, Charlie's one night in the hospital would cost her the earth! The best insurance Lin Su could afford had a high deductible and poor coverage.

In short, no matter how you looked at her finances, money

was tight. Yet she made too much money to qualify for assistance. County or state assistance was a double-edged sword—it made her feel ashamed to accept it and deprived when she no longer qualified.

It was on nights like this that she spent wakeful hours thinking about the strange journey her life had taken.

Lin Su's adoptive parents insisted it was not possible for her to remember her early childhood, but that was merely their denial. She remembered some things vividly. She lived with her mother and several other Vietnamese immigrants in the Bronx in an apartment that was so small they literally slept on top of one another. Lin Su's mother was born in 1965, the daughter of a Vietnamese woman and an American GI, that's how she managed entry into the United States when she immigrated. A church sponsored many refugees, Lin Su's mother among them. Lin Su was born in America, her American father unknown. Lin Su's mother, Nhuong Ng, moved from a refugee camp to New York. And after three years of that, her health failing, she gave Lin Su into adoption.

But Lin Su remembered her mother. At least snippets of her—young, beautiful, sweet. She remembered playing with other children in their small rooms. She remembered her mother's singing and crying. There was a swatch of cloth—six inches by nine inches—embroidered with silk thread that Lin Su had clung to, her adoptive parents unable to sneak it away from her. Lotus in spring, her mother called it. Eventually she hid it because she knew they wanted to cut her off from her past. She remembered the day she was taken by the man in the suit to a building and given to her parents. Her new mother, Marilyn, brought a dress for her to leave the building in and shoes that hurt her feet. She remembered crying loudly and her new mother yelling at her to stop, and her voice was so brittle and harsh that not only did she stop crying, she stopped talking altogether for a long time. She remembered she spoke a little English and expanding on it came hard but her new family hired a teacher who visited her—they repeated words, read, wrote, cyphered. She was not allowed to speak Vietnamese. They began to call her Lin Su, though her name was actually Huang Chao. For many years she did not understand—they wanted her to have an Asian name but not Huang. Marilyn said it sounded like a grunt, not a pretty name.

They took her identity. She became Lin Su Simmons.

Then one day she was with her new mother in a store and two old Vietnamese women were whispering about her with her white parents, called her a derogatory name indicating she was an orphan no one would take and her parents had adopted her for status, not for her worth. She thought she was about seven at the time. And without thinking or planning, Lin Su had shot back at them in Vietnamese, *My mother is a queen and my father is American, you ugly hag!*

The women ducked and ran. Marilyn Simmons was mortified and one of her older sisters, a blonde and biological Simmons daughter, laughed hysterically at their mother's outrage.

Her birth mother had told her, *My father is American and your father is American and these men have failed us.* Her heritage was lost, but for the scrap of embroidered cloth and two faux-gold coins given to Nhuong by her father.

Lin Su had two sisters—Leigh was ten years older and Karyn was fourteen years older. Since Lin Su was three when she joined that family in their rich Boston home, that made her sisters thirteen and seventeen. They attended boarding school and from the time Lin Su arrived until she departed at the age of eighteen her sisters were merely visitors. Later, Lin Su would attend the same boarding school, a prestigious academy located in the Adirondacks. There were family holidays together, Karyn's wedding after her graduation from Bryn Mawr, some trips they all took together. But there were also holidays that her parents were abroad or in the islands and Lin Su stayed at school, one of very few students abandoned while most others spent Thanksgiving or Christmas with their families.

She never bonded with her sisters, unsurprisingly. She had liked them, however. She looked up to them and envied their blond hair and amazing style. Lin Su had friends at school— she was quite popular and very smart. But her older sisters were chic and had fabulous taste. They were also complete opposites. Karyn married a man from a rich banking family, divorced him when she was thirty and married a richer man from a more elite family. She had two children she mothered in much the same way Marilyn had mothered—with a nanny. Leigh had not yet married by the time Lin Su left the family, but she had graduated college, done a tour with the Peace Corps and traveled quite a bit. Lin Su often wondered if either of them ever came home to Boston and said, "What? What do you mean she's pregnant and gone?" But then why would they? They had given no indication they loved her.

It was her senior year at the academy that she began dating Jacob Westermann. Jake was a big, sexy athlete and she adored him. She went with some of her girlfriends to his rugby matches at a neighboring boy's academy; they went to each other's dances; they made love on the sly in any private place they could find. He had been her first.

And her last.

Her parents were very firm—she was to terminate the pregnancy and go to college as planned. She had already been accepted by Bryn Mawr, her mother's alma mater, and Harvard. Her parents' charity had extended itself to its limit. They were

not supporting her while she raised a child with no father. To
her shock and horror, Mrs. Westermann was of like mind.
These two upper-class women who spent so many hours drum-
ming up money for good causes from crack babies to animal
rights would not acknowledge Lin Su and Jake's baby. Jake was
little help. *God, I'm sorry—I was careful. I'll get you some money.
You can take care of it.*

She had no option but to leave. She looked for work anywhere and finally was hired in a dry cleaning/laundry shop.
The owner was Chinese and rented her a room in the back of
his house—a converted garage. She worked by day and went to
cosmetology school by night and then found a Vietnamese nail
shop where she was grudgingly accepted, though her language
skills were rusty at best. In retrospect she realized she took that
route to spite her parents—she went back to her roots and before Charlie was born she had polished her language skills. Her
uppity parents had no idea how women like her, immigrants
from a war-torn country, struggled to acclimate in this complicated country.

Though she worked very hard she still had to accept the
charity of those people who would help her. She relied on social services and free women's clinics for medical care for herself and her baby, shared what seemed like a million apartments
with other nail technicians, hoarded her money like a miser,
shared child care and transportation. By the time Charlie was
three she had socked away enough savings to get to a place
better for all his allergies and asthma—she moved to Eugene.
She worked and went to school, studying nursing, and when
Charlie was six she had a degree and a decent job in a hospital.
Charlie was getting allergy shots, and while they still struggled
with viruses because of his weakened immune system, he fared
well. When he was in school, he excelled.

And here she was, sitting at his bedside, asking herself if she'd been the cause of this latest asthma attack. She could do a little better than that shitty trailer park. They were both at risk there, though they'd been lucky so far. Charlie was an expert at avoiding trouble and keeping the door locked. But she lived in fear. Some of those hoodlums in their neighborhood could turn that little fifth wheel on its side if they wanted to. It might be safer to live in the car, except they needed a kitchen, a bathroom with shower, a food source.

She would not leave Charlie home alone again. She would bring him to Winnie's and make sure they were kept apart as long as Charlie had a cough, even if that cough was benign. And she'd get about the business of finding better lodging. At once.

FOUR

When Charlie was discharged from the hospital, Lin Su took him with her to the hardware store, but asked him to wait in the car. There was always a list of handymen posted on the bulletin board and she used her cell phone to call one. She explained about the lock on the trailer door being destroyed by paramedics, thus probably saving Charlie's life. The man she spoke to, being sympathetic, offered to meet her there right away.

Charlie was breathing much more smoothly; there was no rattle and a very infrequent cough. But he was exhausted. An attack like the one he had took its toll, not to mention the strain of so many drugs to get him going again. He was listless. But pumped full of fresh oxygen, his color was good.

The lock operation wasn't complicated or involved and she wondered if she could have done it herself. When the repairman finished and had been paid a whopping seventy-nine dollars, Lin Su took a badly needed shower. She couldn't coax

Charlie to do the same so they agreed on a washup and change of clothes.

"How are you feeling?" she asked him for the hundredth time.

"I'm fine," he said. "Stop asking me."

"We'll go to Thunder Point, then," she said. "I'd really appreciate it if you'd have a quiet day. Very quiet."

"I'm not quiet enough?" he asked irritably.

"You're annoyingly quiet but you know what I mean, Charlie. Stay in, nap, don't even do a lot of talking. Rest your lungs and throat. I'm sure we won't be staying long. I told Grace to call a substitute for me today."

"I can stay home, you know," he said. "It's not like I'll open the door or go for a walk."

"I understand completely, but should there be any kind of problem, like a broken pipe, I'd rather be close to the action," she said. And they both knew she was not in any way concerned about a broken pipe or electrical short, even though that old fifth wheel was a piece of junk. "If we leave early because I'm not needed or if there's a break while Winnie naps today, I'll be scouting around town for a rental."

He said nothing.

"I thought that might get the slightest smile out of you."

"I'm saving my strength," he said.

"Then I will also save mine!" she snapped back at him. Of course, then she felt bad about her tone. He was tired and the sedative probably had not worn off. He was depressed. This was typical. Not only had the attack zapped his energy, it also left him feeling hopeless. He'd snap out of it in a day, maybe two.

She left Charlie sitting in the car and went to the door. Rather than walking in as usual, she knocked lightly. She hadn't seen any vehicle in the drive, but it was possible the substitute nurse had been dropped off. And since Lin Su had asked for a sub, she wouldn't intrude upon the family by walking in.

Troy opened the door. "Well, I wasn't expecting you! How's Charlie?"

"He's doing very well, thank you. I wanted to come by to make sure you knew we're back on track and if you need anything…"

"Come in, Lin Su. Where's Charlie?"

"I asked him to wait in the car until I could be sure we're not intruding on your nurse and Winnie."

"Ah, Winnie wouldn't have another nurse," he said, running a hand around the back of his neck. "I'm staying home today and Grace will close up the shop a little early, bring dinner home with her and settle Winnie for the night."

"Who's there?" Winnie yelled from the bedroom. "Who's at the door?"

"It's just me," Lin Su called back. "Just stay where you are and I'll…"

Before she could say another word, Winnie came shuffling out of the bedroom on Mikhail's arm. "Well, it's about time! I've been waiting to hear from you! You know, as much as I hate the look of those walker contraptions, I think I should have one, don't you? I can't be calling for someone to walk me every time I want to move! Where is my boy? I want to see him! I thought I'd have to force Troy to take me to your house."

Lin Su's eyes got larger than they'd ever been. *The very thought!* "But I called Grace three times! Charlie is with me. If you'll just sit down and get comfortable, I'll get him. For goodness' sake," she said, shaking her head at Winnie's aggressiveness.

Charlie was out of the car before Lin Su could fetch him.

And when she got back to the front door with Charlie in tow, Winnie had not taken a seat, nor had she gotten comfortable. She was waiting right there in the foyer, holding Mikhail captive with her arm through his.

"Well, at last," she said to Charlie. "I don't think I slept one minute last night!"

"She slept like the dead," Mikhail said testily. "Snored like a freight train."

Charlie laughed. It was the first smile Lin Su had seen. "That figures," he said to Winnie. "You better sit down before you fall down. Go on, then."

Grumbling something about ingratitude and having no secrets, she turned and hobbled toward the great room where she lowered herself into her favorite chair. Charlie followed. He sat down on the sofa, backpack on the floor.

"Well, you look decent. I guess you're fine," Winnie said.

"I'm fine," he assured her.

"I'm told you were chased by hoodlums," she said.

"They're druggies from the neighborhood," he said.

Lin Su winced. Could their circumstances sound any worse?

"Thing is, they'd rob a nun on Easter Sunday, they're such lowlifes," Charlie went on. "I think they rip off houses sometimes—a habit is an expensive hobby and we know they don't work. But the cops hang around a lot, trying to keep the neighborhood clean. I was looking for a cop—but you can't ever find 'em when you need 'em."

"Good Lord," she said. "Do they live near you?"

"In the area," Charlie said. "I think they're from those Section 8 apartments on the other side of the road. I've seen them around there. You know—affordable housing for the working poor? It's a HUD thing."

"Really," Winnie said, arching a slim brow.

Lin Su met Troy's eyes and his eyes laughed. How like Charlie to know all about it and Winnie to not have a clue.

"I'm sure you have some Section 8 housing in Thunder Point," Charlie said.

"I think I lived in it," Troy said with a laugh. "I lived in a real crappy apartment complex, old and cheap, right on the edge of town. I added about five dead bolts to my door." He shrugged. "I'm a schoolteacher. Without a master's degree."

"Charlie, did those boys give you a hard time at your old school?" Winnie asked.

Charlie laughed at her. "Winnie, those guys don't go to school. The guy next door to us, Mr. Chester, used to give me a ride so I wouldn't have any trouble on the way. School was okay. Once you got there."

"Have you had breakfast?" Lin Su asked Winnie.

"Yes, of course. Has Charlie?" she asked.

"I ate some sludge they call breakfast at the hospital—it was gross. What have you got?"

"Charlie!" Lin Su admonished.

"Make the boy an egg, Lin Su. I'll have one, too. Thank God you're here—everyone is out of sorts without you. We'll have toast. I'll have tea and Charlie will have apple juice. Milk will just make him phlegmy, right, Charlie?"

"Right," he said, pulling his laptop out of his backpack and opening it up. He began clicking away.

"You should try a cup of tea," Winnie said. "It would be good for you."

"I'd rather have another asthma attack. Hey, look at this. Average pay for a schoolteacher without a master's is about forty-two thousand. I don't think you qualify for Section 8, but if you work at it..."

Troy ruffled Charlie's hair. "Thanks, bud. Well, now that

the first string is on the field, I think I'll go to the shop and see if Grace needs me. Then set up my classroom for Monday."

"Is time for walking the town," Mikhail said. "Thank God!"

Troy headed for the garage to take his Jeep to town while the old Russian went in the direction of the beach to begin his day of wandering. Winnie and Charlie began entertaining themselves with whatever his interest of the day was on his laptop.

With a sigh, Lin Su took to the kitchen.

Ten minutes later she delivered two trays to the living room—each held an egg and toast, on one a cup of Winnie's favored tea and on Charlie's tray apple juice. While they ate, Lin Su checked out the bedroom and bathroom. With no nurse or housekeeper to start out the morning, things were a little upside down. She muttered about the lazy men under her breath as she straightened the bedding, folded clothes, cleaned up the bathroom, started a load of wash. Though it only took her ten minutes, she wondered that no one could even attempt order in her absence.

When she got back to the living room the trays with dirty dishes were sitting on the coffee table and Charlie and Winnie were gone. She spotted them on the deck, just as Charlie was helping Winnie to her chair. *Aeiiiieee!* she thought, holding her tongue, her hand against her heart. She tried to remain calm as she followed them. Talk about the blind leading the blind! A weakened asthmatic boy and a woman with ALS whose balance was horrible at best and her strength flimsy.

"Just what are you doing?" she asked her son. "Why didn't you call me?"

"I told him not to," Winnie said. "Really, I think I must have one of those atrocious walker things. God, I hate them! But I hate landing on my ass more! Lin Su, I want you to go fix yourself two eggs, toast and maybe some meat—there's that microwave bacon or turkey sausage in the fridge. Troy eats both like candy. Then I want you to go to the guest room and lie down for an hour. You're cranky and you have dark circles under your eyes."

"I'm fine. I..."

"I didn't ask if you were fine. I told you to eat and rest. I'm not breaking in another nurse and I want life back to normal."

"I'm not hungry, thank you."

"Charlie said you haven't eaten and I know you haven't slept. Go. Now. We're going to look up some things."

"No moving around until I'm back," she ordered. "Charlie is not trained in assisting patients."

Lin Su pursed her lips in an angry line, but neither of them bothered to look at her. She went to the kitchen and in exactly four minutes she had scrambled and eaten two eggs and a half slice of toast. Screw the bacon, she thought rebelliously. She went to the guest room, angry at being told what to do. She slipped off her shoes. Her eyes got a little teary as she lay down, flat on her back, hands folded over her waist. *I am not tired*, she thought furiously.

Lin Su awoke with a start, heart pounding, the sound of laughter coming from the other room. She jumped up, slipped into her clogs and rushed into the living room. There were Grace, Blake, Scott Grant, Winnie and, on the floor with his laptop balanced on his crossed legs, Charlie. A soiree. While she slept.

"Oh, I'm sorry, Lin Su," Grace said. "We were being quiet!"

"No, we weren't," Scott said. "But we meant to be. I just stopped by to check on Winnie and Charlie, both of whom are well enough."

"I came over to get the latest on Charlie, but seeing your car..." Blake said.

"And Troy took over at the shop for a couple of hours so I could come home and ask Mother if she needed anything. I'm glad you had a little rest," Grace said.

"I wasn't tired," Lin Su insisted.

They all laughed and she looked at her watch. "Oh, God," she said, dropping her gaze to the floor. She had slept for three hours! Lunch! She'd missed lunch! "I'm so sorry. You must be starving, Winnie!"

"No, you will be starving. We've eaten. Charlie made sandwiches for us. Except for Blake, who eats tree bark, seaweed and unborn animals."

"It's not as bad as that," he said with a laugh.

"What you eat actually sounds worse," Winnie said. "You had a very good rest, my dear. How you thought you weren't exhausted is a mystery."

"I didn't realize..."

But her son narrowed his eyes at her. He didn't like that she never expressed a need or weakness.

"You were right, I was a little tired," she relented.

"I'm accustomed to being right about everything. Ask my daughter. Now fix yourself something to eat and join us. There's gossip. Grace can tell you all about her former assistant, Ginger, who fell in love with a Basque farmer and ran away to his farm to marry him."

"I'm going to get back to the clinic," Scott said. "I know this story—I married a Basque woman. Same family. Charlie, you have my number. You know you can call me anytime. If your meds run out or aren't doing the trick..."

"Yeah, thanks, Doc. I got it."

"Lin Su, when you have some time, let's have a conversation

about running a few routine lung function tests on Charlie as a follow-up," Scott said. "We should do an assessment of his progress or the lack. Just give me a call."

"Absolutely," she said. "Thank you."

Lin Su went to the kitchen to make herself a half sandwich. Because the house had an open floor plan, she had no trouble hearing the story. She knew most of it, anyway, if not the finer details. She'd been on the scene since June. That's when Grace and Troy got married; Grace had a little bun in the oven already and her assistant, Ginger, helped set up all the flowers for the wedding. The person who hadn't gotten all the details was Winnie, who was lapping them up.

"When Ginger thought Matt was taking her for granted, not calling her back when he said he would, she just changed her number. That got his attention. After that it was almost smooth sailing until Ginger insisted that Matt confront his own failed marriage and make peace with his ex-wife, who he hated."

"Your father had an ex-wife he hated," Winnie said. "We had no conflict with that. I hated her, too."

"Well, we're talking about different people and it all worked. Matt made peace. Ginger was so proud of him and so touched. I caught her crying in the workroom. So I told her to pack a bag and go! Matt's the man she's been waiting for all her life. She wants nothing more than to make a home for a family, and boy, does he have family. He's one of eight—Peyton's younger brother and a partner in the Lacoumette farm with his father and brother. It's a match made in heaven. I offered to do the flowers."

"Grace, I had no idea you were such a romantic," Winnie said.

"I had no idea I was romantic, either, till I met Troy," she said.

"Gag," Charlie said.

"You wait, little man," Grace said. "Some girl is going to come along someday and twist your tail good!"

That made Lin Su smile. Then she saw Blake coming to the kitchen. He stood beside her and looked at her with kind eyes. Bedroom eyes. His thick lashes hooded his striking blue eyes.

"I think you're feeling better today," he said softly.

"Considerably," she said. Then she sighed, looked down and shook her head sadly. "My apologies. Winnie was right. I was out of sorts."

"Who wouldn't be?" he returned.

"I had the lock repaired, so you needn't worry that we're not safe," she whispered to him.

She could see a troubled look cross his face. That lock was the least of it and they both knew it. If those creeps could chase a defenseless kid in broad daylight they could assault a small woman as she walked from her car to the door. For that matter, they could grab a crowbar and pop open that door.

"My offer stands," he said. "You wouldn't be in the way. In fact, I might not notice you're there."

Oh, she would never! "That's so kind of you," she said. "I am grateful. We'll be fine."

"I've offended you," he said. "I'm sorry. Maybe someday when you know me better... Well, let's just say I would never criticize your choices. Clearly, you're a survivor. But I apologize if my offer..."

"No, think nothing of it." She cut the sandwich in half and transferred it to a plate. "Let's join the party." And carrying the plate, she went to the living room.

Lin Su did consider Blake's offer of housing in spite of herself. In fact, her pride came so hard. She wanted to be safe, comfortable and warm; she wanted the best for her son. There was some ingrained part of her that fought so hard for the pride that made accepting charity a last resort.

On the weekend, the last weekend before the start of school, there seemed to be a lot of socializing on the beach and around Cooper's bar. Families were getting ready to be free of the kids, teachers were preparing for the first week of school. A group of cheerleaders were practicing on the beach and Spencer told Lin Su that the nights of fall were filled with fires on the beach, cheers and laughter from the teens, usually following the football games.

On Sunday while she was sitting on the deck with Winnie and Troy, three familiar women came walking down the beach toward the house.

"There they are," Troy said with a grin. "The belly brigade. I thought they were having lunch with Iris."

"And dessert with Winnie and Mom," Charlie said. He was sitting on the chaise, laptop open.

Lin Su just looked down shyly, but Grace had told her that morning. In fact, Lin Su was invited to Iris's for lunch, but she respectfully declined, saying Winnie might need her. And so Grace had told her to catch up on whatever chores there were so she could join them. It was a beautiful, sunny day and they'd sit out on the deck, so Lin Su went inside to find place mats for the table.

By the time Lin Su was wiping down the table before the place mats were set down, it was obvious that Grace was carrying a pie and Peyton was carrying a grocery bag that probably held ice cream.

"We're gonna want to get out of here, Charlie," Troy said.

"They have pie!" Charlie said.

"Winnie will save you some," Troy said. "Let's go throw

the Frisbee around while they talk about stretch marks, due dates, birthing plans and other boring stuff."

"Will you save me pie, Winnie?" he implored.

"You know you don't even have to ask!"

Before they could make a getaway, the women stopped them on the beach. Iris spent a lot of time talking to Charlie while Grace and Peyton were laughing with Troy. And finally they were on the deck.

"Look at this," Grace said. Lin Su had the table set with dessert plates, napkins, forks and cups. She had brewed two pots of tea and added cream and sugar to the table. "This is so perfect. We're having a tea party!"

While Lin Su was loath to admit it, the time she spent with these women was wonderful fun. They laughed so hard they had to pee. For the pregnant ones, this was an issue—one at a time they were skittering off to the bathroom. Winnie laughed as hard as the others.

They had due date issues—it seemed they were all due within a few days of one another, all planned to go to Pacific Birthing Center, had the same OB and midwife. They described scenarios in which they were all in labor at the same time, ready to give birth simultaneously. Grace confessed she didn't know the gender of their baby—she had a bet with Troy. Iris was having a girl—the Sileskis were famous for making boys so the baby girl would be so welcome. Peyton said she and Scott knew but weren't ready to tell. She wouldn't even divulge the colors of the nursery.

They talked a bit about Ginger and Matt. Peyton had the inside scoop being both close to Matt and her mother. "She's living on the farm in an RV. A swanky RV that Matt says is a rental and he's going to upgrade that to an even nicer model.

They'll be in it for a year while they're building their house near the orchard."

"God, what an awesome place to live!" Grace said. "Lin Su, someday we'll take you and Mother to the Lacoumette farm—in the spring when the orchard is in bloom."

"Late spring," Peyton said. "When the planting is in full swing, when they're shearing and lambing and Mama's garden is ripening. When the pear trees are in full bloom. Winnie, you will be amazed by the beauty!"

"Is it handicap accessible?" she asked wryly.

"There are so many big men," Grace said. "You'll think you've died and gone to heaven. Mikhail will be so jealous."

"Lin Su, we'll bring Charlie—and his EpiPen! There are insects. And we'll bring Scott—he's almost as good as an EpiPen. We'll have a caravan," Peyton said.

"Ginger came to get the rest of her clothes last week. We had a dinner out to say a proper goodbye to the girls. It was not sad," Grace said. "I've never seen anyone more in love, more ready for the next phase of her life. Hey!" she suddenly exclaimed. "She came to gather up the last of her things! The loft is empty again!"

Everyone just looked at her, not understanding.

"Lin Su, didn't you want to get closer to town? Well, it's there if you want it." Grace bit on her lower lip. "It's very small, probably much smaller than you're used to. There's only one bedroom, but it's a pretty big bedroom, and the couch is a pullout. Oh, and the kitchen is hardly anything—tiny—but if you and Charlie are having a lot of meals here, maybe that wouldn't be too inconvenient. I lived in it for over a year. It's kind of great actually."

"I wouldn't want to impose…"

"Impose?" Winnie asked. "If someone doesn't live in it, it

will sit and mold. Troy and Grace put the furniture and TV from his apartment downstairs. That loft is like an adorable little tree house. I've seen it exactly once—I was charmed."

"Well, Mother. You never said that!" Grace said.

"I think we weren't getting on at the time. But it is darling, Grace. Lin Su, you should consider it. At least look at it. Small but comfortable."

Lin Su smiled and nodded. They thought she couldn't live in a small space? That made her happy—they didn't know how little it took to make her happy. "I have a very tight budget. Single mothers all do," she said. "But I'd love to see it."

"Maybe later?" Grace said.

"I would love to, but today I'm leaving right after Winnie is settled for the night. Charlie and I have a few things to pick up for school—just incidentals—and I want to get him home for a good night's sleep. Maybe tomorrow? When I have a break?"

"Perfect!"

The girls and Winnie enjoyed themselves so much that Winnie's nap was cut short. While she rested, Grace and Lin Su tried their hand at a meat loaf, mashed potatoes and asparagus dinner. The rolls came from Carrie's deli; the asparagus was contributed by Mikhail, who purchased it at a farm stand; Troy peeled the potatoes and the meat loaf recipe came right off the internet, thanks to Charlie.

Soon after the table was cleared Grace sent Lin Su on her way. "I know you have a little shopping to finish on your way home. Let me get Winnie settled tonight. You and Charlie go on."

"I'll take you up on that," she said. "We're both excited for the first day of school. I'll see you in the morning."

Lin Su and Charlie drove to the nearest Target. She had already taken care of his clothes and shoes but still needed school supplies and a new jacket. She wasn't sure if this was a happy coincidence or if Grace was doing a good deed. She was aware that Ginger had moved out and that Grace wouldn't be living there any longer, but what she didn't know for sure was whether Grace could use the space for her business and decided to sacrifice it because Lin Su was looking around. Also, although it was said to be very small, Lin Su was aware—Grace and her mother had very high quality possessions and excellent taste—it might be an expensive rental and out of her reach so she didn't even mention it to Charlie.

But then they pulled up to the fifth wheel and Lin Su's heart sank.

"Oh, my God!" Charlie cried. "Shit!"

Lin Su didn't say anything about his language. For a moment she didn't even know what to fear. The trailer had been broken into—the door stood open. Just six inches, but still. It was dark and ominous.

"Stay in the car," she said.

"Don't go in there," Charlie said. "You never go in a building when you don't know who's in there." He pulled out his cell phone and dialed 9-1-1, reporting that the padlocked door had been pried open.

All Lin Su could do was look into what was her home. She didn't recognize it. It was torn apart, things she didn't even recognize strewn everywhere. Her mind raced—she didn't have anything of real value, just the most necessary articles of daily living—linens, clothing, pots and pans, dishes... She'd always felt safe from burglars—there wasn't much to steal. But there were pictures! She ran to what served as her bedroom, turning on lights along the way. She pulled out the drawer under the bed and it was still there—her album. She wasn't just frugal with money, she was also frugal with space. She had kept some pictures from her childhood in Boston and there were the pictures of Charlie as a baby and toddler. And they were safe.

Then she spied the small closet, the door literally ripped off—and it was gone, her box of treasures. It was a wood and ivory box, not very big. It didn't hold much and the street value would be nothing. Less than nothing. It held the hospital bracelets she and Charlie wore after his birth, his first tooth in a small envelope, two faux-gold coins, a chain and pendant given to her by one of her sisters. And the swatch—the lotus embroidery. The only thing she had of her biological mother.

She fell to her knees and started searching the floor of the closet, the backs of the shelves, under the bed. "No no no no no," she whimpered. Why take that? It was worthless. Even the box itself couldn't be worth twenty dollars! She crawled around the room, stretching her hands under shelves, into corners, even under the bedding. She reached into drawers that had been rifled through and, without realizing it, she was speaking Vietnamese. Rapidly. Breathlessly. Mournfully.

She cried. Then she began to hum softly as she searched.

Charlie stood in the bedroom doorway. "Send someone, please," he said into the phone.

Then he disconnected and found another number, one recently put into her directory. He clicked on the button. The man answered, "Blake Smiley."

"Yeah, it's Charlie. Need a little help here, Blake. Our trailer—it got ripped up, torn apart, and things were taken. Things my mom really loves. I don't know what to do."

"Did you call the police?" Blake asked.

"Yeah, but… They'll send someone when they can. They

said we should file a report. It could be a long time since there's no imminent danger—no robbers here. But I think we have a problem. My mom. She's broken."

FIVE

When Blake pulled up to the trailer it didn't look as though anything was amiss. When he went to knock on the door he could see the lock was broken and the door was closed but not latched. Still, he knocked.

Charlie opened the door. "Sorry, Blake. I guess I could've called Troy and Grace, but my mom, she worries a lot about people feeling sorry for her, especially people she works for. She's the caregiver, y'know? She always has to be the strong one. The together one. I'm the only weakness in her life."

"Don't start that," Blake said. "You're her kid and she takes good care of you. That's not a weakness."

"All I'm saying is I'm the only thing that keeps her from going to work. Like if I get sick or something. And I know you offered us a place to stay overnight if we needed it so I thought..."

"You did the right thing. I'm glad I was able to take the call. Now what's happening with your mom? You said she's broken?"

"Look," Charlie said, nodding toward the bedroom.

Blake could hear soft humming. He was a little perplexed, but he looked. Lin Su was kneeling on the bed, folding clothes, rocking and humming as she did so. He looked a little more closely—they were mostly Charlie's clothes and it appeared some of them might have been damaged. He wasn't sure if these were just clothes hard worn by a fourteen-year-old boy or if the vandals had done it.

"Was anything taken?" he asked Charlie.

"It's kind of hard to tell, it's all such a mess. A couple of things for sure, my mom's winter coat—she hung it in the bathroom. She said it stayed fresh that way as there was no room in the closet and she wouldn't keep it near the cooking. And her treasure box. It was little." He demonstrated, using his hands. "It just had a few things in it—no jewelry or anything. There were two gold coins she said came from her grandfather, passed to her mother, passed to her. It was rumored he was an Army officer, but there's no proof. She said keeping them safe in a refugee camp was a miracle. Our wristbands from when I was born—hers and mine. A crucifix and beads given to her by a Catholic sister at a hospital once when I was a patient. But the most important thing she had was a swatch—her mother embroidered some lotus flowers on a cloth and it was the only thing she had of her mother's."

"Have you talked to her? Is she in shock?"

"I think a little bit. She's been talking in Vietnamese— she only knows a little. She was adopted when she was a real little girl, like two or three, so it's amazing she remembered any. But she worked in a couple of manicure shops that were owned by Vietnamese and picked some up again. She was born in America. I think this Vietnamese stuff... I think it's stress."

"Okay," Blake said, rubbing a big hand down his face. "What is it you want me to do?"

"I don't know. We have to get out of here—the door won't close. I wasn't sure I could convince her…"

"Right," he said. "Go try to make some sense of the mess in the living room and kitchen. Do a little straightening, figure out what's missing if you can."

"What if they come back?" Charlie said.

"That would make my day," Blake said, eyes narrow, jaw clenched. "Those three dopers who chased you the other day?"

"Seems like. But you gotta wonder why they didn't do it sooner. I mean, we've been here nine months."

"Maybe we'll figure it out later. Right now we have to get this place under control, pack up some things, leave. You work out here. Let me see to your mom."

Blake went into the bedroom. He scooped up a pile of clothes off the floor, dumped it on the bed, knelt by Lin Su and began folding. There were jeans and board shorts and T-shirts and sweatshirts. Some looked as if they were stained with paint and he instinctively knew they hadn't been like that before. Some were ripped. Slit. It looked as though a pocket knife could've done the damage. He tossed those in a pile. And some were all right, completely salvageable. Those he folded.

She didn't speak; she just carefully folded clothes from her pile, then began taking clothes from his pile. They proceeded like that for a few minutes before she looked up. "Why are you here?"

"Charlie called me," he said.

"He shouldn't have called you. We can manage."

"Either you're a very messy housekeeper or you're not managing that well. We should pack a few things."

"I can take care of it," she said.

"I don't know you very well, Lin Su," he said. He continued to fold. "But I know you like to do your work, pay your way, take care of your son and responsibilities. But sometimes you have to be humble. Sometimes when you have an opportunity, you have to be gracious and not stubborn. You are so stubborn."

"Stubborn is strong," she said.

"Stubborn is also pigheaded and counterproductive. Tomorrow is Charlie's first day of school and you really shouldn't stay here tonight—it's obviously not safe."

"There's a motel…"

He put his big hand over her forearm, stopping her from her task. *Was she talking about that shithole down the street?* He couldn't stand to even think about it. "Save that money—you're going to have to buy a new winter coat. They ripped it off. And some of these clothes will have to be replaced."

She stopped, holding a pair of jeans in her lap, looking at him suspiciously. "Why do you have a house with so many bedrooms and beds? Are you opening a brothel?"

A short burst of laughter escaped him. "Good idea!" he said. "I have a team and associates. I have a coach and trainer. I usually have a couple of people staying with me two weeks before a race. We travel together for the race and I always give myself a couple of days of training in either a different time zone or altitude. I train almost year-round but hit the training hard before a big race. I used to rent space for my team. I told you, this is my first house. The bedrooms, it turns out, will come in handy."

"I can afford the motel," she said. "I have savings."

"You're a mule," he accused, but he grinned when he said it. "Let's make sure Charlie is comfortable—tomorrow is a big day. Most of all, let's lower his stress if we can—he's very worried about you. And if you stay here or in a seedy motel tonight, he won't sleep."

"I am always there for Charlie. He can depend on me."

"Awesome. I don't suppose you have a suitcase?"

She glanced around. "I had a couple of large duffels—I don't see them."

"I have a couple of gym bags in the car. I'll dump them out so you can borrow them." He looked at her and just shook his head. "You know, I usually do well with the girls. I make them laugh. I'm charming."

"Perhaps the problem is that I'm not a girl," she said.

"Perhaps the problem is that you're obstinate and inflexible," he suggested.

"If you find me so thoroughly flawed, why offer all this assistance?" she asked. "It's a little invasive, you know. I've been through worse. It's a temporary setback, that's all."

"This is an emergency," Blake said. "You'll stay the night so Charlie can get some sleep and have a good first day of school. Then we'll look at the options. Do you own this trailer? Can we move it to the property? Cooper has a hookup beside the bar. He has a trailer he brings out of storage for a guest room when family visits and we could put yours…"

She was shaking her head. "I rent it."

"Then gather up as much as you can and we'll put the padlock back on the outside. Maybe you'll come back for more of your things when Winnie is resting. If you need help, I'll help you. Let's do this," he said, getting off the bed.

He went to his car to dump out his duffels. He took a great deal of time on the easy project so that Lin Su could talk to Charlie if she was so inclined. While he was standing there he heard someone yell. It wasn't a bad yell, more of a whoop, as if there'd been a touchdown on the TV. Then he heard bottles being dumped in the trash. He saw movement and caught the motion of a person skittering around the cinder-block building. He pulled out his wallet, slipped some bills into each pocket, then threw his wallet in the trunk.

He reached into the trunk for a tire iron and a large industrial-strength flashlight. It had been a very long time since he felt he could be in danger from a bad person. Fifteen years at least. Really, since he was thirteen or fourteen he hadn't rubbed up against many scumbags who just flat-out *enjoyed* hurting people. In fact, in all his years, if he ever had anything that could pass for a weapon in his hands—a brick, a bat, a broken bottle—it was because he was in defensive mode, staying alive.

He slammed the trunk, turned on the flashlight and headed across the drive to that brick building. The smell of urine and feces was disgusting. Chances were good that it hadn't been cleaned in years. For the first time he noticed a ramshackle trailer that had a small sign posted. Manager. M–F 10:00 a.m.– 4:00 p.m. He'd check that out later.

He walked around the brick structure, shining his light, and came face-to-face with one of the thugs he'd seen the day Charlie was chased. The guy grinned. His teeth were black and he had a couple of sores on his face. Meth teeth, meth sores. It was the kind of leer that made Blake want to look behind him but he wasn't falling for that one. The guy slowly pulled his hand out of his pocket, gave a small flick, and the blade of a switchblade zinged into view.

Blake took a fast step closer to that knife, swung the tire iron and came down on the guy's wrist. The meth head screamed, dropped the blade and grabbed his wrist. Before he could run or call for his backup, Blake had him up against the bricks, the tire iron against his throat. "Where is it?" he asked as threateningly as he could.

"Ach. What?"

"You know what. The box."

"Let go and I'll tell you."

Now it was Blake's turn to grin. "Not a chance in hell. Where?"

"Bruster's got it!"

"Who's Bruster?"

"You know. The manager."

And probably the biggest dealer in here, he thought. Some things were as predictable as sunrise. It was always the one in charge, the one who seldom got his hands dirty. "And did it get you a hit?" he asked.

"Not even." He choked and Blake stepped back a little. He was an addict; it could get messy.

"Let's go get you a hit, loser."

"You gonna roll me?"

"I'm gonna buy you a hit if I can get my box back."

"You'd do that?"

"I want the box!"

Blake turned him around, twisted his arm up behind his back and counted his blessings. If this charged-up idiot decided to fight him, he might have a real problem on his hands. He'd seen three and four cops have trouble bringing down a one-hundred-and-twenty-pound meth addict when he was high. His flashlight was under his arm, light pointing forward, and the tire iron in his hand, ready.

"Let's go get it," Blake said, steering him in the direction of the manager's trailer. When they stood outside the door, he saw a little trash on the ground right outside the trailer door.

"There it is," the guy said, looking down.

He saw what looked like a small amount of smashed teak wood on the ground and a little unidentifiable trash—paper, cloth, picture, chain. "That's my box?" Blake asked, incredulous.

"He wasn't impressed."

"What's a hit go for in your neighborhood?"

"Twenty," he said. "I mean, forty. Fifty."

Blake felt himself smile. It had been a long time. He had forgotten how much drugs rotted the brain and what liars addicts were. "Here are your choices," he said. "I can give you some money and you can run, get out of sight, or you can stay and talk to the manager with me. Or I can beat you stupid with this iron, but I think you already are stupid."

"You kidding me? Give me fifty and I'm gone."

Without turning the guy around, he pulled one bill out of his pocket. It was a twenty. He shoved the man away from him and he stumbled a few feet. Blake braced himself, wielding the tire iron in one hand and flashlight in the other. The twenty fluttered in the hand that held the iron. "Do you want to disappear with twenty or would you prefer to negotiate?"

As if by magic, his two compatriots stepped out of the darkness and they were a little bigger. But they were ratty and pale. They were vampires; they lived by night. He was one on three. Reasonably, his chances were zero and it was stupid to engage them. This was the time to run. They were high and strong; he was sober and his strength wouldn't matter. So he smiled as though he had confidence, twisted the iron and flashlight, worked his shoulders a little bit and took a couple of wide swings with the tire iron.

The junkies separated, one left, one right, one head-on. One picked up a rock, one produced a knife, one held his pained wrist. Blake didn't waste any time. He took out the knee of the guy with the rock on his left, then hit the arm holding the knife with the flashlight. He jammed the guy in the gut with the tire iron, then gave his ankle a hard whack before shoving the tire iron into the gut of his first boy. He whirled and caught one in the neck. There were a couple more whacks to legs with the iron, then higher. With any luck he'd injured a couple of ribs. Hurt leg joints and bruised ribs could really slow you down, provided you could feel pain. He hit one under the chin with the flashlight and the man sprawled, groaning. His first aggressor limped away while the other two were in the dirt.

He was surprised. He wasn't much of a fighter anymore. He was lucky or they were impaired. And he was out of breath. He tried the manager's trailer door but it was locked. So, tit for tat, he applied the flat end of the tire iron to the door and popped the lock. He peered inside.

Bruster appeared. He was fat and wore a wife-beater T-shirt. *Why are they always fat?* Blake asked himself. The biggest crook and dealer on the block was a lazy, fat blob. With a gun.

Blake put up his hands and backed away a little, though he still held the flashlight and the iron. "You can shoot me if you want but it'll make your life miserable, I swear on the Virgin Mary. It'll bring down the wrath of every Catholic cop in the state because I'm... I'm a priest. And all I want are the two gold coins and the other contents of that box."

"Who the hell are you?" Bruster asked.

Blake straightened proudly. "Father Blake Smiley."

The guy laughed. "Get outta here," he said, reaching for the door.

Blake put the flashlight against it. "I want the stuff."

"I don't know about stuff. I found the coins. They're not valuable," Bruster said.

"Then I'll make 'em valuable. I'll buy 'em from you. I have to have them. They were blessed in Versailles. They're holy.

And your flunkies told me you have the coins. Now come on—let's just deal."

Bruster looked around Blake in time to see one guy limping away, one struggling to his feet and the third lying on the ground holding his knee and rocking side to side. "You did that? And you say you're a priest? You're no priest!"

"They send all priests to defensive tactics training now. You want a search warrant or do we deal for the coins? I told you, they're holy!"

He didn't put down the gun, but he did dig out two small gold coins from his pants pocket. "Now I've seen it all," he muttered, holding the coins. "Two hundred bucks," he said flatly.

"I don't have two hundred bucks! I'm a priest!" Blake glanced over his shoulder, then slipped the flashlight under his arm and pulled forty dollars out of one pocket and another twenty out of the other. He tossed the money into the trailer. "Now, what are we gonna do? You stole them, after all. And I do still have a cell phone, if you don't shoot me."

"I wouldn't mind shooting you," he said. "Here." He tossed the coins one at a time.

"I need a bag or something."

"I don't have a bag!" he shouted. "Get outta here!" He pulled the door closed.

Blake looked at the losers he'd just done battle with. They weren't coming at him, but he had to keep an eye on them. That meant kneeling with his legs almost under the trailer and his weapons close at hand. He began scooping the remnants of the small teak box into his pockets along with the items on the ground, which may or may not have been the contents. He recognized the hospital wristbands and swatch, both very dirty. There was a cheap chain, perhaps once silver in color.

A broken locket, a shred of paper, a cross. He shone his flashlight around for a rosary, but didn't see it. He ran his hands
through the dirt, coming up empty. There was some loose
change—he scooped it up in case it had meaning. A hair clip,
a flat silver ring, an old watchband. Finally satisfied that he'd
looked enough, he went back to Lin Su's trailer.

When he opened the door to go inside he was stopped by
what he saw. Lin Su and Charlie were stuffing piles of clothes
and other possessions in large trash bags. He had forgotten
the duffels.

He started to tremble. He had a flashback and saw himself
as a small boy, seven or eight years old, helping his mother
stuff their meager belongings in plastic bags. That was how
they moved from place to place and they moved all the time
to keep ahead of dealers, pimps, junkies and social services.
When he was thirteen and they came for him, removing him
from his mother's guardianship, he left with a bag of clothes.
A small bag of clothes.

He shook himself. "Hey. We gotta get out of here fast. I
mixed it up with a couple of your hoods and we gotta go.
Now."

Lin Su and Charlie looked at him. He knew what they saw.
He was glistening with sweat even though the night was cold.
He was panting a little—equal parts fatigue and nerves. He
shook a little from some adrenaline and the flashback. He wondered if the flashbacks would ever go away. He held his flashlight and tire iron like weapons. He put them on the ground
by the steps into the little trailer.

He stepped inside, grabbed a full bag and took it outside,
throwing it in his car. He went back for another, then on his
third trip Lin Su and Charlie each had a big bag to stuff in the
backseat of her car.

"Charlie? Backpack and laptop?" he asked.

"In the car," he said.

"I'm going to follow you, Lin Su. If you have any trouble, I'll be right behind you." He picked up his weapons and took them to the front seat of his car.

After Blake had pulled into the garage at his house, Lin Su backed into the drive for convenience's sake. She wasn't pulling four giant trash bags of clothing and miscellany into his house; she wasn't planning to stay long. But she would move the bags he had into her trunk, leave the bags she and Charlie brought in the backseat, and they could pick through them for usable clothing. She was now very grateful for that last-minute shopping run for Charlie's school supplies and jacket. She took her Target bags with her into the house.

Blake held the door for her to enter through the garage.

"Can you leave the garage door open for a little while? I have to get into some of those bags and find clothes for bed and the morning."

"Sure," he said. "I'll leave my car keys on the kitchen counter so you can move your things from my car whenever you like. And you're welcome to use the washer and dryer if necessary. There are clean linens in the loft bathroom and on the beds. The kitchen is all yours. There's tea on the counter, drinks in the fridge, muffins, frozen yogurt, fruit. Have a snack. I'm going to get a shower but I'll be awake awhile. It's not very late—help yourself to the TV."

"You won't even know we're here," she said.

"I want to know you're here," he said. "I want to know you're both here and no more of your belongings will be taken or destroyed or... Oh," he said. He reached into the cupboard for a ceramic bowl and began emptying his pockets into it. The shards of teak and contents of the box were mixed with dirt. "The guy smashed it and I think most of the stuff was lost. The pieces of the box are too small to put it back together, but..."

She stepped closer. The dust from the dirt rose in a miniature cloud. She recognized the hospital wristbands, then heard the clink of two gold coins. She stepped closer. The swatch, filthy, joined the other detritus that comprised her treasures. She grabbed it, unfolding it, gently brushing it. It was going to take a miracle to restore its color, but it was whole.

She lifted her eyes to his. "This is what you were doing," she said in a near whisper. "This is what got you in a fight."

"Yeah. Well, I saw one of those guys, the ones that chased Charlie, and it pissed me off. I knew they'd done it." He grunted and shook his head. "I'm psychic."

"Mr. Smiley..."

"For the love of *God*!" he snapped. "Call me Blake!" He calmed himself. "Or Father Smiley. But no more Mr. Smiley!"

Her eyes were startled. "Father Smiley?" she asked.

"I told Bruster I was a priest so he'd give me back the coins. And not shoot me."

"Awesome!" Charlie said from the back door. "He had a gun?"

"Yeah. I was pretty safe. He's a dealer, you know. The head thug in the trailer park. He wasn't going to shoot me—someone would call the police. If it had been anywhere else he might've, but not where he does business. Too risky for him." He looked at Lin Su. "I probably didn't get everything," he said.

"You shouldn't have risked it," she said. "Thank you, it means the world to me, but you shouldn't have risked it. What if something worse had happened to you?"

"Worse?" he said.

"You're hurt. If you like, I could clean that up. You need an ice pack…"

"Nah," he said, ducking away from her. "I'm fine. Get settled. Have tea. Eat something…"

Then he turned and went down the hall to his room.

Blake closed his door and turned on the shower, hot. He looked in the mirror and almost jumped back in surprise. His eye was swollen, his chin was cut, a lump was rising on his cheek and his nose had bled. It appeared he'd absently wiped it across his cheek. His shirt was torn in two places. And he'd never been aware of taking a single hit.

He'd blacked out. It had been a long time since that had happened.

It wasn't that he didn't remember anything. He could be so single-minded, so focused, the only important thing was his mission and survival. It had started when he was a kid—he could force himself to act without thinking. He'd be chased by some hood and he'd run and hide, then he'd catch his breath and realize he was two miles away. He could do that in a race—concentrate so hard on the task at hand he had no memory of the landscape. He'd know where each competitor was and what he had to do. It didn't happen to him all the time, just when the stakes were high. He gave the credit to his discipline but it was probably more than that. One of his counselors when he was much younger said it was a form of PTSD. As long as he was functional, the therapist wasn't too worried about it.

He stripped and got into the shower.

He'd been very stupid; he could've been hurt. He was always careful; he didn't even ski. Triathlons were his career and he didn't take unnecessary risks. But after seeing that destroyed little trailer, after hearing from Charlie what had been taken from Lin Su, after seeing that meth head ducking behind the building, he was utterly driven. He went after them, equal parts revenge and quest to get back that little box. He was incensed. Taking her useless little treasures had been so cruel. Men like them enjoyed being cruel.

Really, he didn't think any of them had gotten off a shot at him, but his face bore the truth—he'd been hit at least three times. He'd been grabbed hard enough to tear his shirt. He was filthy as though he'd rolled around in the dirt. Maybe that came from scooping up the contents of that broken box? He'd never really know.

He put on a pair of sweats and a clean T-shirt and went into the kitchen. The bowl was gone and a dim light from the loft came down the stairs. There was a light over the stove left on. He checked the garage—the door was down.

He got ice for his swollen eye and turned on the TV. He put his feet up and did a little channel surfing, volume low. He hoped Charlie would hear and come downstairs. He'd like an update on how Lin Su was doing.

He didn't see them again that night.

SIX

Lin Su crept around like a thief; she didn't want to disturb Blake. He'd looked as though he needed sleep. She kept shushing Charlie. She lifted a chair at the kitchen breakfast bar rather than sliding it and warned him to be extra quiet. She didn't want to avail herself of Blake's food but there seemed no other option unless she wanted to walk with Charlie to the diner. His first morning at a new school was now awkward enough.

And how did you spend your summer vacation, Charlie?

Well, let's see, I was chased by drug dealers and landed in the hospital and then my buddy, who is an Ironman by the way, beat them up after they ransacked and vandalized our trailer. He got hurt, but he got back my mother's little treasures…

"Are you nervous about the school?" she asked in a whisper.

"A little bit," he said with a shrug. "I don't expect to have a hard time. I have my schedule. Cell phones have to be off and computers aren't allowed."

"Are you allowed to turn the phone on at lunch or anything? To text me that it's going well?"

"You're going to have to be very brave and wait for me to come home," he said. Then he grinned his goofy grin.

She found granola in a canister on the counter and yogurt in the refrigerator. There was fruit in a bowl, blueberries in the fridge. No milk. She mixed granola and fruit with the yogurt for Charlie. Since she was going that far, she decided to help herself to tea and a muffin. She sniffed the tea cans and voilà...he had green tea! She didn't make a sound as she filled the kettle and got out dishes.

She felt a giggle come to her lips. This Ironman on a training diet with all the überhealthy food didn't live like any guy she'd ever known, not that there were many. Neat as a pin, all organic, healthy and pristine food... Where were the beer and chips?

"Try not to crunch so loudly," she whispered to Charlie.

He moved his mouth very slowly, mocking her. How could his chewing wake Blake?

Then she heard footsteps and after just a few of them, Blake appeared coming up the stairs from the basement. He was sweaty, a towel draped around his neck.

"Good morning," he said.

"You're awake!"

"I've been awake for ages. I was on the bike for over an hour."

"You were right down those stairs? Don't you grunt or pant or anything? Doesn't the bike make noise? Didn't you have any breakfast?" she asked. There were no dishes on the counter or in the sink.

He waggled a banana skin at her. "The bike is quiet, isn't it? It better be." He mopped his face with the towel. "I didn't hear you, either."

"I thought you were asleep and warned Charlie to be quiet."

She peered at him and then winced. "Ew," she said. "I'm so, so sorry. If Charlie hadn't called you…"

"If Charlie hadn't called me, we don't know what might've happened. Except, we both know you wouldn't have your things back. Charlie and I have an understanding—if he needs me, he'll call me. It would be all right for you to do the same."

"Please, could we not mention this to my employer?" she asked softly.

"No," he said, shaking his head. "No, we have to be honest about this, Lin Su. These kind of secrets—they just don't work. The fact is your house was broken into, damage was done, things were taken—it wasn't your fault. You have a place to stay here for now. Be straightforward about that. It's also not your fault I got a couple of bruises—that's my doing. And it was really stupid of me to chase down those guys. I shouldn't have. After seeing the mess they made I was so pissed off I did it without thinking."

As usual, she was hiding all the wrong things. She didn't want to talk about the fact that her treasures included a baby wristband, swatch of cloth, hair clip and two faux-gold coins given to her mother by her GI father. It made her feel like such a peasant.

"You're right," she said. "I'll explain. Charlie, brush your teeth. I think Winnie will want to see you before you start your first day at a new school."

"Can I leave my laptop upstairs? Or should I put it in the car?"

"Leave it upstairs," Blake answered for her. "I'm going to swim, then run, but I should be around when school's out. You won't be separated from it any longer than necessary."

"Thanks," he said, jumping off his stool.

When he was gone, Lin Su began rinsing his dishes. "Mr.…

Um, Blake," she corrected. "I don't expect you to understand this, it makes no sense, but when something goes wrong, like our trailer being vandalized like it was, it somehow makes me feel incompetent. Like a failure. As if I'm not capable of taking care of myself and my son. And Winnie is too generous. I guess she can afford to be, which is wonderful for her, especially now as she battles ALS. But just like it makes me feel like a failure when I can't keep trouble from my door. I don't like to take handouts."

"I do understand, as a matter of fact. Your stubborn pride is familiar to me. But there are times—when the need is genuine and certainly not due to laziness or entitlement—you have to go with humility and gratitude, get on your feet and pay it forward. I've been there, Lin Su."

She tilted her head. "You say things like that—that you understand being poor, that you've had your own hard times. Someday you'll tell me what you mean by that."

"Someday I will," he said. "We actually have a lot in common even though I don't have children. One of the things is this—we don't get along all that well but I think we have a common mission and respect for each other. If I found myself suddenly homeless due to some misfortune I couldn't control or prevent, you would offer to help me. You'd offer me a place to stay out of the cold and rain, no matter how little space you had to share. So let's leave it at that. You're no beggar. You had a bad day—I had extra room."

We really should get along better than we do, she thought. "I'm very grateful," she said. "Thank you. And if I get any more humble, I will be an ant."

He grinned at that. It made him wince.

"You really got pummeled," she said.

"Yeah," he said, ducking away from her perusal. "I'm an

idiot. Those guys are on meth. That means they have no brains and extraordinary strength. I knew before I chased the first guy what that could mean. I'm going to work on being smarter."

"Do you get in many fights?" she asked.

"I can't remember ever provoking one before, but if anyone asks, it was self-defense." When she began adding dish soap to the water in the sink he stopped her. "Stick them in the dishwasher, Lin Su."

"Listen," she said. "I'm looking at a small loft in town today but I haven't told Charlie. It's very nice and might not fit my budget—we'll have to see. I don't want him to get his hopes up."

"You can stay here while you need to," he said. "It really doesn't disturb me."

"You said something about a team, a trainer…"

"My coach will be here in a week—there's plenty of space for her without disrupting you. We'll be all about business and training. After a week of that, I'm going with my trainer and part of her team to Lake Tahoe where I'll train for a week at altitude before the race. I'll be back immediately following the race. By myself."

"But if I'm still here, where…?"

"There is a guest room beside my room and one downstairs. I have my equipment and an office downstairs. I don't need the loft. We could disturb you but you couldn't possibly disturb us."

"Hopefully this small space in town will work out," she said.

Charlie, no longer concerned about waking Blake, came pounding down the stairs, jumping the last four and landing with a loud thud. "Ready?" he asked his mother.

Blake smiled at him. She wondered if Blake had any idea how good-looking he was, even with a banged-up face.

"Ready," she said. "Let's go."

★ ★ ★

The woman has no idea how exquisite she is, Blake thought. He was used to women who *knew* how beautiful they were, knew how powerful they were.

Lin Su was proud, gentle, as strong as steel, as soft as a cloud, stubborn as an ox. He'd seen her care for Winnie with tender strength. It was true Winnie wasn't a large woman, but she was slightly bigger than Lin Su, yet the nurse handled her as if she were weightless. She could be firm with Charlie, and with himself for that matter. Yet he'd seen in her a sweet kindness unlike anything he'd known. And she was breathtaking to look at.

Their rapport was a little edgy, stumbling along, looking for a way to become friends. He could tell they had a great deal in common and maybe that was why they didn't quite trust each other yet. But even though they weren't exactly friends, or maybe they were very cautious friends, he was impossibly attracted to her.

Alone in his house, he laughed out loud. He couldn't have conjured up a more complicated scenario—she worked next door, she had a boatload of secrets she guarded with a kind of stoic tenacity, she didn't trust him because it looked to her— looked to a lot of people—as though he had it easy. On top of all that, she had a fourteen-year-old son who had health issues and regarded Blake as his champion—a boy who wanted an active and adventurous life despite his limitations. Blake thought Charlie was right to want that. He also thought it was possible. He, with no parenting experience whatsoever, thought Lin Su was too protective. He thought Lin Su would keep Charlie from growing and testing his limits in an effort to keep him safe—polar opposite of what Blake believed was in Charlie's best interest. That alone would pit Lin Su against him. And, in a way, him against her.

He was pretty sure they'd never work out the kind of easy, affectionate relationship he'd like. He was convinced the passion he fantasized about was out of the question. He just hoped they wouldn't kill each other and bang up Charlie in the process of discovering what kind of relationship they'd have.

He took his swim—an hour. He showered and cleaned up and it was still early. He could've gone for a run, but he passed. Instead, he walked next door. Mikhail appeared to be out on the deck so he went by way of the beach stairs. Might as well get it over with—he couldn't hide out for a week while his face healed.

He clomped up the beach stairs to find Mikhail sitting at the table playing solitaire. The old Russian looked his way, did not say anything, but lifted one bushy eyebrow. Blake went to the table and sat down.

"I see you've taken up hockey," Mikhail said.

"Fell off the bike," Blake said.

Mikhail grunted. "Bah. Your jig is up. The little one told us what happened."

"Charlie?"

"Lin Su. She said she wouldn't want Winnie to have a fright. So, you lost your cool, is that it?"

He gave his head a tilt. "That's pretty much it. You should've seen what those fools did to the trailer. I'm sure they turned it upside down looking for jewelry or money, none of which the girl had. They left her in a mess."

"And you avenged her," Mikhail said. "A knight."

Oh, boy, that was the last thing he needed her to think, that he'd be hanging close to protect her, take care of her. He had a hard enough time taking care of himself. On the outside his life looked very well ordered and carefully planned, but right beneath the surface things were a mess. Always had been, always would be. It was a constant balancing act.

"Where is everyone?" Blake asked.

"Her Majesty had the physical therapy this morning so she's having a rest. The little one is in town with Grace, looking at the apartment on top of the shop. Maybe it solves the trailer problem, eh?"

"That's the place she's looking at?" Blake asked. "That's good! That's perfect!" And Grace would be sure it was affordable for Lin Su. "Is it a nice place?" he asked.

"Small but good."

He laughed. "She doesn't take up much space."

Lin Su drove to the flower shop even though she would have preferred a nice long walk. She didn't want to leave Winnie for too long in case she needed something. She hadn't been in the shop before—of course, having no need for floral arrangements—and the moment she stepped inside she regretted that. It was charming yet sophisticated, reflecting Grace.

Grace peeked out of the workroom, her green florist apron stretched over her growing belly. "You're early."

"I hope I'm not interrupting anything important," Lin Su said. "Winnie was tired after her therapy. Mikhail is sitting watch."

"I'm up to my elbows in flowers so why don't you just take the key and go upstairs. Look around. You'll see I left a lot behind when I moved out—Winnie's kitchen is much better stocked so whatever is in my little kitchen can be used or packed up and stored. There are extra linens, too. It's tiny, Lin Su. But the sofa pulls out." Grace handed her a key. "I'm afraid the back stairs is the only entrance but at least there's parking. And I'd be happy to give you a flower shop key so you can go through the shop if you want to enter from the front of the building."

"Thank you. I'll only be a minute."

Lin Su let herself into the loft and just stood inside the door for a moment. It was, as she expected, beautiful. Yes, it was very small, but not much smaller than the trailer, which she had hated so much. Yet this space was furnished richly. There was a dark wood wall unit of cupboards and shelves that held a large flat-screen TV. The sectional was soft leather, the two accent tables were dark wood. No cheap blinds in Grace's loft—the only window had custom wooden shutters. The little kitchen was perfectly functional—small refrigerator, two-burner stove top, microwave, sink and a table that could seat two comfortably. There was no oven.

The loft was long, divided in two. One half was the small kitchen and living room. An arch separated it from the other half, which was a bedroom and bath. Between the sections was a closet on one side and a little stacked washer and dryer plus utility closet for the vacuum cleaner, ironing board and other supplies.

She looked around the bedroom—it was very economically designed—a queen-size bed on a wooden frame, a small foldout desk, an armoire, tiny closet, two bedside chests with drawers and more drawers in the wooden platform under the mattress. She touched the wood of the headboard—again it was rich and fine. It reminded her of the home she had grown up in—the furnishings were tasteful and expensive. She sat down on the bed. The mattress was firm. When she stood again, she smoothed the comforter.

She stayed a little bit longer than she intended. She looked in the bathroom—it was large and comfortable. She sat in the living room facing the TV. She opened and closed the shutters behind the sofa. Well, there was no question about it—she would love to live in such a place. She'd lived in larger homes and apartments, but they were invariably in poor repair in bad neighborhoods. Often, she shared them with roommates to cut the rent. Her first few years on her own with Charlie had been very difficult—there was school and a job and a baby who had frequent bouts of upper respiratory illnesses. Then things calmed down a bit but the past five years with the recession, scarce jobs and rising costs had been difficult. She and Charlie had lived in some real dumps, that little trailer taking the cake.

But this—this beautifully decorated, compact little loft—was not only lovely and comfortable, it was right in the center of town, two doors down from the deputy sheriff's office where Seth Sileski worked. It was not really a place to raise a family but it would be so ideal for a single woman and her son.

Too bad it was impossible. Even if it was priced reasonably it would be hard for her to afford. The furnishings alone made it even more valuable. And Lin Su had already made a decision—she wouldn't negotiate with Grace. Over the years, she'd become a fierce haggler. Even used-car salesmen quaked when they saw her coming. But Grace was her employer. She might take care of Winnie but she knew she worked for Grace.

She went back downstairs. Grace was still busy at her worktable, constructing an arrangement. Lin Su handed her the key. "Grace, it's very beautiful. It's small but so expertly arranged."

"You should have seen what I started with—a completely unfinished attic, full of junk left behind by Iris's mother. She was the last owner of the flower shop, and when she had something she didn't know what to do with, she shoved it upstairs and it never came down again. Iris and I had a field day poking through her stuff. Not much was worth keeping."

"Did you do it yourself?" Lin Su asked.

"I only helped. I had to hire tradesmen—there wasn't even a bathroom up there! But the plumbing was in the right place. I painted, papered, sanded, but no way could I install a tub or toilet. And that arch? That was indulgence—I really didn't need a door that closed for just me." She clicked her teeth. "I suppose that could be a problem with a fourteen-year-old son."

Lin Su laughed a little. "I think he'd like it if I didn't live with him at all. Boys his age resist mothering. But we manage. Our trailer didn't offer much by way of privacy—one pocket door to the bedroom and a pullout screen to close off the bathroom." She shrugged. "It was manageable. But, Grace, I'm not sure we can make this work."

"Ah," Grace said. "Just too small? Not enough storage space?"

"Grace, it's beautiful. It's first class. I'm afraid I have a tight budget. But I'm sure something will..."

"Lin Su, I wasn't thinking of charging rent! If it works for you, use it!"

"Now wait," Lin Su said suspiciously. "You can't mean to just loan it to me."

"Why not? I didn't charge Ginger rent."

"But she worked for you!"

Grace laughed. "And who do you work for?"

"But I don't work in this flower shop! The loft is part of the flower shop!"

"You could help me with the electric bill, but I use so much more than the loft ever uses. Does a third sound fair? It could be as high as a couple hundred dollars. It's the refrigerated flower case—it's a big energy suck. Maybe we should say a fourth? But even though that's a lot, you'll save on gas over time. Not much of a drive to your job."

"But, Grace, the furnishings alone…"

"You like the furniture? Oh, I'm so glad! This is the lucky result of two people who have had their own homes combining households. Troy and I took what we wanted from each apartment. It left some nice things in the loft so it's ready to live in. Of course, if you have your own things and it gets too crowded, we'll just store some things."

Lin Su took a breath and reminded herself—gratitude and humility. She had been honest with Winnie about the break-in, the destruction. "After last night, that isn't going to be a problem."

"Oh, Lin Su, was the loss terrible?"

"Actually, no," she said, giving her head a little shake. "The things we really need, we took. I'll drive back over there in the next day or two to make sure there isn't anything important that I forgot, but all things considered, we were very lucky. And thank God Charlie wasn't home while I worked!"

"Well, if you choose to live upstairs, I can promise you Charlie will be safe when he's at home. I'll be in the shop until closing. We have as many issues as any small town but it's pretty safe around here. If you have any concerns you can always talk to Seth. He's such a wonderful deputy—I just love him."

Lin Su just shook her head. "You all have been so generous."

"Generous is good," Grace said. "But really, I don't happen to see it that way. You're better than the best nurse my imagination could conjure up. And I think Charlie is very good for my mother. They're like best pals. I suspect they have secrets and plots but don't let on. Winnie needed someone like Charlie right now—he's completely honest all the time and Winnie gets a little more life in her when Charlie's around. And Charlie doesn't take any of her shit. Refreshing. Between Charlie and Mikhail, Winnie is kept human!"

"And the women come to her house for tea or a drink," Lin Su said.

"She's never had that kind of life," Grace said, shaking her head sadly. "She's always been somewhat apart from the mainstream of life. Oh, she had friends, don't get me wrong. But where are they now, these society women Winnie socialized with for years? They don't visit and rarely call. Winnie needs to feel family right now and that's exactly what she has. We're an odd family—me, Troy, Winnie and Mikhail—but people act as if we're perfectly normal. If you and Charlie can be part of our strange little family it would make me so happy."

"You really do so much for us. You've only known us three months!"

Grace laughed a little wildly. "By the time I knew Troy for three months I was pregnant! I have pretty good instincts. So? You want the place?"

Lin Su nodded. "I'll treat it with great care."

Charlie was not as thrilled about the use of the loft as his mother was, but then he didn't crave independence for his family, just for himself. He liked staying with Blake right next door to Winnie, Mikhail, Grace and Troy. He couldn't see any reason why his mom wouldn't take Blake up on his offer to give them the two bedrooms in his upstairs for a while. For some reason she had a hard time accepting a gift like that from Blake.

He wasn't disappointed in the loft in town, not in the least. It was clean and nice. Lin Su insisted on settling Winnie for the night before taking Charlie to the loft, their new home, and then she brought in their clothes, one garbage bag at a time. She was busy with the washer and dryer, folding and putting things in drawers, until after midnight. He slept in spite of her fussing around.

His first day of school was fine. He met a couple of people who were nice to him, his teachers all seemed cordial. Lee Downy, Frank's younger brother, sought him out and said, "Hey, bud, if you need anything, let me know." Lee was a big guy and if Charlie needed a good bodyguard, Lee was a definite contender.

A girl who sat next to him in Algebra groaned through the whole class and Charlie finally asked her, "This hard for you?" When she admitted it was, he said, "If you ever need help, let me know." And she asked for his number. It wasn't a girlfriend thing, of course. But Frank was right—be a teacher, a tutor. It couldn't hurt.

This was a red-letter day in Lin Su's mind because Charlie had a new school that he didn't have to walk through bad neighborhoods or run from druggies to get to and they had new digs at an affordable rent, practically free. But that wasn't what was foremost on Charlie's mind. He had a bigger, secret project in the works. He knew his mother had fictionalized some of her past, *their* past, and he was making some headway in finding the facts. First of all, he located his grandfather's business address—Gordon Simmons. He was, as Lin Su had said, an attorney in Boston.

Lin Su checked Charlie's computer regularly to be sure he wasn't getting into any trouble—she'd look through his browsing history, his apps and programs; she probably even read some of his emails. They never talked about it but she told him he used the computer by her consent and she would be checking. A couple of times he saw her with his laptop and knew she'd been snooping—once when he came out of the shower, once when he woke up after being asleep awhile. And she asked to use it a few times to pay bills, something she could do as easily on her smartphone.

He didn't mind. He was smarter on the computer than she was and covered his tracks. He joined a couple of professional networking links that were free; he joined Facebook but didn't have an accessible page. He had a lot of Google searches but his surfing tracks weren't visible in his cache.

Once he found Gordon Simmons he started poking around for Lin Su's adoptive sisters—Leigh and Karyn. Karyn was tough—she'd been married a couple of times, changing her last name each time, and he'd had to search public records. But Leigh Simmons was easier. She was either single or had kept her last name. She was a professor of anthropology at Rutgers. She'd done a stint in the Peace Corps and was a big supporter to this day. He liked her face and he thought she might respond to him if he got up the nerve to get in touch.

All this would hopefully lead to two things. One, he didn't think his biological father was really dead. Charlie wasn't sure of his name. Just asking would get Lin Su a little riled up. She said his name was Jake, that there was no family, that it was unimportant to discuss and it had been such a hard time for her. Charlie bought the hard time, but not the rest. You don't love a good man and not even keep a picture!

The second thing, Lin Su said his grandmother had been in such ill health, she gave Lin Su into adoption, but that didn't mean she had died. Lin Su never knew for sure what became of her. She had that one picture—his grandmother as a little girl, sitting on an American serviceman's lap. It was taken in the sixties. Lin Su had no other pictures of her mother, just her name—Nhuong Ng. She would only be around fifty if she were alive.

Charlie wanted to find his roots.

SEVEN

It took Lin Su only a couple of days to get herself organized and comfortable in her new small space, working on laundry and sorting in the evenings and early mornings. She felt the need to make a run back to her trailer to look around in case there was something she forgot. She asked Mikhail if he'd be around the house while Winnie napped so she could do that and Winnie said, "Take Mikhail. Or Blake. But please don't go alone."

"I'll be perfectly all right in the light of day, Winnie. After all, I lived there for nine months without any issues."

"And now there have been issues. Don't fight me on this. I don't need a keeper at naptime—I'm going to rest for two hours. I won't even be answering the phone."

"I'll go," Mikhail said, standing up. "Is good to be safe."

When they were in the car Lin Su tried pleading one more time. "Mikhail, I mean no offense, but I don't think you could protect me if we had a problem. And I don't want you to even see the awful mess left behind—you'll think I lived like a dirty peasant."

"I *am* dirty peasant," he shot back. "I had no bed till I was eleven and then I shared with two brothers. Her Majesty calls me 'scrappy little Russian.'" He pointed forward. "Drive. I hope little bastards give me trouble. I'll bite their noses off."

Just what I need, she thought. But she drove.

As if to hammer home the point that her time in the little trailer was at an end, she pulled up to see the padlock had been broken. The premises had been invaded again, except now that there was nothing of value left it seemed to have been taken up by squatters. There were only a couple of things that had come to mind to fetch— Charlie's nebulizer machine for his breathing treatments, a couple of pans, her old Crock-Pot, the teakettle, miscellaneous junk, stuff she really didn't need to get by or that she could replace cheaply. She stood just inside the door and looked around. There were beer cans here and there. A beanbag she didn't recognize had appeared in the little living room. Beside it on the floor, a syringe.

"Touch nothing," Mikhail said. "We are finished here. We start over. When you think on that it will fill you with a glorious renewal."

She sighed. "It filled me with a feeling of renewal the first ten times I had to start over…"

He looked at her with tired eyes. She didn't know Mikhail's history except that he emigrated from Russia when that was not easily done. And now his best friend, Winnie, was dying, though very slowly and without much suffering. With deep sincerity he said to her, "I know this to be true."

Mr. Chester was standing by her car when they left the trailer just a minute later. He was holding his rake, his weapon. She suddenly realized she had rarely seen him without it. "This place wasn't always like this," he said sadly. "The wife and I put our new mobile home here twenty years ago right before my retirement. It was a pretty decent place. Clean. Safe. Everyone had flowers bordering their patios and the laundry was scrubbed clean. There were good people, friendly like us, but all the good people left. I don't know what happened to it."

"Was the same property manager here then?" she asked.

He shook his head. "We been through a few of them, each one worse than the one before. Do you have a place to go?"

"I do, a nice place."

"Go there, then. Tell that boy of yours I'll miss him."

She gave the old man a hug. "I'll miss you, too, Mr. Chester. Take care of yourself."

She drove away, Mikhail silent beside her. She left the graffiti-filled park, passed the motel, stores, run-down homes and apartments, the fenced-in industrial parks. She was very glad to leave all that behind. *Is it true that you can be poor anywhere?* she wondered. And she decided not to think about that place again.

That was the day her life began to really change. Rather than driving to Winnie's house, working and then driving home, she was now part of the town because she was seen there several times a day. She'd met lovely people before moving above the flower shop but now she was in the mainstream and not a nurse escorting Winnie here and there. People stopped her on the street if they saw her, asking about Winnie, asking about herself and Charlie. Now she had coffee and a pastry at the diner before walking across the beach to her job, and more often than not someone from town would sit beside her—maybe Seth, sometimes Carrie or Peyton or even Grace with her two cell phones, one for work and one personal. She started many days chatting with Gina, who had been working in that diner for almost twenty years. It was Gina who could give her the oral history of the people she knew, starting with how Cooper came to Thunder Point to find out how his long-time friend, Ben, had died so unexpectedly. Cooper stayed on, turning Ben's old bait shop into a nice establishment on the beach, thus the name Ben & Cooper's.

One of the things that surprised Lin Su was learning that she wasn't the only person in town, nor the only newcomer, who had fallen on hard times. It seemed even Gina hadn't had the good life handed to her. "Me?" Gina had said. "Girl, I got pregnant in high school, only sixteen, had to drop out of school to have and take care of Ashley. We lived with my mother until Ashley was sixteen and that's when I married Mac and we combined single-parent households. As for Mac, he had his own struggles—married young, had three kids right away and then his wife left him with the kids, the youngest still a baby. His aunt Lou lived with him and helped raise those kids. That's really how we became friends—we had daughters who have been best friends since they were twelve. We joined forces to get them around and share chaperoning responsibilities."

Then she learned about Devon, the office manager in the clinic. She had been homeless and without family when she was drawn into a cult. A few years later, penniless and terrified, she escaped with her three-year-old daughter, and Rawley found her and brought her to Thunder Point. She had been working to get on her feet and in a position to raise her daughter alone when she met Spencer.

There was really nothing to compare to learning that all those things Lin Su kept quiet—the fact that she was a single mother who had never been married, that she was now without family—were in no way unique. It felt remarkably like a *real* fresh start. So when Mikhail asked her, "How does my little nurse do these days?" she was happy to answer, "Renewed."

As Blake's lumps and bruises faded over the week it gave Lin Su peace of mind. It seemed to not hamper his training schedule. She saw him all the time, taking to the ocean for his swim, riding out on his bike, stretching and then running down the beach road and back hours later.

Charlie was certainly capable of going to the new loft after school. Lin Su always left a snack for him and it would have given him quiet time to finish his homework. But he didn't do that. Instead, he walked to Winnie's where an after-school gathering seemed to become swiftly established. Winnie was refreshed after her nap, Mikhail had returned from his daily meanderings and Blake was done with his workout and wanted to hear about Charlie's daily experiences with the new school and student body. The next to arrive was always Troy and finally Grace. Sometimes Spencer or Cooper would wander down to Winnie's to get an update on the school day. It was like happy hour. The cooking was traded off between Lin Su in the kitchen or Grace bringing home something from the deli. Sometimes Troy or Mikhail planned and executed a meal. Her days were long but fulfilling.

Charlie was getting to his homework at about eight o'clock at home. And he was as happy as she'd ever known him. For Charlie that was saying something as he had always been a very congenial child. She'd often thought that kid, even with all his problems, would be happy no matter what. Yet he was now even happier.

Iris tapped on the back door to the flower shop on Saturday morning and Grace let her in. "There's been a big event in the Sileski home."

"Bigger than that?" Grace asked, pointing at Iris's growing belly.

"Maybe not quite that big, but momentous. Yesterday was my mother-in-law's birthday and last night we had a nice birthday dinner with the whole family. I helped Gwen make some of her own birthday dinner but my sister-in-law also brought her contributions and it was lovely. Her sons brought flowers and stuff. And my turd of a father-in-law gave her a *card*. A card? He showed up at the table as usual in his mechanic's shirt with his name monogrammed on the pocket, sat like a bump, complained the potatoes were lumpy. I was ready to kill him. Everyone bought her such nice gifts. Carrie baked her a beautiful cake and of course Gwen would never complain that her husband of over forty years gives her a stinking card. Then Norm says, 'Aren't you going to open the card?' So finally she does and what do you suppose was in it?"

"I'm breathless," Grace said, still arranging her flowers.

"You aren't going to believe it. A *cruise*. Norm is taking her on a cruise. A long cruise to Vancouver and Alaska. In three weeks. My father-in-law, Norm Sileski, is actually going to spend quality time with his wife."

For a moment Grace just stared widemouthed. "Do you think he'll wear the mechanic's shirt?"

"He wears it to Christmas dinner some years, so why not?" Iris asked with a shrug.

Iris had grown up next door to the Sileski family and last year married the love of her life, Seth, the youngest of three boys. Norm had owned the gas station in town, sold it a couple of years ago, but he still went to work every day. He said Eric, the new owner, needed him. Whether or not that was true was questionable. The more likely truth was he wasn't going to waste his time and talent on bingo and cruises with his wife. He didn't play golf, there wasn't anywhere he particularly wanted to go and he liked his routine. He had seen the merit of selling the station while he could get a good price, however.

"I hope Gwen doesn't live to regret it," Grace said.

"Try to imagine being held captive on a ship with Norm for over a week! I think Gwen should have been more careful what she prayed for. But for just a moment last night, when Gwen opened her card and got happy tears in her eyes, Norm's expression was downright sweet." Then she shook her head. "But he recovered quickly."

Iris pulled out a chair across from where Grace was working. "How are you feeling?"

"Great. You?"

"All right. But I wanted to ride my bike to school and Seth had a fit so I'm driving. I guess he has a point—if I fell, it wouldn't be good. I was always awkward to start with. Now I'm a total tripper."

"Well, now that you mention it, my ankles are already getting fat. And I have a backache. But what should I expect when I'm standing all day."

"Grace, what are you going to do without Ginger?"

"I ran a couple of ads but have only had one call so far and she didn't sound qualified. Ginger spoiled me—she stepped into this shop and ran it. So this time instead of advertising for an assistant, I'm looking for a manager. I suppose that means I'll be giving her most of the income from the shop but at least I can take time off to have the baby and get days off here and there." She sighed. "The hours are going to have to change. No more of this all-day-all-week jazz. Now all I have to do is find someone half as decent as Ginger."

"With Winnie, a baby and your own business…"

"I know. Things will have to change somewhere…"

"I thought Ginger would be here at least another six months," Iris said.

"It's that loft. It's a love nest. First me, then Ginger and Matt."

"Have you warned Lin Su?" Iris asked.

"Warned me of what?" Lin Su asked, just coming in the front door.

Iris and Grace exchanged looks, then burst into laughter. "The loft—someone cast a spell on it," Grace said. "Once a man and woman are alone together up there they tend to fall in love. So if you have plans that don't include love and all its hassles, be careful who you invite upstairs to spend a little time."

"Oh, thanks for the warning!"

"Um, was that a genuine thank-you or do you have someone in mind for the spell?"

"Me? Oh, hell, no! But I'll be sure Charlie isn't alone with a girl up there!"

"Come on," Grace said. "What about your love life? Or at least your fantasies!"

Lin Su shook her head. "Not on your life. I've not only been too busy for a love life, I don't even have time for fantasies. It's me and Charlie."

"Aw, that seems kind of lonely," Grace said.

"It might be lonely for Charlie, but not for me. I'm afraid he's the only guy I'm willing to take a chance on."

"You know what the problem is," Iris said to Grace. "We're off wine, that's the problem."

"We used to meet here once in a while just to catch up. I kept a nice white wine chilled in the cooler, a couple of glasses in my office. It was usually the two of us but if someone else wandered in for a chat with wine, they never left here without telling the whole story."

Iris leaned her head on her hand. "I miss those days…"

Lin Su laughed. "They'll be back, ladies. I have to run upstairs to get something. I have a meeting with Scott."

"Is it about Mother?" Grace asked.

"No, no—I wouldn't meet with him about your mother and not tell you, you know that. Charlie had a couple of breathing tests and the results are in. I want to get my folder of his medical records."

Lin Su usually carried the briefcase of records around with her as if it was a baby. There were always copies of records somewhere, but she feared losing her own file. And thank God she was so protective—she might've lost them in that madness of the destruction of her trailer.

But with the loft, she had no fear of such calamity and kept her briefcase next to the desk in the bedroom.

Lin Su had told a little white lie. There was *always* time for a fantasy or two. She'd had an attraction here and there over the years but not so much as a date. When the man you love and believe in offers you enough money to terminate your pregnancy, it's a slap in the face that doesn't go away quickly. Plus, Lin Su often worked two jobs or was between jobs. And there was always Charlie—there was very little time for socializing. When the opportunity did present itself, she often found herself with people who had children close to the same age or with nurses she worked with.

She'd had a brief fantasy about Dr. Grant, as a matter of fact. She was working in the Bandon hospital, he was on call and Charlie had a bad cold. Scott was always so encouraging, so positive, and there was the small matter that he was handsome and fun. With her usual great timing, she recognized her little crush just shortly before Scott announced he'd found a great new physician's assistant. When Lin Su saw the way Scott looked at Peyton, she knew he was off the market.

She was actually relieved. There was no room in her life

for a man, not even a man as wonderful as Scott. But she was deeply grateful for his friendship.

It being Saturday morning, there wasn't anyone there, just Scott. When she walked in he was waiting and of course Scott asked where Charlie was. "He's more interested in a game of chess with Mikhail than another doctor's appointment. Especially just for test results."

"Can't say I blame him," Scott said. "Well, the results are good. Not excellent but improved. We gave him a lung capacity breathing test before discharging him and another a week later and there was marked improvement once he was fully recovered from his asthma episode. Of course, Charlie will never have the capacity of a healthy fourteen-year-old who has never suffered asthma and bouts of pneumonia. But he's in pretty good shape. His problem is—he isn't going to fare well if he's thrust into the need for a burst of physical stress like he was. It's time for him to change that as much as possible, Lin Su. Charlie has to train. A steady buildup of physical exertion to strengthen his circulation, muscles and breathing endurance. It's important he grow stronger."

"Oh... I don't know... We live in a better place right now."

"Don't think in terms of keeping him safe from bullies and a doctor's pass from PE—think of other situations he could find himself in that can create the same disastrous results. What if he comes across a person in peril and has to run for help? Or what if he's chased by a dog? Or what if he wants to test into a police academy? If he improves his stamina he can be ready for anything."

"You mean, no more medication or inhaler?"

Scott shook his head. "Charlie will probably be on medication at least into adulthood and might be reliant on an inhaler forever, at least as necessary. But he can get much better than he is. More independent."

"He already romps around the beach! He plays volleyball, he hikes."

"He needs more training in controlling and understanding his asthma. I have a booklet for you—it's really just an average overview for the typical asthma sufferer and…"

"But Charlie's not typical!" she said, feeling a little panic set it. It felt like turning him out, setting him free—free of her care, her help. "He landed in the hospital, almost intubated! Very recently!"

Scott was shaking his head. "Not because his asthma is more critical than most, because he's out of shape. Listen, an average kid with good lung capacity could exert himself and be weak and winded for a while, then recover. A kid with exercise-induced asthma is going to collapse, maybe suffer worse consequences. Charlie has been kept still too long, Lin Su. It was necessary, I understand. Now he has to build his strength, then he has to maintain his stamina. He stays on medication, uses his inhaler once a day, or maybe before or after some monitored exercise, improves his capacity slowly…"

"I have no idea how I'm supposed to do that," she complained. "I'm working, and he's in school all day…"

"Stop," Scott said. "Charlie can have a better experience, a safer life. There are Olympic athletes with asthma. They control it with medication and training. Charlie can…"

"Oh, it's *him*!" she said. "This is *his* idea!"

"Whose?" Scott asked.

"Blake Smiley! That first day Charlie rode his bike and got severely short of breath, Blake told him to research famous athletes with asthma! This is his idea! Why doesn't he stay out of my business?"

Scott frowned. "It wasn't Blake's idea, as a matter of fact, but if it had been I would have agreed. I know Charlie and his asthma is the center of your universe but we have many patients who have to be rehabbed, build their strength again to avoid relapse—heart patients, patients with muscle and bone repairs, transplant patients. I guarantee if you sit in front of a TV for two years, even you will have to start over with rehab to get back in shape. Charlie needs to be stronger. And if you have trouble figuring out a plan, Winnie's house sits between two professional trainers—Blake and Spencer. Spencer is the athletic director at the high school and I volunteer as his football team doctor. Either one of them would help you develop a program for Charlie. You could consider it professional help."

"Will you be monitoring this program, as well?" she asked.

"I'll always be around. I'll continue to look in on Winnie every week and if you'd like I can try to time my visits for afternoon, when school is out."

"That might help. Let me read about this a little," she said, holding out her hand for the pamphlet.

"Read about it. And maybe talk to either Blake or Spencer about beginning a training protocol for a kid who hasn't been active all this life."

"Sure," she said. "Thanks."

"You're not losing control, Lin Su. You're helping to manage a chronic condition."

Somehow that wasn't how it felt. "I understand," she said.

Sunday morning Charlie saw Blake go out on his deck with his bike, pick it up and carry it down the stairs to the beach and lean it against the stair rail to put on his helmet. When he looked around, Charlie waved.

Perfect. Blake would be gone at least two hours, probably

more. His mother was in Winnie's bedroom. The door was ajar, which meant they weren't doing anything too serious—probably some exercises or morning tidying. She expected him to keep himself quiet and busy. He grabbed his laptop and slipped out onto the deck and down the stairs.

Since he had to leave his laptop home and was always in very close company with his mother and others after school, his espionage was really suffering. Besides that, Lin Su was seriously researching something about asthma on the laptop when he wasn't using it. Whatever she was learning was bound to restrict his activities—that was always the end result.

He walked down the beach stairs about halfway. Troy and Grace were in their little apartment, windows open to admit the cool fall air, so he went to Blake's house. He went up the stairs almost to the top and sat down. He didn't have to be out of sight, but he didn't want his mother or anyone sneaking up on him. What he was doing took time and concentration. He flipped open the computer and logged on.

Charlie had already established a free email address with a password his mother would never guess. When he researched public records and other sites, like *Finding Your Vietnamese Family*, he always cleared his cache so if his mother checked his browsing history, it wouldn't show up. He'd also set up a phony Facebook page with some picture he'd lifted off the internet and a name she wouldn't recognize. He'd sent an email to Gordon Simmons, his adoptive grandfather, but had not received a response. Gordon would be at least seventy now and he certainly hadn't turned up on Facebook.

But his younger daughter had. Leigh Simmons, college professor at Rutgers, was apparently beloved by current and former students. She was also on sabbatical for the fall semester. He'd tried to "friend" her, but he couldn't reel her in—she didn't know him. Or maybe she wasn't paying much attention to her Facebook page while she was away. He'd sent her a message, which he understood would probably be lost in a buried file or ignored. He'd sent it to the faculty email address on their website.

Dear Leigh Simmons, my name is Charlie and I think my mother, Lin Su, could be your adopted sister. She was adopted when she was three, is Vietnamese and Caucasian American. She left home at eighteen. Do we have a connection?

An answer came back right away.

I'm sorry I missed your email. I'm traveling on sabbatical until late October and will only have limited access to email. If you need information directly, please contact my assistant...

He hadn't bothered the assistant and hadn't heard back from Leigh, of course. He was surfing the internet in search of old family pictures or news from the Simmons family. From newspaper clippings he'd learned that his grandparents divorced shortly after he was born and found pictures of Leigh Simmons in yearbooks and newspapers—her work in anthropology and writing on international human rights was apparently lauded. Even if she turned out not to be an adopted relative, she sounded like someone he'd like to meet.

"Looking at porn?"

Charlie almost jumped out of his skin and slammed the laptop shut. Blake was standing right behind him. He was helmetless now and in his stocking feet, eating an apple with one hand and holding a plastic bag of fruit in the other.

"Jeez, you *are* looking at porn!" Blake said.

"No, I'm not!"

"Well, then, what's up? You panicked just then."

"Never mind," Charlie said. "What are you doing sneaking up on people like that?"

"Aren't you on my property? Not that I mind, but Jesus, cut me a break. I'm not exactly spying on you."

"What are you doing here? I saw you leave!"

He held up the apples. "I rode to the orchard on the other side of 101. The fruit stand." He sat down next to Charlie. He fished an apple out of the bag and handed it to him. "What-cha doin'?"

"Nothing," he said, taking the apple.

Blake laughed. "You sound guiltier by the second."

"I don't need my mom to freak," Charlie said.

Blake chuckled. "Okay, there are some things a guy wants to know that he can't really ask his mom, that's understood. Unless you're researching building a bomb, I'm pretty trust-worthy."

"You're saying you can keep your mouth shut? If it's not a bomb?"

"Or a crime," Blake said. "If you ask me to keep a confidence about something that's not dangerous to yourself or oth-ers, I'm good for it."

"You sure about that?"

"Yeah, probably," he said, taking another big bite of apple.

Charlie gave him a kind of naughty smile. Blake must think he was looking up things like testosterone and wet dreams and the average age a guy loses his virginity. He'd already done all that. "My mother is Amerasian. She doesn't want to talk too much about her family history. Or mine. I don't think my bi-ological father is really dead and I think it's possible her Viet-namese mother isn't, either. Vietnamese refugees were scattered all over the place. A lot of countries accepted them and families didn't all go to one place. Some spent decades finding each other. My mother's father couldn't have been a soldier—she's too young for that. Saigon fell and all the Americans left by 1975 but her grandfather could have been a GI. I'm trying to find out who I am."

Blake stopped chewing for a moment. He started again slowly, finally swallowing. "Whoa."

"Yeah, you can't tell her. When the Vietnamese part of her goes nuts, it's really scary. I'm not real sure how much Vietnamese she really knows, but I'm sure she knows all the swear words. Her temper is stored in the Asian parts."

"Listen, Charlie, she probably just wants to hold on to that information until you're a little older, more mature and able to deal with the facts in a grown-up way."

"No, I played that card. She said there are some things better left buried, and she said a lot of it in another language."

"Aw, man," Blake said, resting his head in his hand.

"Well, it's not a bomb," Charlie said.

"It sort of is," Blake corrected. "Why can't you just look up stuff like how often a guy thinks about sex in a day? Like a normal fourteen-year-old."

"How often does he?" Charlie asked.

"It's perfectly ridiculous how often," Blake said, sounding a little weary.

EIGHT

So, there was a lot more to Charlie and Lin Su than a struggling single mother and a kid with asthma. Blake decided to get his own laptop out and do a little research. Saigon fell three years before Blake was born, eight years before Lin Su was born… The United States had evacuated all military and civilian Americans in 1975; almost all POWs had been returned before that and only a small number didn't make it out with that group. By 1980 there were only a handful of Americans left in Vietnam.

Lin Su had told Charlie that her mother immigrated, sponsored by a church. Lin Su was born in the United States. She didn't know who her father was but her mother said he was American. Her mother, in ill health, gave up Lin Su and she was adopted by an American family at the age of three. That same family, disapproving of her pregnancy at eighteen, told her she was on her own if she insisted on having the baby—Charlie.

What Charlie said made sense—if Lin Sue was born in 1982

or '83 her father could not have been an American serviceman. Her mother's father could have been a GI, however, if
Lin Su's mother had been conceived between 1960 and 1967.

From the time of Lin Su's mother's birth till now, fifty years
of mystery? Or cover-up?

I think people deserve to know where they came from, if possible,
Charlie had told Blake.

Blake couldn't argue with that logic. But he knew a little
too much about where he came from and it hadn't done that
much good. Though he had loved his mother devotedly, help-
lessly, there had been so many times he had wished he'd been
given up for adoption. He might not be who he was today,
however, had that happened.

*Listen, I can keep my mouth shut but I can't help you with this
because you're defying your mother,* Blake told Charlie.

*I understand. Just don't tell her. It could take me years to figure out,
especially behind her back, so don't tell her and jam me up.*

Now the information, what little there was, sat like a boulder in his gut and he couldn't look at Lin Su in the same way.
She wasn't just a single mother of a sick kid soldiering on despite debt and difficulty. Now she was the daughter of a refugee
who had been spirited out of a war-torn country as a teenager
who then became a mother who couldn't care for her child.
Lin Su had been adopted by the new family who took her in.
And then she was cast out when the same thing happened to
her. When she found herself alone and pregnant. Oh, God,
she wasn't just a little complicated like he thought. She was as
complicated as he was, and probably in a lot of the same ways.

He tried to behave normally around her but was conscious
of the fact that meeting her eyes wasn't easy. He tried to be
around as much as ever, which meant at least showing up for
a few minutes after school to check in with his neighbors and

get the latest updates from Charlie and Winnie, but covering his concern wasn't smooth. Even though her laugh seemed to come quicker these days, which probably had everything to do with being out of that crappy trailer, his laugh was a little stunted.

"Blake, are you feeling well?" she asked him.

"Fine, why do you ask?"

"You're a little quiet. You seem preoccupied."

"Ah, that. It's just the race coming up. I think that happens to me."

"Oh, of course," she said, smiling. "Tahoe, right?"

"Right."

"Charlie can't stop talking about it."

It was at the end of the week, Friday afternoon while Winnie napped, that Lin Su paid Blake a visit. She went to his front door and rang the bell rather than adopting their casual habit of trotting up the beach stairs, something they only did as neighbors if someone was out on the deck. "Well, this is a surprise," he said. "Need a hand with something?"

"No. I mean, possibly. If you have a minute, I'd like to talk to you about Charlie."

"Is he okay?" he asked, holding the door open for her.

"He's great actually. The new apartment, new school, new friends here on the beach—it's all working very well for Charlie. For me, too. But I could use some advice. Assistance?"

"Come in and tell me what's up," he said. Then he held his breath. What was he to say if she was concerned about Charlie researching his roots? He pulled out a chair at his dining table for her and pushed his papers aside. He'd been gathering up some of his records, getting ready for business meetings next week.

"Well, Scott Grant had a talk with me. A pretty stern talk. He said Charlie has to start strength and endurance training. Charlie has to get control over his asthma to avoid serious attacks like the one he had when he was chased by those creeps from the trailer park. I've been reading and it appears this is good advice. I have some ideas and I think I've learned plenty, but I'm no expert. Plus, Charlie isn't always happy to take my advice. It was Scott who suggested I ask you, so if this is a huge imposition you have him to blame. And please be honest."

Blake started grinning by the time Lin Su had the first sentence out of her mouth and just couldn't suppress his delight. "Where would you like me to start?" he asked.

"I don't know," she said. "I've read suggested protocols for this kind of thing but..." She shrugged. "Look, I'm okay in rehab, following instructions, but this is different. It's Charlie and my instincts want to keep him still and quiet."

"Then let me work up a protocol for him. I'm good at that sort of thing. All you have to do is explain what Dr. Grant suggested and send him to me. I'll be here next week, then I'm gone for a week but we can get Troy as a backup. I'll talk to him. We just have to monitor workouts, take times, keep a running record. Not complicated."

"Maybe I could do that," she said.

He shook his head but he was smiling. "Step back, Mom. You're not doing anything wrong." He stood and went to the refrigerator, pouring her a drink and taking it to her without asking. "Tea and lime. You'll love it." He put it in front of her. "Send Charlie over to see me sometime before he has dinner. I'll talk to him about a routine."

"I should come with him..."

"Let him do this, Lin Su. Let him manage his program, his routine and his goals. Let him have control of this."

"But you have to be in control!" she insisted.

"I won't be in control, I'll be a trainer. A coach. I'll watch his vitals and reactions, slow him down when it's warranted, push him harder when that's warranted. But Charlie should feel this belongs to him."

"What are you going to do?" she asked.

"Nothing fancy," he promised. "Treadmill, bike, elliptical. We'll work up to some weights. Your timing is good—my trainer is coming on Sunday. She's very talented, especially with young people. She runs a training institute in Boulder and gets Olympic contenders in their early years for workshops and summer sessions."

"You're preparing for your race! This must be inconvenient!"

Blake couldn't help but laugh outright. "You'd do anything to get out of this, wouldn't you? I just told you it was perfect timing. I'll be starting at 4:00 a.m. every day. Charlie isn't going to intrude on my training at all. I'm excited about this. I think this is an excellent thing to do."

"I wouldn't want to take your focus off your race…"

"Lin Su, this is what I do. When I'm done racing, it's part of my long-term plan to be a full-time trainer, maybe with a training facility of my own."

She frowned. "I'm not sure I know what you do. I mean, I know you're a professional athlete but…" She shrugged.

"Well… I do a lot of things now, but…" He took a breath. "I was on the high school track team and was able to use that to get help with college tuition. I thought that would be the extent of it but I kept racing. I raced after college, picked up some medals, kept racing. I got a job in a lab where they liked athletes so I trained while I worked, kept entering races, won a few, took a couple of years off work to go to the world championships, picked up a couple of medals and moved up to training for the Ironman races. That's where I started making a living at it. Racing has been my primary job for five years... more like six."

"Charlie says you have world records," she said.

"Not in the Triathlon, just in some individual events," he said. "But I haven't set any triathlon records. I hold a couple of running records, but I didn't win the full race. I'm going to before I retire, though."

"What would that be?"

"The best Ironman time is eight hours, three minutes, fifty-six seconds," he said. "Someone's going to break eight hours."

She gasped at the thought. "Maybe it will be in Tahoe!"

"It won't be there," he said with a chuckle. "Not at five thousand feet. But we'll get there."

"Is that your ultimate goal?" she asked.

He could see he had her complete interest. "That's a short-term goal."

"Why? It sounds so monumental!"

"Oh, it is," he said. "But I can't take that one and retire. And I can't do this forever. At some point my joints or back or something is going to get hurt, slow me down. I'll probably always race, but not as a full-time job, not as a way to earn a living. I'm transitioning. I've done some public speaking and I've set up a nonprofit foundation with a partner."

"Your trainer?"

"No," he said, and then he laughed. "Gretchen has her own business and our goals don't exactly match. No, there's a guy I kind of grew up with. Jimmy. He's the brains of this operation. We come from similar beginnings and we're both driven by similar ideas."

"He's an athlete?" she asked.

"Not even a little bit. Oh, I think Jimmy walks toward the

coffeepot at a good clip and he has a powerful focus but he's a legal weasel. We did time in a couple of foster homes together as teenagers. Then we landed at the same college for a while. He's brilliant. I'm a jock."

He could tell she was trying to take it in, still not sure what he was getting at. That was okay. There was plenty of time. He put his hand over hers. "Lin Su, this is a good thing you're doing for Charlie. I think I know kids pretty well—he's ready for a little independence. Ready for a challenge. If you let go a little bit, he'll thrive. Don't be scared—we'll keep a close eye on him, make sure he doesn't get in over his head. By Christmas you'll see a big change. Give him a good ninety days and everything will be better—not just his asthma but also his frame of mind. His confidence will get a good shot in the arm, too."

"Do you know anyone more confident than Charlie?" she asked with a laugh.

"Around us, yeah, he's solid. We don't know how he is around other people, especially kids his own age. It's a constant uphill battle for a fourteen-year-old boy, trust me."

He gave her hand a squeeze, reluctant to let go. Her hand was small in his, warm and soft. She turned her hand over and held his for a moment.

"Thank you for doing this," she said. "Thank you for everything you've done. You've been very kind to me and Charlie."

"It's a privilege," he said. *It's a privilege?* Where the hell had that come from? He wanted to say something much warmer, much more intimate than that. He wanted to say something sexy.

She pulled her hand away from his. "Should I send Charlie over this afternoon, then?"

"Sure. I mean, give him time to unwind after school. I'll stay here today instead of coming next door for the afternoon report. Charlie won't want to discuss this in front of everyone. We'll do it one-on-one."

"You do have good instincts about kids, don't you?"

"I'm interested in kids and athletic programs. In some cases it can save their lives. You know?"

"Like in Charlie's case?"

"That would be a good example. It can also get them out of trouble, build self-esteem, help them sleep at night and have something to look forward to in life."

She stood from the table. "I hope all of that works for Charlie. I'll catch up with you after you've had a chance to talk."

He let her out, softly closed the door behind her. And leaned his forehead against the door.

Crap.

She was controlling, manipulative and secretive. She was fiercely determined to have her way, and beneath that beautiful face and little body, she was powerful. There was an iron will in there. Almost unnaturally strong. She obviously had identity issues that she'd unwittingly passed on to her son and he'd put his money on some serious abandonment problems, as well. She had calm hands, a gentle step, was sweet spoken when it suited her and had a sharp tongue when it didn't. He hadn't even witnessed this crazy Asian temper Charlie referred to, yet he had no trouble picturing it. There was a Zen-like serenity about her, unless she was pissed off, then look out. Don't turn your back. She was a very complicated woman. Untangling her would take a lifetime.

And he didn't care. He *wanted* her.

Lin Su entered the house quietly. Mikhail was sitting on the deck alone, his feet propped up on the deck rail on this sunny afternoon. She checked on Winnie, sleeping restfully, then went into the guest bath, closing the door softly behind her. She looked in the mirror. Her cheeks had a slight rosy blush. She reached up and pulled the stick from her bun, letting her hair fall down her back. She pulled it over one shoulder and combed it with her fingers.

He was so tender with her, she thought. Gentle and kind and sweet. But there was no mistaking the firmness in his resolve—he would not weaken under duress. Never. Instinctively she knew this was a man who wouldn't change his mind. When he first moved into that house she thought he was just another rich guy, self-indulgent and pompous. Over time she began to think of him as prudent and steady, someone who knew his mind, was mature and comfortable in his skin. Solid.

She splashed cold water on her face. She would be very careful around him, cautious that she didn't betray the slightest desire. If she could rein in her feelings, control her actions, perhaps they could be friends. She didn't dare even entertain a single romantic notion; it could be her undoing. She made up her mind a long, long time ago—it would take every breath of energy and resourcefulness she had to be a mother first, then a nurse, then a friend. She would never again be a lover.

But, oh, it was hard. He was magnificent.

When Charlie got home from school, home to Winnie's, Troy was not yet home and Grace was still at the shop. Lin Su took him aside. "Spend a little time with Winnie, tell her about your day and I'll listen in. Then I'd like you to go next door and see Blake. He has some very good ideas about an exercise program that can help you build strength and stamina so it will be less likely you'll have an asthma attack if you exert yourself."

"Huh?" Charlie said. "You mean work out?"

"Well, a monitored program, but yes—work out."

"He wants to do this?" Charlie asked.

"Yes, he does. I asked him for help. He's a professional athlete and trainer."

"You asked him?" Charlie asked, awestruck.

She made a face. No one thought her capable of letting down her guard long enough to share control of her son. It irritated her that people found her thus. So she lied. "I asked Scott Grant about it and he's pretty convinced, as am I, that much of your asthma is exercise induced. Scott confirmed what I already suspected—your asthma is not severe. But you can't control it without building up endurance." *There*, she thought. That should show her in slightly better light to her son. "Of course, if you get an upper respiratory infection or have a severe allergic reaction..." She just couldn't seem to stop herself. Warnings seemed to come more naturally than encouragement.

"I *told* you!" Charlie said, ecstatic.

"Now look, never be without the inhaler and do not skip meds—this is an experiment! We all expect it to be a successful experiment, but remember, that's up to you. Several gold medalists live with asthma and, believe me, they can't afford to take chances and neither can you."

He was grinning like a fool. "You almost made it," he said. "Almost made it through the whole lecture without getting your Mama on."

Lin Su sighed wearily. She wondered if she'd survive his teenage years. The onset of testosterone was seriously impacting his sweetness.

Charlie went to where Winnie was sitting in her favorite chair. He plopped down on the sofa and said his day was fine and he was going next door right away to talk to Blake about a workout program to help control his asthma. And out the door he went with Winnie's blessing.

Two hours later he was back, his eyes sparkly and his cheeks rosy. If Lin Su hadn't been aware of the circumstances and Charlie's excitement over this new project, she'd have taken his temperature. Troy and Grace were home and Lin Su was in the kitchen, making a salad to go with their dinner, and he called to her. "Mom, come and see what we figured out today."

She could feel her smile reach way down inside her and it lifted her heart. Lately he had become more protective of her, especially when they had some crisis like the break-in, but he was less likely to include her in the rest of his life. They all gathered around the dining table and passed around a booklet that explained the effectiveness of different aerobic exercise and a notebook that Blake had created for him to monitor his activity, times, pulse, whether he had to use the inhaler.

"He's going to monitor the first week, starting tomorrow. Then when he goes to Tahoe to race, Troy can. Troy, will you?" Charlie asked.

So much for him not wanting to do this in front of everyone, Lin Su thought. She couldn't imagine him more excited if she'd gotten him a puppy!

"Be happy to," Troy said.

"I will help. I am coach!" Mikhail insisted.

"I think Charlie is supposed to use some discretion," Grace said. "You have a reputation for being the most difficult and demanding coach on the circuit."

"Pah! You are baby! Princess!"

"You are brute," Grace said, a slight Russian accent involved.

"This is going to be great," Charlie said.

I must find an appropriate way to thank him, Lin Su thought.

Blake was a true hero, over and over. This was the kind of man she hoped her son would become.

She didn't realize she was massaging Winnie's hand, holding it lovingly, gazing at Charlie with glowing eyes. It got her attention when Winnie looked at her. "You're very smart to start this," Winnie said. "You're a good mother." Then Winnie lifted her arm and put it around Lin Su's shoulders, pulling her in for a hug.

"Ah, Winnie, I have so few shining moments as a mother."

"Obviously you have enough," she said.

Seth Sileski gassed up the police SUV at least once a day, sometimes twice. It was a good opportunity to spend five or ten minutes talking to his dad, if Norm could pry himself away from other more exciting things, like explaining to Al how to better tune an engine or educating Eric on the best way to change out brake pads. Self-serve gas pumps were not allowed in Oregon so Seth had to wait for an available attendant even though he grew up pumping gas in this station. He was hoping for a moment with Norm. He hadn't talked to his dad alone since his mom's birthday dinner.

It was his lucky day. Norm came shuffling out of the garage, wiping his hands on a rag that he then stuffed in his back pocket.

"Morning, Dad," Seth said.

"Son," he returned. Seth already had the tank cover open so Norm went straight for the gas nozzle. "How's crime today?"

"It's an easy day so far. I wanted to congratulate you—your present to Mom was a big hit. Cruise, huh?"

"I thought I could make the sacrifice. A lot of the fishermen have history with Alaska. Sounds like I might be able to stand it. I sure ain't going to some island with all topless hula dancers."

"They're topless?" Seth asked.

"Ain't they?" Norm asked in return.

"I don't think so, Dad."

"Then what's the point?" Norm asked.

That was his dad. He couldn't help but laugh. "Well, it was a classy thing you did. Mom's been dying to go on a cruise."

"Aw, she deserves to get some of the things she's been praying for. After the way she took care of me when I nearly died of the gallbladder."

Seth suppressed his laugh. He had not come even close to being in serious condition, but Norm was still getting a lot of mileage out of his one and only gallbladder attack. "She must be very excited."

"She's spending money like crazy, buying all kinds of clothes. I don't mind, of course. Gwen's never been a spendthrift. But she's buying stuff for me to wear and I don't know that that's going to work. I like my clothes just fine. Don't need anything new. I'll pretty much just stand at the rail for ten days."

"Now that surprised me," Seth admitted. "You could've gone for four days or even a week, but you took on the whole ten days." He whistled. "That's quite a plunge," he said. "No pun intended."

Norm shrugged. "I hope she don't have any high ideas of dance parties and shuffleboard. Could be bears, though. And there's a glacier. You don't even have to get off the boat."

"I hear the food is good."

"Food's good right here," he said.

"I'm sure you'll have a great time," Seth said.

"I'm sure I'll throw myself overboard after the second day," Norm said.

"That's it," Seth said. "Attitude is everything."

NINE

Charlie wanted to begin his training program immediately. "Blake says I have to be patient because we're going to start slow, but if I get started right away it'll be no time at all and I'll be able to run a mile. Ride five miles," he told his mother.

Lin Su could work as much as she wanted to and if she needed time off, all she had to do was make arrangements with the other members of Winnie's household to make sure she had all her meals and wasn't trying to get around the house without supervision. So, if Charlie was going to be working out with Blake, Lin Su was going to be right next door, taking care of Winnie. It was all she could do not to beg Charlie to let her observe.

Of course, on Saturday Grace was at the flower shop all day. Troy and Mikhail took the opportunity to go somewhere. It was just Winnie and Lin Su when Charlie went next door at three, a prearranged time. Blake had his own training schedule to keep, mostly in the morning. While Charlie was next door, Lin Su was busier than usual doing chores that were rarely done on weekend afternoons—laundry, cleaning, linen changes, running the vacuum. Winnie sat in the living room, a book in her lap. Then she wanted to go to the deck since the sun was shining brightly. Then she wanted to be back inside.

By four o'clock Winnie started asking questions. "What's taking him so long? He's not supposed to do too much the first day! Lin Su, go next door and see what's keeping him."

"Uh-uh, no way. If they need me for anything they know where I am."

"Oh, don't be so tough! You've cleaned the kitchen five times!"

"A kitchen can never be too clean," Lin Su said.

That first workout, which was supposed to be moderate and easy, lasted a long time. Charlie didn't show up at Winnie's until almost five. He was flushed and sweaty, not at all what she expected. She thought he would be bored and disappointed!

"You should see all the stuff he has," Charlie said excitedly. He now had two books plus his notebook. He sat down in the living room with Winnie, and Lin Su joined them there. "He has heart monitors, breathing equipment, scales, speedometers, you name it. He can run a lung capacity check that's almost as sophisticated as the hospital's. It's amazing!"

"Tell us about it," Lin Su said.

"It was awesome. We started with some resting readings but I was too hyper so I had to lie on the massage table and..."

"He gave you a *massage*?" Lin Su nearly shouted.

"No, the table moves and vibrates and massages. Jeez, easy does it, Mom. So then when I was calmer, he did some resting readings. Then I took a hit of the nebulizer and he had me walking, then at an incline, checking vitals all the time. I thought I was ready to quit until he pushed me a little bit." Charlie laughed and his face was bright. "I didn't think I'd get to run—I got to run! Well…jog. My vitals were good. Then I had a rest and got on the elliptical for a while, till I started to sweat pretty good. Then he gave me a fruit drink and some power bar thing—tasted like shit… Oops, sorry, Winnie. But it did. Then I got on the bike. Just for a little while. Then he has this lifting operation—cables, pulleys and free weights. That wasn't so much endurance—he was just checking my strength. Then I jogged a little—real slow. Just fast enough I couldn't walk, just getting my heart rate up to an aerobic level for a little while. Then he stopped me, took my blood pressure, did some more readings. He listened to my lungs. He's a physiologist and trainer—he has a stethoscope. My heart rate and breathing recovered in just ten minutes—I didn't need another hit of the inhaler."

"You were gone such a long time," Lin Su said.

"It took a long time to do all that. We won't have to do it all forever, just in the beginning. He does that for himself, you know—checks his heart rate, his breathing, his recovery time, his strength. Big muscles don't swim very well but no muscle won't get a bike up a hill. He's always looking for exactly the right balance—a strong and lean one-fifty with good endurance. Timing is everything in a triathlon, did you know that? He can't start out too fast or he won't end in the money. He rations his strength and endurance perfectly—that's what wins the race."

"My word," Lin Su said. "You got quite an education in one afternoon."

"I have to read these two books," Charlie said, holding them up. One was about anatomy and physiology and the training of athletes and the other was about asthma and training. "He has other ones—diet, weight training, body building, one called *Speed*. He said we'll get to that someday. But the best thing?

The absolute best thing? He said when I'm in a little better shape, he's going to teach me to swim."

Lin Su's eyes widened. It took every fiber of her being to keep from yelling, *No!* Hopefully Blake would have all those heart rate monitors and other equipment at his disposal.

"Blake said it's all looking good, and that last attack might've been worse because those guys who chased me scared the crap out of me. Half the battle is mental, he said. Did you know athletic competition is as much about mind-set as muscle? That's what he said."

Lin Su leaned closer to him. "You smell gamey."

"That's called sweat, Mom!" And there was no mistaking his sparkle.

It wasn't long before Troy and Mikhail returned and Charlie's experience was recounted again. Next came Grace bearing chicken parmesan, salad and garlic toast from Carrie's. Charlie went through his story one more time and showed no sign of coming down to earth.

Lin Su was tired. Just worrying about the first day of this new program, the waiting and wondering, left her exhausted. She asked Grace if she could manage the bedtime rituals; she wanted to take Charlie home for a shower.

Bedtime wasn't a demanding chore and Grace was more than happy to step in. It required just a little freshening up after which Winnie was content to read and watch TV in her room. But Grace would not let Lin Su leave without a generous portion of Carrie's dinner to take along.

Charlie was still wound up when they got home to their loft; he was starving and ate as though he hadn't been fed in days. He showered off the sweat, though Lin Su suspected he wanted to bask in it awhile longer, a kind of badge of glory. Then while Lin Su took to her bed to read, Charlie was reading in his own bed. His was the pull-out couch and he was completely absorbed in one of the books Blake had given him.

It took willpower not to tell him it was time for lights-out.

Sundays were often Lin Su's own, the day she caught up on shopping, cleaning, laundry. But given that Charlie would be working out with Blake, Lin Su said she'd be more than happy to spend a little time with Winnie and the family, making sure everything was caught up.

"I bet you'd be happy to," Winnie said.

"I wasn't trying to fool anyone," she protested.

The workout at Blake's was not quite as long as on the first day, not quite as much discussion, Lin Su assumed. But in all other ways it was the same—Charlie was lit up like a lightbulb, happy, excited, feeling very proud. And smelling very gamey.

Lin Su wanted to take him home, fix him an early dinner and make sure he was ready for school the next morning. But she wanted to return to Winnie's. "Now that we're so close, after I have dinner with Charlie, I'm coming back. I'll see you at about seven o'clock for your bedtime rituals. It won't take long at all and I'd like to do it. Grace, you can take a night off."

There was more to her mission than getting Winnie settled for the night. After the little time it took to accomplish that, she walked next door and knocked softly at Blake's door. This could wait until the next day, but she remembered his trainer was coming to town and he might not be alone. For this she didn't need an audience.

He opened the door and the house behind him seemed pretty dark, as though the lights were turned down. He wore exercise pants and a snug T-shirt but his feet were bare.

"Lin Su, this is a surprise. Is it my birthday?" he joked, grinning.

"If you have a moment..."

"Come in, please. You're not worried about Charlie, are you? He seemed to be doing great."

She shook her head. "Not at all. He's home, reading his books, ready for a new week that now includes at least an hour in your gym every day and I've never seen him so enthusiastic. I want to thank you, Blake. This is made possible by you and your generosity. I could never have managed it as well."

"I'm happy to do it. It's not going to take that long, you know. He'll be on his own in no time."

"And I'd like to apologize," she said. "You've been on Charlie's team all along and I stood in your way."

"Nah," he said. "I understood your concern. Charlie's not the first kid I've known who needed all the right circumstances to fall into place to get going. It's too bad it started with an ambulance ride. But that's the past. Onward."

"I didn't mean to stand in his way. I really didn't."

"It's not your fault. He's your boy. You want to do what's best for him."

"Some of it is just… I could never have gotten him to read a book about asthma. He didn't even want to talk about his asthma."

"I know. It felt like a ball and chain," Blake said. "Besides, you're his mother. He'd be more willing to listen to a coach— it's that simple."

"I barely know you, yet you've been such a help to us. There's really no way to thank you properly."

"Pay it forward," he said with a shrug. "I got a lot of help when I was his age. But I didn't have a parent resisting—the resistance was all mine." He chuckled. "I was somewhere between an angry victim and a delinquent."

"And who helped you?" she boldly asked.

"A foster mother, a couple of teachers, a coach. That's just a start. Just as I needed something, someone appeared with the next challenge. I didn't have asthma like Charlie, but I had a hard time growing up. Charlie's going to be fine."

"He's such a great kid," she said. "Sometimes he acts like he has to take care of me and I wish he didn't. But he's such a good son."

Blake put his big hands on her cheeks and bent down, placing a gentle kiss on her brow. "And you're a good mother. I know this was hard for you. You were very strong, letting him set his own limits."

"Oh, I don't want him to set his own limits. You're there, you're the coach!"

"I'm only there to catch him if he falls," Blake said. He ran one hand down her arm and briefly took her hand in his. "He's going to do this. He's going to do it on his own and the feeling that will give him will fuel him for years."

And then he let go.

"Well," she said a little nervously. "You know what you're doing. I just wanted to say thank you."

"Anything you need, Lin Su. Just let me know."

It was just as she remembered—a shiver that ran right up her back to the base of her neck, a fullness in the breast and a little gasp on her lips. It was the way a desired man's first touch reached inside a woman and filled her with expectation and excitement. Her senses were consumed with the scent of him— soap and wind and musk and a little of the salt in the air. He had that unique scent that never seemed to change; if he was sweaty from exertion it only magnified his scent. His sweat, she had already noticed, smelled clean. How was that possible?

Lin Su was not that surprised. She was a bird in a snare. From the first moment she laid eyes on him she had been stimulated and intrigued. Then he became their hero and the intrigue took on speed. When a man protects you and your child, he owns a part of your soul. But then when he touches you with affection, he takes a piece of your heart.

She wished to ignore him and feel nothing but it would be difficult. After all, he embodied the qualities she admired most—strength, kindness, tenderness and power. And there was courage—he chased down those thugs to get her meager treasures. Maybe it was his foolishness she admired? She didn't swoon for gladiators but she had a huge respect for a winning spirit, for a man willing to test his abilities. She happened to like his fearlessness. And she appreciated his humility. He wasn't trying to win her with muscle but with softness.

He probably wasn't trying to win her at all, but a part of her was won. He might not know that, of course. And if it was up to her, he *wouldn't* know!

Well, she was good at concealing her emotions; she always had been. She knew how to take small steps and move with an economy of motion. Her older sisters would tease her and call her "little geisha." She liked to think her mother had walked, talked and moved in the same way. It was also a holdover from her early childhood fears, from that time she was trying so hard to be small and invisible.

It would be hard to remain aloof, especially with Charlie spending so much time with him. It would be wrong to remain aloof. He deserved her gratitude and friendliness.

She would make sure he thought she was open and agreeable. She would laugh at his amusing comments and express her appreciation. But she would not be alone with him when the lights were turned low and he was feeling affectionate.

It would be dangerous.

★ ★ ★

Blake was waiting in the baggage area of the Eugene airport right after lunch. He had already secured a cart for the bags— Gretchen Tyrene would bring a lot. She had equipment and supplies she liked to tote everywhere. Sometimes he thought it gave her credibility more than served her needs. All he really needed for his own training was a stopwatch, a distance calculator, a heartbeat monitor, wet suit and bike. He had a lot of fancy equipment in his gym—he liked testing it and testing his readings to gauge the impact on his race. But he never carried all these things to races.

But he didn't travel light, either. There were the special dietary supplements, the bike plus repair kit and spare parts, the clothes and shoes. The bike was always a big issue. It was specially designed and worth a lot of money. He liked to watch it loaded, something that gave airlines fits. Always a hassle.

Gretchen was walking toward him, tall and long-legged in her tight jeans. Heads turned as she passed by. She wore platform shoes and a leather jacket and her blond hair was cropped short and sexy. She had a healthy tan.

She was a runner but she didn't have a runner's body. Oh, she was slim, but she had good-size breasts and a nice ass. Gretchen was more of a trainer with a sculpted body than athlete made up of bone and sinew. But she had endurance, he'd give her that. She could almost keep up with him on a run.

When she saw him, she beamed. He'd last seen her a few months ago; she hadn't joined him in Sydney for his last race. She put her arms around his neck. "I've missed you!" She held him close for a moment and he reciprocated, embracing her. But he knew at the first contact. She was thinking about sex.

"We're in touch almost every day," he said.

"It's not the same as seeing you."

"We're going to be busy. This isn't exactly a pivotal race but it's important."

The luggage carousel started turning. There weren't that many people waiting and he recognized the large red trunk. Then came her red duffel. He started loading them onto the luggage cart. A third bag appeared a few minutes later and finally the bike bag, an enormous contraption that padded and protected the vital parts. And then, surprisingly, a second bike bag. One bag was red and one was black.

He peered at her. "Couldn't make up your mind?"

"I'm checking out a new bag, supposed to be better. It packed up about the same and it has as much quilting and padding yet is lighter."

"New bike?" he asked.

"I'm trying one out. And I've decided to race. We have several clients in the race. Nigel is coming out to Tahoe next week with the support crew. You'll be his priority, don't worry."

"And what about you?" he asked. Elite racers should have support in the crowd, just in case they ran into serious trouble—damaged equipment, injury, a hold on the race due to freak weather. Not to mention crew support such as fluids, towels, help with transitions in the race, readings for the record to enable training for the next race. The race personnel would provide stations along the course and the support crew would look after individual racers. Rules were strict on just how much personalized support a competitor could receive; the playing field was kept strictly level.

"We'll have enough crew to manage," she said. "If you have any critical needs, of course I would drop out to make sure you're taken care of."

But Blake knew that was unlikely. In all his years of racing he'd had only two serious problems on the circuit. Once he had a muscle injury and could barely finish and another time he'd had an epic equipment failure—the bike had practically collapsed after a minor collision. It led to the development of the custom Smiley bike, on which he held a patent.

"You won't have to drop out," he said.

On the drive to Thunder Point they talked about the upcoming race. "What makes this race so important? Besides a chance to set records or win a purse?" Gretchen asked.

"I'm not going to be setting any records in Tahoe," he said. "Running is my best event and there's so much uphill track that would be tough for anyone, but the runners who live at that altitude have a definite edge. I could do well in the water, but... But what's important is that I have an excellent performance because of McGill. He's not racing—he announced his retirement and I want anyone who cares to know I'm in it to win it. I'm the guy to beat—and I'm not going anywhere."

"And if you get beat?"

"That's always a distinct possibility, but I'll kick ass in Kona."

"You ready for Kona?" she asked.

"I was ready for Kona last year," he said.

And she laughed loudly. "I brought a new supplement for you to try—a B12 with a better delivery system and extra B6 and E packed into a kale and grain formula that one of the interns worked up a year ago. We've had excellent and fast results so let's see if it's right for you. It's just a tweak of the protocol. I've been looking at the red blood cells of some of our runners and not only is there a noticeable difference, the times have come in stronger."

"Let's see what happens," he said. "I'm in for a trial."

"You're the best," Gretchen said.

"Only because you are," he returned.

And all this was true. She was an excellent physiological

scientist and had founded the Tyrene Institute in Boulder. Many athletes thought Gretchen and her staff were the team to align with, had the most up-to-date equipment, made the most significant strides in athletic training and were showing arguably the best results.

She had also been his lover for a while.

They'd met five years ago. Blake had bet the farm on her, she was that expensive. He researched her science, her training program and her institute and paid her a ton of money to give his training program a workup. His improvement was marked. Though he visited her institute several times, their contact was mostly long distance and virtual—he'd send her his times and readings, she'd meet him with a support crew at significant races. He won a couple and set some race records. That took two years.

Then they slept together. And it was powerful. Good.

During that year they were together he realized they had very different views on love, sex and commitment. Gretchen was married to her work and wasn't interested in a permanent, long-term relationship that might include family. He went along with that. Not everyone felt like getting on the baby train. He wasn't even sure he was interested in that. After all, his career was pretty all-consuming. And since he was about twenty-three he'd felt there were a lot of kids out there who could use someone like him in their corner. He had put considerable focus on them.

But Gretchen, who worked with some of the finest athletes in the world, was also not into exclusivity. She wasn't loose by any means, but if the spirit moved her and the man was someone she knew and could trust, she'd sleep with him. And why should it matter? she argued. After all, wasn't he doing the same thing? Women came on to him in droves—he was handsome, mildly famous, fit and nice.

But no, he didn't. A couple of times since first meeting Gretchen, before they were intimate, he'd had relationships of very short duration, women he met, saw briefly, kept in touch with for a matter of weeks before determining there was no foundation to support a long-distance relationship. But the racing circuit was tight; all the same people ran into one another all the damn time in all the same places.

Since he started having sex with Gretchen, talking to her almost daily, there had been no one else. They had something of a standoff as he insisted they decide what kind of relationship they were going to have moving forward. Friends? Lovers? A couple? A long-distance couple? A serious and committed couple? A family of two?

Gretchen liked it the way it was. He should know how important he was to her—she put him first. They were in constant communication. They saw each other regularly. Was she ready to be tied down to one man permanently? Why? she asked. What's the difference? She wasn't putting him at risk and all she asked was that he not make another woman more important or put her health at risk. She described that as being adults about this.

Blake, who was clearly not on the same map, chose to be honest and told her that wouldn't work for him. There was a vast area between platonic friends and business associates and a committed couple, and he wasn't comfortable in that uncertain middle ground. He decided not to move to Boulder, something he'd been considering. He rented a place in Truckee for a while during the summer while he looked for real estate that would suit him better. But in his mind, he and Gretchen had been, for over a year, friends and colleagues. Not lovers.

At first, that had stung. He had enjoyed having a steady woman in his life, something and someone to look forward to; there hadn't been many of those in his adult life. There had been too many when he was much younger, when he'd just been following his dick as young men will do, and once he figured out that wasn't going to bring him the satisfaction he really craved, he had more time for his sport. But having a woman in his life, he liked that. The right woman at the right time. He had thought he probably loved her.

Then he realized *he* had uttered the words. She had been touched. "Oh, Blake, that's so lovely. You are the most wonderful man." But she had not said them back.

He was over the romantic illusion now. He didn't love her and their parting wasn't causing him any distress. He'd like to continue to work with her on his athletic performance, but there were other trainers if that wasn't possible. Other trainers who would give a lot to get him for a client.

When they were at his house and had unloaded the luggage and bikes, she looked around his house and gym. "Wow. I tried to envision this from your descriptions but this is really beautiful. You did an amazing job on the house. It's just too far away."

"I didn't build the house, Gretchen. I just picked out the appliances, paint color and fixtures. That was enough work."

"How about something to drink?" she asked. "Any chance you have a cold beer?"

"Knowing you like your beer, I bought a six. Your brand. Sam Adams?"

"Will you have one with me?"

"Sure," he said, sensing she was leading up to something. He opened two bottles and handed her one.

"To us," she said, toasting.

"Which us?" he asked before drinking to the toast.

"I'd like to talk about that, if you're open to a conversation."

"Go ahead," he urged her.

"I've given it a lot of thought, Blake, and I'll agree to your terms. We can be exclusive."

"Why do I get the feeling this is a major concession for you?" he asked with a smile.

"Not at all. I miss our relationship. If the price is remaining exclusive, you're worth it. I meant it—I miss *you*. What I'd like? I'd like to have a beer, share a shower, roll around in the bed for an hour, then take a ride before the sun goes down. Like old times."

He put his bottle on the counter. He knew he wore a pained expression. "I'm sorry, Gretchen. You gave me too much time to think. We're not right for each other. It was pretty clear—we're looking for different things."

"So. Have you found what you're looking for?"

"I'm not with anyone, but that's really not the point. I was hoping we'd be a couple, but that was two years ago. I thought being a couple meant living in the same house, having common goals, working together and relaxing together. When that was off the chart I bought this house. My first house. It's not in Boulder—it's not anywhere near your house. I wasn't intentionally putting distance between us, but when being close was no longer a priority, I found a place and house I like."

"We made it work before," she said. "Not living in the same town much less house."

"Yeah, I was ready to make something a little more serious work. You weren't. That's okay, Gretchen. We have to be honest with each other. But now that we've made the break, this is what we have. And I really don't want to be a casual fuck if it's all the same to you."

"I never saw you as a casual fuck," she said, growling a little.

"At the end of the day it felt like that. Committed people share space. They share feelings and goals and time."

"We have the feelings, goals and time covered," she said. "We've always been rowing in the same direction, that's how we ended up in bed together."

"Is it?" he asked. "I liked you. I was attracted to you, wanted you. Wanted a future with you. When you said that wouldn't work for you, I moved on."

"Is it my age?" she asked.

He laughed. "You're forty-four! You find that old? Too old for *me*?"

"I spent a couple of decades building this life, this business. I'm not going to settle into being some cute little wife. I'll never be a mommy."

He frowned and shook his head. He had never suggested such a thing. "I was thinking *partner*."

"*I* built that business."

"*Life partner*, Gretchen. Not business partner. But never mind all that—it's in our past now. We were connected for a while but it didn't work. We'll always be good friends, I hope."

"Maybe after the next couple of weeks…"

"I want to work on the race, not our relationship," he said. "You were pretty clear where you stood on relationships and I'm not interested in concessions. Let's focus on the sport."

"Right," she said. And he could see her regroup internally, setting her mind on the appropriate track.

But he had no illusions. Gretchen was strong-willed, which was what had made her successful. If she wanted him back, she would be applying her best strategy to that end. She would be careful and clever because he had a deal with the institute. Not with her, but with the institute, and he was adamant about that distinction. He had allowed his name to be used to promote the institute and, in return, the training fees had been sharply reduced while he maintained a priority-client position. She would not want him to take his business elsewhere.

So, while they finished their beer, she got out her laptop and showed him some charts and graphs worked up to highlight where he stood with major competitors. These competitors weren't clients of hers, of course; that would be unethical. But their times had been carefully recorded so that Blake had all the necessary information. During the week Gretchen was here they would have one triathlon run and after that he'd work on individual events with plenty of time and nourishment to fully recuperate. He'd enter the race at his strongest and healthiest.

Meanwhile, there would be a lot of spiritual preparedness—envisioning the track, the route, the events. He also practiced yoga and Tai Cheng; Gretchen totally approved and preached the mental aspect of the sport. It was said running was 90 percent mental and the other 10 percent was…mental. But there was a significant difference in the way Blake and Gretchen practiced this aspect of the sport. She was powerfully strong and demanded of her mind that she focus, that she be present only in the race.

Blake practiced by letting go. Trust.

A tai chi mentor had run with him a few times and had said, "Your pace is choppy. Stop running on the trail. *Be* the trail. Your chi will decide the pace. Trust."

He had no option but to trust. Really, he shouldn't be alive today much less a winning triathlete. He learned to run to survive. He ran to live. He was a small kid in a terrible neighborhood filled with pimps and dealers and gang members, and if he couldn't run, he'd be at least beaten to a pulp.

He still ran to live.

It was nearly five by the time they'd changed clothes and assembled Gretchen's bikes. It was not a workout but a casual ride, a rejuvenation and a chance to get Gretchen acquainted with the landscape and moisture in the air. When they took the bikes out through the gym door and down the beach stairs, Blake noticed that Winnie was on her deck with company—the ladies of a certain age: Ray Anne, Lou and Carrie. Lin Su was also there, of course.

Charlie would be home from school by now and either doing his homework or secretly searching for his roots, but he was not in sight.

Blake waved and the women waved back, yelling hello.

"Who are they?" Gretchen asked.

"A neighbor lady and her friends. They get together sometimes. They call it a hen party."

"Attractive," she pointed out. "Particularly the blonde."

"That would be Ray Anne, who is probably in her sixties, fighting back age. Winnie is the lady next door. She suffers from ALS so her friends often come to her after work. A little happy hour."

They set up their bikes on the beach road, pointing toward the town. Gretchen put a hand on the back of Blake's shoulder as he got astride and slowly moved that hand down his back to cup one firm butt cheek. "Ready?" she asked.

He put a foot on the pedal and shot out, riding down the beach road ahead of her. When he got to the marina, before continuing to the road through town, he stopped. He put a foot down and waited for her. She caught up to him and stopped. "Don't ever do that again," he said. "Especially in front of my neighbors."

"Wow. Little touchy, aren't you?"

"We're not together, remember? You're my trainer. My coach. You don't pat my ass to imply we're lovers. You hear me, Gretchen?"

"Jeez. You bet," she said.

She put her foot to the pedal and rode out ahead of him.

Wherever Winnie was, Lin Su was not far away. While Charlie worked on his homework at the dining room table inside, Lin Su was with Winnie and her friends. Then Blake came outside with a woman, an incredibly beautiful woman, and waved at them.

They all waved back. And stared.

There was the little ass-pat, then off they went. They looked like a Nike ad, riding across the beach road in the late-afternoon sun.

"God bless those biker shorts," Lou said.

"Seriously," Ray Anne agreed. "Do you suppose it's too late to make a play for a younger man?"

"It was too late fifteen years ago," Carrie said.

"I know what you mean, though," Winnie said. "That is one fine-looking man. But given what we just saw there, he's not going to give any of us the time of day. I do believe Mr. Smiley is spoken for."

"Hmm," Lou said. "Then do you think we can get him to jump out of a cake for us?"

While the women laughed hysterically at themselves, Lin Su just looked at her hands for a moment. And she wondered if she would ever learn. She felt so foolish.

TEN

It was only a couple of days until Blake brought his trainer to Winnie's to introduce her to the entire family, including Lin Su. Charlie had already met her because he went to Blake's gym every day and had pronounced her awesome.

Lin Su found that Gretchen was not only beautiful, she was charming. Delightful. Lin Su almost felt relieved in a way. It was a little bit like meeting Peyton—Lin Su's brief crush on Scott was forever cured in deference to her admiration for the wonderful physician's assistant. Thus it was with Gretchen. She instantly felt she couldn't hold a candle to the beautiful, athletic blonde. Not only could Gretchen keep up with Blake, she advised him on how to improve his skills. His already staggeringly successful skills.

The visit of the gorgeous coach took Lin Su's mind off her idle fantasies and she was reminded of a couple of things she wanted to do. She asked to run an errand while Winnie napped and Mikhail watched television. She drove to North Bend to pick up the walker she had ordered for Winnie, and while she was out, she dropped into a craft store and department store. She had finally thought of a proper gift for a bachelor—towels that she would embroider with his initials.

Winnie was ambivalent about the walker. "Thank you," she said dourly. "I know I need it. I hate the look of the bloody things, however."

"But while you can walk, it's important to keep walking. The wheelchair is a cop-out and we both know it. Fortunately, it's too soon for that."

"Not so much a cop-out as giving up," Winnie said. "And by damn, I know there's no going back but I'm not quitting yet."

"Good for you!" she praised. "But for the first days especially, please let one of us know when you're taking a stroll. It's helpful, not foolproof."

They practiced for a while and in no time at all Lin Su was begging Winnie to slow down, make every step a careful step.

Lin Su often heard Blake and Gretchen laughing if they were on the deck or the beach or even if the windows were open. She tried not to imagine what was happening at his house after the training was done. Unfortunately, she couldn't stop the images. She knew in her heart that Blake was with the woman of his choice, a woman he'd been coupled with for a long time. He had explained they'd worked together for five years.

Finally the day came that the house next door to Winnie fell silent and this was a great relief to Lin Su. Of course, Charlie still used Blake's gym with Troy monitoring his progress and taking all his readings for his notebook, but they didn't hang out over there. They went over for their hour. Troy took advantage and indulged some of his own workout while keeping an eye on Charlie.

Charlie was so proud of his progress. He was gaining momentum in no time. He was only into his third week and he was running. He wasn't running too far but there had been no serious shortness of breath and not a hint of an asthma attack. He was going to try some training without the nebulizer when Blake got back from his race.

At the words *back from his race* Lin Su tried to forget the way he'd touched her, kissed her brow. They would have to start over. He was Charlie's friend and supporter, her neighbor in a sense. Nothing more.

Once in Tahoe, Blake drove the event track. He insisted on doing this alone. There was one section of the run that was incredibly grueling with a steep climb of two thousand feet around a mountain curve. Then the next four miles were at over five thousand feet, a challenge for anyone who had not trained at that altitude. Then, even harder for some, a decline of three thousand feet. Down was hard.

Go to the track in the morning when you're fresh and well rested, his mentor had suggested. *Walk that part of the route at a slow and leisurely pace. Take it all in, inhale it deeply, listen to all sounds, remember how it felt when you were not depleted. Recall these details in the race and put your mind there. Be the trail.*

There were a lot of triathletes out on the route, looking it over, some running or riding parts of it, some just examining it. Blake wondered how many were doing what he was doing—committing it to memory while there was no stress so he could recall and replicate the feelings. And float.

Blake was happy in Tahoe. He saw Gretchen every day but she had rented her own condo, one with space enough for some of the support crew and trainers, and she was busy with her own training. He wanted to be alone, to have no distractions.

She had proven to be a distraction. He was both surprised by this and unsurprised, if that was possible. She was the one who was not flexible about their relationship, yet now she was the one who wanted him back. She didn't understand about "too late." Before they made the drive in his SUV to Tahoe, she had begun testing him, wandering around his house in only a towel, a towel that slipped. Touching him in suggestive and affectionate ways. Making comments about what a good pair they were and how something seemed missing now.

But when it came to the training, to tweaking his program and nudging better times out of him, she was a master. He would hate to give her up. It would cost him but the price of keeping her could be higher.

He crouched on the trail he would run on Saturday. He picked up some loose dirt and gravel and let it drift in the breeze. By four Saturday morning Gretchen would have all the temperatures, wind velocity and approximate location of gusts around curves and passes. She would tell him where he'd get his next food and water and the support crew would be standing by to report endurance times and stats. He carried gel packs in his pockets, protein supplements he could use on the track; he shaved his legs.

Blake loved the marathon; it was his favorite part, even when he was tired. His legs were long, his stride wide and his pace even. Sometimes he thought of his childhood and sometimes he felt like Forrest Gump—someone who could run forever. Moving ahead, moving away from the pack, going forward, had always brought deep satisfaction. And during the race he exercised amazing control, not giving in to the urge to change his pace or up his speed—that took confidence. He trusted his rhythm, his heart rate and respirations; he believed his timing was close to perfect. He was rarely beat in the marathon; he knew what he was doing. Those runners who were desperate to make their mark and pass him dropped back before long because they didn't trust their training, their pace. Maybe they didn't know their best, most dependable speed.

This morning as he crouched along the trail and felt the breeze on his face, inhaled the scent of pine and sunshine, he wasn't thinking of the race. He was thinking of Lin Su. He knew she had seen Gretchen's saucy move. He knew Lin Su would take that in, weigh it and hold it silently in her head, judging it to mean that she meant nothing to him. She would decide his gentle touch and soft kiss was just a neighborly thing when it was more.

He looked at the sky above the pines. He couldn't think about that now. Now he had to think about this trail, this breeze, this scent. He would be in a pack of a dozen at this point in the race and he wouldn't be ahead. He filled his lungs with oxygen; last year this race had been canceled because of smoke in the air. This year the air was clean. He would be ahead after the ascent of two thousand feet, and he would be barely ahead. The descent, if he could hold his heart rate and pace, that was his chance to get ahead if he didn't screw it up by going too hard or fast. Going down was not easy; it was a trick. Those runners who took advantage of the plunge down and went with it, they got breathing too fast and their respirations huffed and they wore themselves out. You can coast on wheels, not legs.

He'd done this a hundred times. He'd run this race five times; it was a good race. The purse was small but the sponsors were all here. Unless there was a dark horse, he might actually win it.

How could he show Lin Su that he admired her? That he was attracted to her? That he thought maybe they came from the same place and would understand each other?

Don't expect too much of the future, his mentor would say. *Live in the present and let the future evolve as it will and trust.* It was a fancy way of saying, You'll know what to do at the time. Or, Everything will be as it should be.

He went back to his condo and prepared for his race. He rested, meditated, practiced his breathing. He envisioned the race and worked on his nerves. Funny how after this many races, this many years, his nerves could still jangle. It made him very quiet and introspective. For obvious reasons he always had this feeling, deep in his gut, that if he wasn't the fastest, wasn't faster than everyone else, he wouldn't survive. Intellectually he knew that wasn't true, nor was it the real purpose of his race, even though he was a competitor through and through. That was his baggage.

He was up at four, ate his kale, oats and quinoa, banana and jerky at five. Got his gear set up, anything that wasn't ready the night before. There was a support crew of eight for the Tyrene clientele but Nigel, Gretchen's right-hand man, was personally looking after Blake's equipment and would have his bike ready in the rack for after the swim and would be responsible for it before the marathon. They operated like a pit crew at the transitions—transfer of equipment, quick report on times, et cetera. Blake swam in his cycling shorts, changed shoes, ran in the same shorts. Along the way there would be water; Blake added small gel packs now and then. Occasionally they'd substitute a shot of sugar, a candy.

In the chaos of race setup—all the athletes gathering, collecting their numbers, getting final instructions from buddies, coaches, partners—Blake always went numb. He started hearing all the voices as if they were speaking in a tunnel—muffled and slow. He nodded now and then and there was no point in arguing, but by now it was too late to introduce any new instructions. He was busy inside his head remembering everything and nothing, trusting his experience and instincts, reminding himself from this point it was just a go. The gathering in divisions lasted for over an hour. Being in the pro men's class, he had to wait for his wave to be called, so he stretched and did his breathing. He was hot even though the air was cool, and he paced. Paced and stretched with Nigel in his ear. *Wind at ten knots, temp is sixty-four, water temp is sixty-two. Your event times are ranked fourth but you have the highest number of races in this event. We'll be ready with numbers, wind and temp readings...*

He lived for the sound of that horn because the waiting was almost as hard as the race. Once he heard that horn, ran and dove into the lake, all anxiety was gone and all he thought about was the race.

He was surrounded by swimmers who would soon be behind him and for right now all he heard was the rhythm of his breathing, his arms gliding through the water, the silence of the water and the smooth kick of his feet. Funny that this would be his best event, the thing that could've killed him once when he couldn't swim. Now he thought swimming was the most relaxing part of the race. His time on this segment was always excellent.

He was gliding quickly, efficiently, and there was a little tension at the thought of the bike, his hardest segment. For some people it was the easiest, but for him, so tough. The length of his legs, even with a custom bike, made that segment too much work. But the swim was good; his time was right where he wanted it to be minus fifty seconds.

He had hours left to this race.

Out of the water, he dried his feet and got into the cycling shoes. He bent to adjust the tightness, took a gulp of water, got on and shot away. And although he tried, he could not get the number out of his mind—one hundred and twelve miles. His quads would begin to ache twenty miles in and burn at fifty miles. Running somehow set him right. His long legs fell into an easy, fluid stride and a relaxed, fleet pace. No matter how much he trained, the bike was his challenge. No matter how light and customized the bike, his legs would rather run. He was convinced it was all mental.

He had an image of Charlie taking off on his bike at warp speed. The kid who might've grown into adulthood without ever owning a bike, never really appreciating one or riding one. He saw the joy on the kid's face even while he was huffing and puffing. He caught a glimpse of Lin Su glowering at him, pretty much telling him to butt out of her business, her son's asthma, her life. And it made him smile. The first time he'd ever smiled on a ride. He wasn't aching or burning; he wasn't pumping. He was gliding almost effortlessly, so he assumed he was falling behind.

Someone sailed past him. Griffin. Australian. He had a reputation for taking early leads and had never won a race, though he'd placed very well in a few and was going to win one pretty soon. But Blake decided to just indulge himself, let himself think a little about a kid with asthma so damn grateful to be able to ride a bike for a little while, so apparently unaffected by the trouble in his 'hood, so protective of his mother.

The kid who wanted to know who he was.

His pace steady, he passed Griffin and shot out ahead, so of course he worried that he'd lost his pacing, but it was too late now—you don't drop back unless you're out of steam and he felt strong. He had some tough competition for the run, though. Those hills.

He was gaining on the last curve, feeling a little disoriented, grabbed his bottle of water and squirted some in his mouth, swished, swallowed and bore down. He could hear a dozen cyclists on his tail and forced himself not to think about them—this was traditionally his worst event and he'd make up for it in the run if he didn't totally deplete himself. His legs were always quivering after the ride. But before he could even think about it, he came up on the transition and his support crew was ready to intercept him.

"You shaved two minutes!" Nigel whispered excitedly.

Blake used his toes to peel off his shoes, wiped off his feet, stuck a few gel packs in his pockets, tied his running shoes quickly but carefully. Nothing worse than starting a race with a shoe that pinched. He swallowed some water, stretched out his legs and off he went.

And yeah! This was his home turf. He fixed his pace, moved his arms all over the place to stretch them out, then got comfortable. Within ten minutes seven runners had passed him and he just thought, *Go for it, boys, go for it. You'll regret that…*

An hour and a half in, he got to the climb—two thousand feet in five miles. This would take out the best of them so Blake remembered the smell of pine, the softness of the breeze, then the ferocity of the wind through the mountain pass and he told himself he was just visiting this place. His pace slowed because the work he did here was monumental, so he congratulated himself on staying steady and strong. Then it was level and his pace moved up just slightly—it was tempting to take advantage of the level track and push too hard. When he did that, the last five miles were deadly. Just before the trip down, there was a water station and he stuck out an arm. Five miles more and he stuck out his arm for water again. Then he was headed down and he maintained his constant speed. He could feel the pain in his heel and he concentrated on fluidity of movement and reminded himself not to hit the trail but caress the trail. And the hours moved by steadily and his long legs ate up the distance.

There were three runners ahead of him. He nudged his pace up a notch, then another. He passed an Austrian he'd raced before, then an Italian whose legs were too short for the trek, so he was moving them like mad at the end, pumping his arms and panting like bloody hell. The finish line came into view, three-quarters of a mile down the track, and he thought he could hear those pimps and gangbangers on his heels and he pressed into a solid canter, stretching out his stride, flowing over the ground. He wondered where he was in the pack; he wondered how many had crossed the finish line. Then he heard the screams, the shouting, the chanting, the cheering. He stretched it out, pushed into the nearest thing to a sprint he had in him and, arms over his head, he crossed the line and tore through the tape.

Holy Jesus, he wasn't supposed to win this one; he was just supposed to scare the living shit out of the rest of them. But what happened?

"Nine-fifteen!" Nigel bellowed. "Nine-fifteen! On a fucking *mountain*!"

He braced his hands on his knees and leaned down for a second, concentrating on not puking, and when he was sure he wasn't going to, he slowly stood and began pacing, walking it off, pushing his way through an encroaching crowd.

He had a towel around his neck, a bottle of electrolyte-laced water in his hand, Nigel in his head telling him how close he'd come to a Tahoe record, people crowding him with congratulations. *He'd done that?* Someone said Griffin had come in fifth; Abraham Cadu, a well-known African athlete who was the favorite for this race, was behind him by a minute and a half, which meant had he not trimmed two minutes from the bike he wouldn't have won.

Which meant watching Charlie and Lin Su in his head had been like holding a carrot in front of a stampeding horse.

Someday he might tell them.

Charlie was sitting at Winnie's dining room table with his laptop open. He had it plugged in because it was going to be a long day. It was Saturday and he'd been there on and off all day. It wasn't easy to follow the race via computer because it wasn't live, but there were regular updates complete with pictures and some video streaming that was pretty reliable. Finally, while Lin Su was in the kitchen trying to put together a chicken divan recipe that Winnie wanted her to try, Charlie erupted.

"You are not going to believe this! He won! At least, I think he won! They're doing the awards tomorrow, but there's a live video stream of... Yeah! That's him! That's Blake! First one over the finish line. Nine hours! He raced for over nine hours!"

"Dear God," Winnie said. "Who does something like that?"

Lin Su was just making her way around the breakfast bar when she noticed that Winnie was reaching for her walker and struggling to stand. Before Lin Su could rush to her to help, Mikhail was beside her.

"You worked very hard when you were competing," he reminded her.

"I practiced, and yes, it was hard, but in competition I skated a two-minute program," she said. "Let me be! Let me do this!" She wrestled the walker away from him and moved steadily toward Charlie. "I hate this god-awful thing, but at least I can get around without always needing help!"

"If you don't go slowly you will need help getting off floor,"

Mikhail said. "But do as you please. You can always get new nose after you fall on your face."

"Charlie, push out that chair for me," she said. She sat down beside him. "Let me see what you see there," she said, leaning toward the laptop.

"Yep, that's it, he has the best time," Charlie said. "When's the news come on? This should be on the news, right? Or ESPN? Let me look it up? Where are Ironman triathlon results reported? Aw, come on," he said impatiently to the computer. "When did he say he's coming home?"

"Certainly not immediately," Lin Su said. "Charlie, he can't be in any shape to drive from Lake Tahoe tomorrow! It's a long drive. Maybe eight hours."

"Eureka is only four hours away but he'll go straight up 5," Charlie insisted. "But Tahoe… I'm going to text him."

"Honey, don't bother Mr. Smiley," Lin Su said. "He just raced for over nine hours! And you know he doesn't have his phone with him!"

"Text him," Winnie said. "He'll catch up with his phone."

Lin Su sighed heavily. "Did it ever occur to you to be a good influence?"

"I am. I'm training Charlie to trust his instincts. He should text. After all, the rooting section is right here and we've been waiting all day."

Charlie's thumbs started clicking away wildly. Lin Su found herself thinking that if he learned to do his homework as rapidly, he would be president one day. But the clicking went on…and on…and on…

"Charlie, what are you saying to him? For heaven's sake, don't you think he'll be a little tired after today?"

"I think he won't look at his texts until he's recovered a little," Winnie answered for Charlie. "What did you text?" she then asked Charlie.

"Asking if he really won, saying we're all watching and tracking the race, waiting to hear the official results, that we hope he feels okay and was it a good race and when is he coming home and does he want me to fly down to Tahoe and drive him so he can rest." And at that last, he grinned his best boyish grin.

Lin Su finally coaxed Charlie home just before eight. She suggested a movie and popcorn, but he wasn't interested. He wanted to read one of his training books and keep his phone and laptop open in case there was any news from Blake. Feeling like a movie for herself, she told Charlie to go to her bed with his book and electronics and she would keep the volume down.

Grace had introduced Lin Su to her stash of chick flicks and she had selected two. Troy had added two DVDs that Charlie might find tolerable—one action, one spy drama. Since Charlie was into his training program, Lin Su popped in *The Holiday* and pretended to be Cameron Diaz falling in love with Jude Law. At about the time she was going to make a commitment to Jude, she heard Charlie's phone chime with an incoming text. She waited and listened but didn't hear anything. Then the phone, in the other room, chimed again. She put the movie on pause and got off the couch.

Poor Charlie. He was sprawled over his book, his glasses all wonky, his laptop sleeping as soundly as he. So she picked up the phone and read the text.

Just got your text. Yep, I took it—surprised me as much as anyone. I want to come home tomorrow, but we'll see how I feel after awards in the morning.

She picked up the phone and took it to the couch. She began to text.

Congratulations. Lin Su here—Charlie fell asleep but he was waiting to hear from you. I'll tell him about your text in the morning.

She was barely finished when her cell phone began to ring and she answered in surprise. "Hello?"

"What's a fourteen-year-old kid doing asleep at ten o'clock on a Saturday night?" Blake asked.

"I think following your race, the excitement of it and all, just wore him out. He's sprawled on my bed, his training book under his head and his laptop... Wait a minute. What's a tri-athlete who just completed a nine-hour race doing up?"

"Nine hours and fifteen minutes, thank you very much. I was a little too wired after the race. And there was a little celebrating to do. I'm winding down now. I should sleep well."

"I'll bet. Was it awful?"

"It was awful good. I never expected to win that one. In fact, I was planning on not winning, but I wanted to do well. Well enough so that when the front-runners for the Kona talk about contenders they'll notice how well I did on the mountains and speculate on how that translates into the island race and fear me." He laughed. "That's what I was going for. I'll have to remember that. Obviously good strategy."

"Are you sore?"

"I had a rubdown, I'm all right. The morning after a race is always a little creaky, but I'm feeling good. And you? You're all right?"

"Me?" she asked. "Oh, I'm fine. Very well, thank you. I got

Winnie a walker and she's now a speed demon. We're going to have to keep an eye on that."

"Charlie's workouts are going well?" he asked.

"He's very happy with his progress. You said six days a week, less than an hour each day, but I'm afraid he's impossible to stop—he's at it every day and has to be bribed off the equipment after an hour. I haven't seen him this excited about anything since the day he inherited that laptop from one of my patients a few years ago."

"No problems with his asthma?" Blake asked.

She was reminded that's what their relationship was all about—Charlie's training program. "No problems at all. Be sure to tell Gretchen he's doing well. He was quite taken with her."

"No doubt," Blake said with a laugh in his voice. "I'll try to remember if I talk to her."

"But she's there," Lin Su said. "That's her job, to be there while you race, isn't it?"

"Gretchen decided to race in the women's division. She finished very well. I haven't seen her since the race. We all went in different directions. I had acquaintances here, and she had other clients and the support crew from her training facility. They're all going back to Boulder together, probably tomorrow, but I didn't ask. No worries, I'll be talking to her this week—she runs statistics for me routinely."

"Statistics?"

"Race times, winners, weather conditions, everything. Plus she keeps my personal statistics logged, just like what Charlie's doing for his training, though for a slightly different reason."

"Slightly," she echoed.

"I haven't talked to you too much since you moved into

your loft. Gretchen was in residence and I was getting in that uncommunicative race mode. So, is it good? Your loft?"

"Grace's loft," she corrected. "When she was renovating the flower shop she finished off the upstairs, which had been used for storage. Now it's a small apartment. It has as much of a kitchen as I had in that trailer but is so much more comfortable. And I guess I don't have to tell you about the neighborhood..."

"Plus you're close to your job," he said.

"And school. Charlie seems to really like the school. He's getting phone calls from girls about homework."

"That always helps a guy settle into a new school, a little notice from the girls."

"He says he took Frank's advice and is offering to help the kids with their studies. Um, Frank... Frank's a kid from town Charlie met last summer. He's a genius, Charlie says—going to MIT on a scholarship. But as Charlie tells it, Frank was a nerd in glasses and kind of small when he was Charlie's age, so they bonded."

There was quiet for a long moment. "That kid," Blake finally said. "Never underestimate that kid. He has great insight. His instincts are on target."

"You're right," she said. "He amazes me. Um, I should hang up now. You should rest—you've had a very long day."

"Yeah," he laughed. "Yeah, I have. Hope I've unwound enough to sleep. These races—you either crash afterward or are too wired to sleep. Tell Charlie I'll text him if I'm on my way tomorrow."

"I will," she said. "It was nice of you to text him. Thanks."

"Of course I would. You're friends of mine. Bye, then."

ELEVEN

Grace was putting out her fall sidewalk displays, though the first holiday, Halloween, was weeks away. September was growing ripe, football season was in full swing, leaves on the surrounding hillsides were changing, fall rains were cold and unpredictable and people had begun to decorate their front doors with stalks of Indian corn and fall wreaths of colored leaves and pinecones.

Grace and Troy had each begun winter projects. Troy had hired a stonemason to finish the outdoor hearth. It wasn't too complicated because the foundation and gas pipe were already installed. It was too complicated for Troy, however. Between Grace and Winnie they had convinced him not to play with gas or electricity. So the fireplace man was called.

Putting a metal frame over the base and building around it with the stone Grace and Winnie selected appeared to be a simple process, though time-consuming, and work stopped for rain because of the outdoor location of the fireplace. There seemed to be activity around that project every day.

During the construction of the fireplace, Grace couldn't stay away. She closed the shop twice a day to check on the progress; Troy used his lunch hour to drive home and look things over. The mason was an older, seasoned man in his sixties who had told them to expect at least ten days for the construction, did not show up every day and was not open to suggestions. His name was Keebler, like the cookies. It was never clear whether that was a first name, last name or only name. And he was highly recommended and grumpy as all hell.

"But what if I don't like it?" Grace asked him.

"You'll like it," he said. "Everyone likes my work."

"And if it doesn't seem to fit? The appearance of it, I mean."

"You picked the stone. I reckon you can start over. My schedule is a little tight."

It was obvious if they didn't like the work, they'd be buying a second fireplace. But he'd done Cooper's and it was beautiful. They all held their breath and watched the slow evolution of the outdoor hearth.

Meanwhile, Grace was trying to find a manager for the shop. She interviewed a few women from the area and it was taxing. She came close to hiring one just based on her enthusiasm, but in the end her lack of experience just wouldn't do. Even though the best assistant money could buy had been Ginger, a woman with virtually no experience other than a love of flowers and other beautiful things and a fierce desire to be useful.

She was having an interview that afternoon and she was very hopeful. Ronaldo Germain had owned his own shop in Grants Pass, which he lost to the woes of recession. The last thing she expected was a slim blond man named *Ronaldo*. But it was rare for a man she didn't know to come into her shop, so when he entered she stood from her place at the worktable and said, "May I help you?"

"Ronaldo Germain, here to see the owner," he said. And he looked around her shop, his nose definitely in the air. As if her adorable little shop was somehow inferior!

For a second it occurred to her to say the owner wasn't available today. She didn't have a good feeling.

"I'm Grace Headly, Mr. Germain," she said. "This is my shop."

"Lovely," he said insincerely.

"Come into the back," she said. "I'm working on a piece and we can chat while I finish. I've already read through your very impressive résumé."

He followed her and when they were in the back room he said, "Call me psychic, but I think I see the reason you're in the market for a manager. You're not one of those modern mothers, planning to bring the baby to work, are you?"

"You don't like children? Babies?" she asked.

"Not in the workplace, no, but it's your business, not mine."

"Right. Well, I saw in your cover letter that you owned a shop that fell on hard times and had to sell. Are you employed as a florist now?"

"I am a barista," he said, again the lift of the chin.

It was really at that point that Grace realized she'd struck out again. So, Mr. Lovely had lost his shop and now worked in a coffee shop yet looked at her shop with obvious disdain. But she continued with the conversation, now a little out of curiosity and a little out of fun. She wasn't going to hire him but she wasn't forgiving him for commenting first on her pregnancy and second on her plans for child care. It was her business, after all.

"Tell me, Mr. Germain, what led to you working in the floral industry?"

He sat down at an angle to her and folded his hands on the

tabletop. "It was sheer luck," he said. "I started to work with flowers through a friend who owned a shop and then, a few years later, opened my own. I discovered there's a need for more creative designs, particularly for formal weddings. You do create for weddings, don't you?"

"Of course. I won't be serving weddings in December and January unless I find a skilled and talented florist, however. For obvious reasons. And then, of course, I will often be bringing my baby to work. Because I *want* to." She smiled indulgently.

He glanced at her arrangement. He sniffed. "You might want to trim the stems on those mums and find a better color for the orchids. Is it supposed to be a birthday arrangement or something for the house?"

She ground her teeth and narrowed her eyes. "The customer was very specific. It's for an open house—anniversary. Fall-themed anniversary, thus the rust and gold mums, yellow oncidium, dried maple leaves, curly willow and larkspur."

"Hmm," he mused, taking a slanted view. "I'd opt for some coral Asiatic lily. And Queen Anne's lace. Maybe miniature gerbera."

"That would be very pretty," she said. "And not what the customer asked for."

"I'm sure the customer would like it," he said. "I can assure you, after ten years in the business, I can make a decent bouquet."

"Of course," she said. "I have a digital program that shows the price of each stem and stalk and illustrates their images on a computer screen. That way I don't have to guess when the customer says, 'Oh, just give me something pretty my wife would like.' Though sometimes, depending on the customer, something pretty at the right price is safer."

He stiffened. "No one has such a program."

"*I* do. I helped design it with a programmer when I started out in flowers in Portland. The software writer was a friend of mine. We worked on it together. It's wonderful. And it's patented."

"And you use this for events? Weddings? Funerals?"

"Not funerals. People either have specific desires or are too emotional to listen to a lot of explanation. I use the program for weddings mostly. Sometimes for event centerpieces or arrangements for businesses. I can email images to the prospective client along with a bid. It's very convenient."

"Are there a lot of business events in this, ah, Thunder Point?"

"Not so many, no," she said. "I've been known to cover much of Coos County and beyond for specialty arrangements and accessories. Bandon Dunes plays host to many business meetings and special events and they seem to like my work."

"Who helps you now?" he asked.

"My last assistant just left to get married. She'll be living near Portland, which leaves me shorthanded. Why don't you tell me what you're looking for, Ronaldo."

"Well, I was hoping for a management position and a larger shop, but I suppose this will do. If you're willing to let me have a free hand with some design. Computer program or not, there's no substitute for artistry and experience."

"Really?" she asked.

"Sometimes people have to be encouraged to take a few risks for the sake of beauty, for innovation and creativity."

"Is that so?" she asked. "Most of my customers, ninety percent of my customers at least, are more interested in deciding what they want and not paying a dime extra for it, no matter how creative. It's enough of a challenge to keep the price within their budgets."

"Well, maybe I've spoken out of turn, but my shop was much larger and served a much wider area. My clientele were looking for something very special."

"How lovely," she said.

She asked him a few questions about how he was accustomed to handling billing, repeat customers, what vendors he used for ordering fresh stock, that sort of thing. She wondered if he was accustomed to the upkeep of his own shop or if he hired a cleaning crew and, no surprise, he didn't do any of the cleaning himself. He had assistants who helped with everything. It sounded as if he didn't like the grunt work.

Finally she couldn't think of another question. "Well, thank you for coming in, Mr. Germain. It was a pleasure to meet you, and it was nice of you to take the time. I've had a number of applicants so I'll be in touch." She stood and put out her hand, but it was of course dirty and green from the stems and florist's tape.

"Have you had any applicants who are professional florists?" he asked, also standing.

"Actually, no. Not a one. But my last assistant, who was amazing in every respect, was trained by me. So of course there was never any controversy—we were always on the same page."

"You speak as if you're already convinced we won't work together well," he said.

"I think that idea began with no babies in the workplace," she admitted.

"I'm much more flexible than I let on," he said.

"Ah, but I'm not looking for flexibility so much as an assistant who sees things the way I do. Still, let me consider all the data, taking into account your amazing résumé, and I'll be in touch. It's a very small shop, Mr. Germain. Small and simple and hopefully beautiful, and my clientele has been happy so far. And it's a profitable store. I wouldn't want that to change."

"And if you don't find a productive assistant before..." His gaze dropped to her belly.

"I'm not worried," she said. *A lie.* She was worried. If she didn't find good help, she would have to close the shop for a while. That would probably mean rebuilding her entire customer base when she opened up again. "Thank you again."

He shook her hand. "When will you make a decision?" he asked.

"In a few days," she said. "Have a lovely day, Mr. Germain."

Grace sat again at her worktable, but her heart was a little heavy. That was a disappointing interview. A person like that would never do in Thunder Point. The last thing her friends and neighbors would tolerate was someone who believed he was too good for them. And while her experience in the flower industry had been relatively brief, she'd seen his like before— the artsy-fartsy flower shops that tried too hard to be different, to be chic. Oh, she was familiar with the high-end market, the regionally famous, upscale resorts and hotels, and they were especially appreciative of a hard-working florist who was more eager to please than to be congratulated for her artistry and high prices. Even the fanciest markets wanted good work from talented people and the best price. After all, hadn't Grace grown up with one of the richest women in Northern California? She knew class, she knew style. She knew pretention.

Twenty-year-old Justin Russell came to the shop an hour later for his deliveries. "How you getting by, Grace?" he asked.

"Excellent," she said. "You?"

"Also excellent," he said. "You have a lot of deliveries today?"

"Just five, but they're all out of town. Take the delivery van.

I'm going to close the shop for an hour or so and walk across the beach to check on the fireplace man."

He looked at her doubtfully. "You want to use my car?" he asked.

"The walking is a good idea, Justin. I'm not handicapped, just pregnant."

"Right. But... Well, seems like you're getting real pregnant these days."

"That's the idea, Justin. Then poof! I explode."

He winced. "Don't do that, okay?"

"Okay," she laughed. "Your deliveries are all tagged and in the refrigerator. Lock the back door please?"

"Sure. If you're not here when I bring the van back, I'll leave the keys on your desk."

She really wasn't worried about the stone man or the fireplace, but after that lousy interview, she thought a little fresh air and perspective might help. She needed her jacket because the air on the beach was cool, though it was a beautiful, sunny, fall day. She walked up the beach stairs to the deck and Keebler turned to look at her.

"Looking very nice, Keebler," she said.

He grunted.

In the living room she found Mikhail sitting in Winnie's favorite chair, his feet up on the ottoman, reading his electronic book. She shed her jacket, hung it on the back of a dining room chair and gave him a kiss on the forehead. He reached up and patted her hand.

"How long has Mother been asleep?" she asked.

He glanced at his watch. "Better than hour," he said. "Lin Su folds the clothes."

As Grace went to her mother's bedroom she passed Lin Su in

the hall, pulling linens out of the dryer and folding them. They nodded at each other and Grace went to her mother's room.

Winnie was resting peacefully, lying on her back, her eyes closed and the merest smile on her lips. Grace sat on the edge of the bed and her mother's eyes fluttered open. Winnie yawned gracefully.

Grace pulled Winnie's thin and frail hand to her belly to feel the movement and Winnie laughed. "She's romping now," Winnie said in a faint whisper.

"She's wild. She takes after her grandmother, I think."

"You were very active. I didn't enjoy it as much as I should have. I wanted the pregnancy to be over so I could skate. I was so shortsighted."

"Nah, that was just the place you were in at the time," Grace said.

"Something is bothering you," Winnie said.

Oh, indeed, Grace felt bothered. She had very little hope of finding the right person, someone like Ginger, to run the flower shop while she excused herself to have a baby, to spend the first few weeks with the baby. She feared she'd have to close the shop for at least a couple of months. And, oh! She'd worked so hard to build that store, to stock it, to learn to run it, to make it a good working shop that made money. She'd worked easily twelve hours a day, seven days a week. It was her whole life.

Of course, there had been no Troy then. All there'd been was the shop and her need to be independent, to succeed on her own. That was only a couple of years ago, before she reconciled with Winnie, before she fell in love with Mr. Hottie High School Teacher, before there was a baby in her.

She sighed deeply, pressing her mother's hand on her belly.

"I love this baby," Winnie said softly.

Why worry about a flower shop when you have everything in the world that matters? Grace asked herself.

"Mama, I've been thinking. We need a little more time together before the baby is here. I think we should read something together. I've never read some things that should be read. I have an idea—let's pick a book and I'll read it to you. An hour in the afternoon or something."

"Fifty Shades!" Winnie said.

"Oh, Mother, I'm not reading that out loud! It has too many body parts in it. The private kind."

"Prude. All right, let's do something by that Higgins girl."

"I was thinking something even more tame. And old. A timeless romance. Deeply romantic, rich in language and titillating. *Jane Eyre? Wuthering Heights?*"

"I love *Wuthering Heights*," Winnie said.

"We'll do that! I'll get us a copy and we'll start tomorrow. We'll have to think about when is the best time of day."

"That would be lovely, Grace. Now what's bothering you?"

She took a breath. "I had an unpleasant interview with an applicant. He acted like he was doing me a favor, applying for the job. He looked at my perfect little shop like it was a hovel."

"You won't hire him, then," Winnie said.

"The shop will be hard to manage when the baby comes," Grace said. "When you need more of my time."

"Grace, listen to me. I'm not known for wisdom or unselfishness, I know that. But life is short. Hire more nurses if you must. Get a good nanny or sitter. But follow your heart while you can."

"It's not just a store to me, Mama. I love the flowers. I love taking my flowers to weddings and parties. I love sitting in my little back room at that scarred old table making beautiful arrangements, and though I don't need the money from it, I love that I can earn it. It was the first thing after skating that made me feel competent. And I don't expect anyone to understand, but I'm always happy when I'm doing my job. But I want to be a good mother. I want more than one child."

"That's because you haven't had labor yet," Winnie said, smiling. "Or colic or terrible twos or sass."

Grace ignored her; she wasn't worried about any of that. "I can scale back the hours. My drop-in sales are not the biggest—most of my business comes over the website or phone. But I don't want to be forced to give it up."

"It's going to work out, Grace. If it truly makes you happy, you'll find a way. There is always a way."

Grace leaned over and kissed Winnie's cheek. "A year ago you would have argued that the flower business wasn't worth my time."

"I've decided that I'd like to be missed when I go, after all."

Grace laughed at her mother. "And what can we do that would make you happy?" she asked.

"Me? Well, I've been thinking about that. I'd like to go to one of those football games."

"You? Football?"

"Everyone goes," Winnie said. "The whole town goes. Then half of them come out to the beach and make noise till all hours, dancing around the fires like druids."

"Well, then, we'll take you to a game," Grace said. "Who would've guessed?"

"What? I've been to football games!" Winnie said.

"Really? Have you ever been to one where you didn't view from a private box?"

She shrugged and made a face. "Perhaps not. But I think it sounds like fun."

"Then fun it shall be," Grace promised.

"Only if it's not raining, of course," Winnie said.

"Of course," Grace said, laughing.

In the evenings, Lin Su embroidered the ornate letter *S* onto towels that were very pale taupe in color, just like the walls in Blake's hallway and master bath. She chose a silk thread that was between tan and gold. It was because of her mother's swatch that she taught herself this needlework, not nearly as good as those Vietnamese artisans, but her work was excellent and she was proud of this towel set. She thought he might appreciate it as something he wouldn't otherwise have purchased. And it was personal without being intimate, the perfect gift for a single man.

Lin Su was very grateful to Winnie for her desire to attend a football game because that paved the way for Lin Su to go along, be of service and check out her son as he attended with a few new friends from school. She couldn't go with him; that was too invasive. And she hadn't wanted to go alone.

Charlie and a couple of kids sat near Troy, Grace, Peyton and Iris. Scott was down on the field with the team and Seth was near the field, the town deputy ready for anything, though he was not in uniform. Charlie was considered very cool to have this association with these Thunder Point residents, particularly Troy, considered by many to be the most popular teacher.

But what she noticed during halftime and the end of another successful Thunder Point game was that there were a number of kids swirling around Charlie, high-fiving him, patting him on the back, calling out to him and generally being wonderfully friendly.

Winnie was bundled up and sat in her wheelchair at the base of the bleachers, wearing one of her beloved furs. Her friends swung by to say hello. There was Lou and Gina, Carrie and

Ray Anne. Mikhail and Lin Su stayed near her, Seth and Troy
checking on them regularly, offering to bring them goodies
from the concession stand. And not surprisingly, Blake happened along and chose to stand for a long while with his next-
door neighbors. Then he went into the bleachers and squeezed
in with Charlie and his friends, probably enhancing Charlie's
sudden popularity.

Lin Su couldn't stop smiling. As far as she knew, Charlie had
never enjoyed camaraderie like this before. She had worried
about him almost constantly, fearing he was regularly picked
on by older, bigger kids. But tonight, he was laughing and
cheering wildly. She checked her coat pocket to make sure
she had that extra inhaler and EpiPen, then stopped herself.
He was fine. He was happy.

For once Lin Su wore jeans and boots with a heel, wrapped
in her new red winter coat, her hair loose and flowing down
her back. It was probably feeling good in her civilian clothes
that made her a little more animated, a bit more excited. She
looked like a real woman for once and not so much like the
local nurse. And since she'd been living in the loft in town
for a couple of weeks, people shouted out to her as one of the
neighbors enjoying their favorite entertainment—a high school
football game.

Her relationship with everyone had evolved. She began to
think of many of them as friends. Their acquaintance grew
beyond her work for Winnie and much of that had to do with
the simple fact that Charlie was in school all day and Lin Su
had more time to connect with people. She went to work a
little later in the morning, took breaks in the afternoon while
Winnie napped; she even babysat the flower shop a couple
of times so that Grace could spend an hour or two of quality
time with her mother.

She was spending a little time with Blake because of Charlie's training schedule and because they ran into each other so frequently. She was even invited to come to Blake's gym to watch Charlie work out with Blake. But only once. And, she suspected, only at Blake's insistence.

There were little slivers of time here and there when it was only Blake and Lin Su. It was quite by accident, of course. Lin Su would be out on Winnie's deck for a little while or maybe on the beach road watching for Charlie to get home from school. Blake would always greet her and take a few minutes to talk. Blake liked to take a happy hour with the family when everyone was gathering at the end of the day, though his cocktail would be a lime and electrolyte-charged water. He was always in training. And with a big race coming up, he was more rigid than ever about his schedule.

They were all gathered in Winnie's living room, Lin Su nearby in the kitchen, when Blake asked Troy if he could take over Charlie's workouts for a while.

"No problem. We might have to adjust the times a little, might even have to do it early in the morning before school, but we'll get it done."

"I'm going to be scarce for the next ten days. I'm going to be working hard at getting ready and in three days I'm going to Hawaii. I want to be there six or seven days before the race."

"Kona is a big one," Charlie said. "*The* big one. If I was sixteen and had a license, I'd drive the route with you for practice," Charlie said. "I'd give almost anything to be on the crew."

"Couple of years before we consider that, pal," he said.

"How many people on your crew?" Troy asked.

"Hard to say," Blake explained. "They come from the institute, Gretchen's training facility, and they crew for more than one athlete. There might be two concentrating on me, but as soon as my needs are met, they have another athlete to fix with water, nourishment, transition. Their timing has to be perfect—they know exactly how long it will take each athlete to complete a phase of the race, and if they're not at the right place at the exact time it can cost the race." He started to laugh. "One year a long time ago there was a Navy SEAL in the race and he was a favorite, but his crew ran out of water and relied on beer instead. It might've kept him hydrated but it also slowed him down." He laughed. "But he came in second!"

"I thought the race personnel had water stations," Grace said.

"They do. I've relied on them, as well, depending on the race and the rules of the race, but if I can have my own team it gives me a little more confidence, especially during the transitions. For me, if the timing is right my race is better."

"I'll be watching all day," Charlie said. "I figured out they're live streaming from the race so I can get more coverage."

"Well, my head will be in another place so you can fill me in on the race when I get home." He stood to leave. He put a hand on Charlie's shoulder. "You know who wins the race, right?"

"Right," Charlie said. "The guy with the plan."

"The guy who ignores his plan doesn't do so well. The guy who changes his pace too early gets in trouble." He shook his head. "Some athletes have a reputation for it—they take the early lead even if it depletes them. They wash out. Remember that in your workouts—you have a plan. It works. No fancy stuff while I'm gone, okay?"

"I know. Nice and steady," Charlie said.

"You'll thank me someday," Blake said. Then he shook Charlie's hand and bent at the waist to give Winnie a little kiss on the brow. "Be well, Winnie. I'll see you pretty soon."

"Good luck, Blake," Winnie said. "Bring home the gold."

"I'll do my best."

The house fell silent when Blake left. No one spoke or stirred.

"Hey! He's going to do great!" Charlie finally said. "He's ready! That's ninety percent of it."

TWELVE

It remained quiet while the family ate dinner. "Why isn't anyone talking like usual?" Charlie asked. "This is the one he trains all year for. You're not worried, are you? He's going to do great!"

"Of course he is," Winnie said. "Who is Blake's family? Where are they?"

No one answered for a moment. "He said he was raised by a single mother, like me," Charlie finally said. "And she's gone now."

"Who will be at the finish line for him?" she asked.

"I imagine he has a lot of good friends, Mother," Grace said. "He's been racing this circuit for years. He's been in the top tier for years."

"Yes, I know what that's like. A cheering section made up of your competitors." Winnie snorted.

"He has a team, Mother," Grace said. "Really, he'll be fine. And we can have a little gathering to celebrate when he gets back."

"A poor substitute for having people who really care about you at the finish line."

"It will have to do," Mikhail said. "He's had years to figure out who will be at the finish line."

"One of us should go," Winnie said.

You could have heard a pin drop.

"Due respect, it won't be you, Your Majesty," Mikhail said.

"Pah, I could do it with the right support! All I need is a little help."

"A *lot* of help, Mama!" Grace said. "I can't have you stranded on some island with your health as it is! Besides, you're not up to watching a nine-hour race!"

"I'll just watch him come in. I was there for every competition you had, and even though you hated me, it meant something, didn't it?"

"I didn't hate you," Grace argued. "We were at odds, that's all."

Mikhail said something in Russian. Something passionate. Everyone looked at him. "Was good for mother and daughter, though a challenge for coach."

"I'll take Lin Su, the wheelchair, the walker, everything we need. I'll get Virginia right on it," she added, speaking of her assistant, still based in San Francisco. "She'll find us some superior accessible accommodations not too far from the race."

"The place will be overrun with people!" Grace said. "It's ten days away! You'll never get anything. And if you do, it will be inconvenient. And who's going to drive you around the island?"

"Virginia can do anything. She's been booking my travel for years. Lin Su will drive or maybe we'll get a car service. Lin Su learned to drive in Boston. She can handle a little island traffic. And of course we'll take Charlie."

Lin Su was suddenly all ears. "What?"

"I wouldn't leave him out of this excursion. This could be my last trip. I'm still in relatively good health. If I'm sitting down I don't fall. My only real problem is fatigue and I manage that by planning ahead. Besides, Charlie is probably the most dedicated of all Blake's fans. Charles, when is your birthday?"

Charlie, looking a little stunned, answered slowly. "June thirtieth."

"And tell me, did you have a celebration?"

"Yes," he said. "We went out to dinner and I had presents. A couple of apps for my phone. Clothes for summer and stuff like that."

"This is a belated birthday present."

"Winnie," Lin Su said. "It's too much. Charlie has school."

"We won't go for a week," Winnie said. "Just a few days. We'll have a wonderful time. Of course we can't count on Blake until he's recovered from his race, but that won't keep us from having a good time. And Charlie will learn some important things."

"We might distract Blake," Lin Su said. "We might distract him and do more harm than good. I know your heart is in the right place but remember what he said—he plans to the second. He's not flexible when it comes to his performance. It would be a bad idea. Grace is right—a small celebration when he gets home is better."

"Bull," Winnie said. "We're going."

"No!" Lin Su said. She took a breath. "If you insist I go, maybe Troy can keep an eye on Charlie while…"

"We're going," Winnie said. "I'll speak to Blake to be sure we won't be an inconvenience, to be sure he isn't distracted by us. You, me and Mikhail and Charlie."

"Ah. Madam has included me," Mikhail said, lifting his drink to his lips.

"No," Lin Su said. "I have to put my foot down. It's extreme and indulgent."

"Ma," Charlie said. "Come on!"

Lin Su jerked her head sharply in her son's direction and said something harsh and adamant. The only trouble...it wasn't in a language anyone understood.

It silenced the table again.

"That was interesting," Troy said. "You get that, Charlie?"

"That was another no," Charlie said. "With swearing."

"Sleep on it, Lin Su," Winnie said calmly. "I'll speak to Blake tomorrow if I can catch him. I'll make sure he doesn't veto the idea. If he doesn't want us there, we'll think of another excursion. But damn it, I'm in the mood for some tropical weather. And I'd love to see my friend Blake do some damage in Kona."

While clearing the table and washing up some dishes, Lin Su appealed to Grace to put a stop to this extravagant and complicated idea.

"You've been with us over four months, Lin Su. Does it appear that once Mother gets an idea, you can talk her out of it? And didn't you say in your interview that travel wasn't out of the question as long as you had time to prepare?"

"You said it wasn't likely, that's why I didn't mention Charlie at the time. I don't want Charlie to get the idea people will be giving him things like trips to Hawaii! In the long run, it won't do him any good. Ever since coming here to work for Winnie, things have been handed to us left and right, from the new school to the loft! A trip to Hawaii is so...so... It's just huge, that's all."

"It's actually a nice idea," Grace said. "Listen, I'd intervene for you if she started going completely crazy and suggested taking Charlie out of school for long tours out of the country, but a few days in Hawaii to watch his best friend race?" Grace shrugged. "That's actually nice of Mother. She is, under all her bossiness, a very generous person."

So she appealed to Winnie, suggesting spoiling the boy would make his life more difficult in the end.

"As hard as he's worked?" Winnie asked. "He should be so proud of himself. He's been completely dedicated. Stop worrying so much—it's a few days and we'll have a nice time."

"He shouldn't get any more attached to Blake," Lin Su said.

"You're too late, my dear. He's already attached. To Blake and to all of us. Just as we're attached to him."

She knew this in her heart. It was true. They were all good friends now, though she tried to keep things in perspective. Charlie had always known people she worked with and for, but this took it to the next level. They were almost a family and she was very grateful. What she didn't want was for Charlie to feel what she'd felt when that family that she counted on, her adoptive parents and sisters, abandoned her, as if they'd never been family at all.

She had tried to protect him from everything. She hadn't been able to so far.

"Have you ever been to a luau, Lin Su?"

She had. And she'd been younger than Charlie.

When Lin Su was a girl she'd been on some mighty nice trips. Her parents were well-to-do and they spent a couple of weeks in Saint Thomas every winter; Boston was brutal in the winter. They had a place at the cape for summers. She'd been to Maui with the family twice—Karyn's second wedding was held there. They also traveled to Europe a few times.

Lin Su also went to Europe with her high school class—Italy, France, Spain. She'd had good experiences even if she hadn't thoroughly enjoyed the company of her parents. Well, they didn't happen to be especially enjoyable people. Gordon was only interested in golfing, drinking, living it up with his cronies. Marilyn, focused on status, was more interested in the wives of those cronies.

Lin Su had fun—all the cronies and wives had kids and she went to school with many of them. Then along came Jake in her senior year and those little family trips improved tremendously. Her parents were more than thrilled to invite him along—both to keep her out of their hair and to impress his parents.

Charlie, however, had never been anywhere except the emergency room from time to time. And while they always seemed to be moving, scraping to hold things together, worrying about where they'd land next, he had never complained. Why shouldn't he be lucky for once? Fly to the islands, watch his idol race?

But it wasn't just Charlie she hoped to protect. Lin Su grew to like Blake more every day. There wasn't an admirable quality he lacked and she didn't want to long for him, to long for a life she would never have. She pretended she didn't want Charlie to be let down when Blake turned out to be human. She feared being vulnerable to his touch, his kindness, his devotion to her son; she feared the dark pain of rejection. Ordinarily such fears would be easy for her to mask but Lin Su had strong memories of frolicking on the beach with her teenage lover, Charlie's father, Jake. What more poignant way was there than that vivid memory to remind her that her life would be forever ruined if she let herself be drawn into that sort of romantic idealism again? Charlie was just a kid. She had been just a kid.

After Winnie was settled, Lin Su walked with Charlie along the beach road to the loft. "Soon it will be too cold for this walk," she said.

"I want to go," Charlie said. "I want to see him race. I want to take a trip. On a plane."

"You've been on a plane," she said.

"Not recently enough for me to remember," he reminded her. "You can forbid it, I know. You can refuse and even force Winnie to get a nurse who goes along with what she wants, but that would be so stupid because Winnie makes your life easier than anyone ever has."

"That's not why I took the job," Lin Su said. "The pay is good. She provides benefits we need!"

"I want to go," he said again. "It's safe, it's convenient, it's not expensive, and if you find a way to say no to something so totally cool, it will come between us. In a bad way."

Lin Su stopped walking. "Are you threatening me?"

"I'm going to go places and do things, Mom. I might not be a great athlete but I'm going to do athletic things. I'm going to run and swim and study and travel. I know it's going to be hard but I can work at it and it will happen. Because I want it."

"The sisters I grew up with had everything handed to them and they were incorrigible," she said.

"I don't know very much about them."

"Better that way," she said, walking again. "You can trust me to tell the truth."

"At least part of it," Charlie said. "Just the part that keeps me in line. Why don't you trust me with all of it? I'm not a bad person. I do everything you want."

She stopped again. "Charlie, how can I show you life is not easy? That you have to be strong?"

"You think I didn't figure that out already? You should ask

Blake sometime about how he learned to run, learned to swim. He makes our life look like we're trust-fund babies." He walked a little more. "I want us to go, to see something we don't see every day, to watch him race. Mom, I want us to go."

"Lucky for you, Winnie is stubborn and she won't stop until she gets her way and we need the job," she said.

"Why are you afraid to go?" Charlie asked.

"I'm not afraid," she said. Then she sighed. "It's a thing I have. About my comfort zone. Where I feel most at ease. And secure."

"Where you feel most in control," he argued. "Don't worry, we'll be fine. Winnie and Mikhail have traveled the world. Over and over. Even unfriendly places. This is only Hawaii, just another state, just like driving to California. Except it takes a little longer."

"Over six hours. Over ocean," she said.

"It's beautiful there, Mom. And my friend Blake is going to kick ass."

"Language," she said. "Language."

"Prude," he said, laughing.

Grace asked Lin Su if she'd mind the flower shop for a couple of hours right after lunch so she could read with her mother and run a couple of errands. Lin Su was more than happy to— there were many things she loved about the flower shop. It was quiet most of the time, there wasn't much demand on her besides taking calls and, if she was completely bored, she did a little tidying up. And being around fresh flowers was soothing.

She decided to walk across the beach when a male voice startled her. "Nice day for a walk," Blake said.

She stopped and looked at him. He sat on the bottom step to his deck, drenched in sweat.

"I don't think you were out for a stroll," she said.

"Eighteen miles."

"I thought you'd be gone by now."

"Tonight. So, you'll be there."

"We'll be there," she said. "I hope that doesn't distract you. Winnie insisted we should go."

He shook his head. "I'll be focused on the race. When it's over, when I've recovered, maybe then we'll get together before coming home." He leaned back, his elbows on the step behind him. "I hear you put up quite a fight."

"There are definitely no secrets around here."

"Oh, I think there are still a few," he said. "Slowly, they're giving way. Kind of like the little Dutch boy and the dam."

"We won't interfere with your race, with your team. We'll stay back and just cheer. We can congratulate you later. When you're done celebrating with all your friends."

"Okay," he said doubtfully, smiling at her. "I do think of you, Charlie, Winnie and Mikhail as friends, however. But it won't be much of a celebration, if one is even in order. I'll be tired."

"Charlie says you're going to kick ass," she said.

"I'll give it my best. It's my plan to have my best race this year. Then I'm going to have some downtime—a few months."

"No training?"

"Just maintenance, not endurance training. I stay in shape, keep my times good, relax the OCD a little..."

"Oh, so there is some OCD," she said, smiling.

"You think anyone could do this for a living without it? We're driven. It's kind of a survival thing, I think." He just shook his head at her. "I'm glad you lost the fight. I'm glad you're coming. It's an awesome event, the weather is supposed to be great and the islands are so relaxing when you're done killing yourself in the race."

"Will it be relaxing before the race?"

"A little bit. I'll train, but the main thing is to get my head in the game. That takes concentration and a good dose of serenity. Hawaii lends itself to that." He grinned. "It would be all right for even nonracers to relax a little."

"I'll be working, of course."

"Maybe if I'm lucky you'll have a coffee break at some point."

"Oh, I'm sure Charlie will completely dominate what little time you have after the race."

"He'll try," Blake said. "One of these days you and I are going to spend a little time together. You know, just to get to know each other better."

"If there's anything about me you'd like to know, you only have to ask."

"Let me think about that, then," he said. "I have a feeling if we ever relax and talk, we'll find out things about each other that surprise us both."

"I can't imagine what," she said, completely sincerely. Lin Su thought she knew all she needed to know about Blake Smiley. He was a world-class athlete, a huge success in his world, a legitimate good guy and her son's idol.

"I think eventually we'll find out how much we have in common."

Impossible! she thought. But she wouldn't say so; that would be rude. "That will be interesting," she said. "I'd better get to the shop. Grace needs a break."

"If I don't see you before, I'll see you in Hawaii," he said. "Have a good week."

All the way across the beach she was thinking, *Don't read*

anything into that. He's just charming, that's all. Polite. Accommodating. Delightful.

And next she thought, *I'd better do a little shopping for island wear.*

Grace was looking forward to the weekend with great anticipation. Her mother and Winnie's support crew would be gone to the great race in Kona and she would be alone with her husband for the first time in months. Troy and Grace hadn't even managed a honeymoon. She was thinking about locking up the shop. There were no major events on her calendar and she could take phone orders from home. But she really didn't dare. She was going to have to close the shop in two weeks to attend Ginger's wedding on the Lacoumette farm up near Portland. And there would be a lot more closings in the next several months.

She was hard at work on a gorgeous arrangement for the resort in Bandon, one of her best customers. They had ordered four extra-large floral sculptures with large rock bases inside a clear glass oval bowl, calla lilies, orchids, birds-of-paradise, curly willow and a fine green fern that was almost like moss. They had a very big weekend coming up at the club. A large fall wedding was taking over one of the restaurants and they wanted to put two arrangements in their reception area and similar arrangements in the restaurant where the bride and groom would host over a hundred guests for a seven-course dinner.

A far cry from the way Grace had married Troy, on the beach with their neighbors present, as well as people from town who just felt like crashing the party. Most of the guests were barefoot within an hour.

The bell on the front door jingled and she stood, pasted a

friendly smile on her face to greet her customer, then froze. "Mr. Germain," she said, not feeling at all welcoming,

"Mrs. Headly," he said, giving his head a nod. "Do you have a moment?"

"I sent you an email in response to your interview, Mr. Germain…"

"It was received," he said.

There was no posturing or sniffing this time. Of course she had declined to hire him. His attitude just wouldn't cut it here.

"You were very polite, thank you," he said. "I wonder if you have time to talk?"

"The job is no longer available," she said.

"Still…"

"Come back to the workroom," she said, questioning her own judgment in this. She did not want to endure a lot of time with him. Plain and simple, he was a snooty pain in the ass. "Have a seat while I finish up. What's on your mind?"

"Well, I wasn't myself the day I came to interview with you and I'd like to apologize for that. I think I was…" He lifted his chin. "I was superior. I've been accused of that before."

She tilted her head. "Oh, have you?"

"Once or twice," he said. "Look, I'm an excellent florist. My shop was in demand. I had a great business."

"But what did you tell me? The economy had you upside down?"

"The economy didn't help but that wasn't what went wrong. It was a number of issues that converged like…" He took a breath. "The perfect storm."

She listened but he had stopped talking. "Apology accepted. Of course."

"There I go, being vague again. I had a breakup. My part-ner was also my partner in the store. She'd been pilfering for some time, I learned. I guess in the big leagues we call it embezzling, but I couldn't prove anything since she was doing the bookkeeping. It looked like we were losing money for the first time when in fact she was skimming. Taking money, cheating on me, the store, everything. She didn't pay taxes that were due and left me a pot of bills that should've been paid." He rubbed his shiny forehead. "And I had other things distracting me or I might've caught it. My mother was sick, my sister was in need, my profits had become low when they'd always been excellent. I really am a good florist. Then there were some medical bills in addition to taxes due…"

She? Grace thought. She'd taken him for gay. Apparently not. He was about forty, a little too old to be delusional or closeted. Straight, she decided. With some affectations?

"And the partner?"

"Gone. I looked into a forensic audit, an attorney, a detective, that sort of thing, but in the end I'd be throwing good money after bad. She got away with about a hundred thousand dollars that I'll never get back and I had to let the store go. You obviously didn't do a background check or you'd know—I lost it. That simple. I filed bankruptcy."

She *had* looked at him, for as much as internet research could do. She'd noted the bankruptcy. After meeting him, nothing more seemed necessary. "Would you like a cup of tea, Mr. Germain?" she asked, surprising herself.

"That would be so welcome," he said, sighing with relief.

"Let me put the water on," she said. She didn't have to go far; she had a little electric kettle on her desk. She rinsed it, refilled it and turned it on before going back to him. "I have chamomile, Earl Grey, peppermint and green tea."

"Peppermint would be great," he said. Then he raised a brow and glanced at her round middle. "Stomach issues?" he asked.

"From time to time," she said. "And your mother?"

"She passed a little over a year ago."

"I'm so sorry. And your sister?"

"Melanie is a special-needs adult and my mother took re-sponsibility for her. We've had a little bit of a struggle since my mother died."

"I see. You're right—the perfect storm."

She went back to her desk and fixed him up a cup of tea. She put it in front of him and took her seat again.

"This is lovely," he said, admiring the arrangement that took up a great deal of her worktable.

"Thanks. Listen, Mr. Germain," she began.

"Ronaldo, please."

"Ronaldo, I appreciate your courtesy in coming back, apol-ogizing, explaining, but…"

"I know. You don't need me now. Well, the thing is, who-ever you hired might not work out and you'll be looking again. If that should happen, I'll probably still be available. My shop wasn't the biggest or most important shop in the business, but we did well. And I loved working with flowers."

"How are things going for you now?" she asked.

He took a sip of his tea. "Getting by pretty well actually. I had to sell my house but I'm living in my mother's house. My sister is in a group home right now and she wants to come home so much. My hours at the coffee shop are crazy and she needs some supervision. She's very functional, but she can't live on her own. She will never live on her own. She needs routine, however, and I can't keep her with me, change her schedule every week and expect her to adjust. And she calls me," he said, adding a laugh. "And calls me and calls me and calls me."

"Tell me about your shop," she said.

And he did, from the day he bought it until the day he closed

it. He talked about his biggest jobs, some of his regular customers, pictures of his work that had been published, whether
purposely or because they happened to be in the photograph
of a grand opening or wedding or other major event. When
he'd been up and running for a couple of years his sister began
to work for him. She was a wonderful organizer and helped
him keep the shop clean. His customers loved her.

His sister had been the victim of a near-drowning accident
when she was a young child, been without oxygen for too long
and suffered serious brain damage. He was clearly devoted to
her, if he was to be believed. Finding a good job in a flower
shop didn't materialize, but when he saw the ad for a manager,
he thought he might be able to get back to flowers.

"I miss it," he said. "I miss designing, unruffling the hys-
terical brides, placating the matrons whose parties I provided
flowers for, the churches that came to me first, even the funerals that hoped for something special. I delivered and staged
my own flowers…"

"So do I!" she said.

"I'm not letting anyone else set up my flowers, deliver my
bouquets to events," he returned enthusiastically. "Staging is
half of it. A third, anyway."

"Tell me something, Ronaldo—why don't you move? Go
to a bigger city? Portland would be good. San Francisco would
be better. Somewhere a good florist can make real money."

"There's the magic word—money. Relocating like that can
get expensive. But it's emotional also. I've lived in Grants Pass
my whole life and I'm not sure Melanie can cope with a move.
Like it or not, even with a group home, I'm going to make
sure Melanie has what she needs."

"That's a good brother," she said.

"Have you lived in this little town a long time?" he asked.

"I came here to buy the store. I'd been looking for one. I worked in a shop in Portland, with good friends who trained me." She rubbed her tummy. "Lifelong friends, really. I have to visit them before the baby comes."

"And after. What brought you to the flower business, besides good friends?"

"A very difficult but in the end rewarding journey," she said. And then she told him everything, beginning with once being a champion figure skater, an Olympian. He was thrilled by this; he loved to watch the skating. She explained about her exit from the stress, her flight to Thunder Point, falling in love with the hottest teacher at the high school, reconciliation with her mother who was here now. "A rich dowager who lives with us, or we with her, and this little shop is my haven. I love it. It means so much to me."

She was completely oblivious to the time as they compared mothers, flower shops, friends, favorite work projects. And then the back door opened and Justin stepped inside. He grinned his lovely boyish grin. "You have my deliveries ready?" he asked.

"Justin!" She looked at her watch. "Oh, my God, I lost all track of time. Yes, yes—just about. There are five in the cooler and this one is nearly finished. I need five minutes." She stood up. "Ronaldo, I enjoyed the conversation."

"So did I," he said. "If anything materializes for a florist…"

"Absolutely," she said. Justin was taking the arrangements for delivery out the back door.

"There's something I should probably explain…"

She laughed at him. "If either one of us explains any more, I'll miss my deadline."

"I'll be quick. You should know, on the off chance your new hire doesn't work out… That partner. It was not a woman."

She raised her eyebrows. "Is that so?"

"If that's a problem in a fishing village full of old-fashioned folks..."

"This is one of the nicest towns I've ever encountered," she said. "If there's one thing I've learned, it's not in your best interest to hide your real self. Besides, it's like dousing your natural flame." She laughed. "No pun intended."

He smirked and shook his head. "Too bad I screwed up the interview. I have a feeling we'd have fun working together. And that business about no babies in the workplace? I actually like babies. And they like me."

"I have no doubt," she said. She put out her hand. "Now go! I have things to do—I've played long enough!"

He picked up his cup and took it to the sink.

"No, no, leave that. I've got it. It was a pleasure. I'll let you know how things work out."

"I'd appreciate that."

Grace hurried to finish her piece, got Justin on his way, then she put in a call to Virginia, her mother's administrative assistant in San Francisco. Winnie was very wealthy and the challenge of hiring for her household staff had always been taken very seriously, given the value of her possessions, her estate, her person. Grace asked Virginia to run a check on Ronaldo Germain, a potential employee. And she asked her to rush it.

A couple of hours later her husband was at the shop, his workday at the high school done. "How's my sexy little mama today?" he asked, wrapping his arms around her.

"I think I've found someone for the shop," she said, beaming. "Provided he turns out not to be a felon."

"No kidding? You mean we can actually have a baby without you stressing out over the flowers?"

"If he turns out to be the kind of person I believe he is. Virginia is researching him."

"When did he turn up?" Troy asked.

"I'd already interviewed him and rejected him. He came back. He wanted a second chance. I told him the position was no longer available, but…" She shrugged. "I hope my instincts are on target. But I promise to take it slow."

THIRTEEN

Lin Su was not prepared for how out of her experience this short trip to the big island was. First of all, a private jet took them to San Francisco and no one had mentioned beforehand that this would be the case. All she knew was that they had a flight to San Francisco from the nearest regional airport. Once there, they went directly to their commercial flight where four seats in first class had been booked. When Lin Su asked her why she'd done this, Winnie simply said, "I wasn't going to stick you in the back. I need this space. And I need my nurse."

Lin Su told Charlie not to get used to this.

Winnie had offered to have a car service available but Lin Su protested loudly. It wouldn't do to have a luxury sedan or SUV pulling up to a triathlon. They would be a spectacle. She insisted on a rented vehicle that could accommodate Winnie, her wheelchair, her walker, all their luggage. Virginia arranged for a rental van with a portable ramp to help Winnie in and out. It was a very big van. Lin Su sat in the driver's seat, Charlie next to her, and she studied the dash and all the controls for a while before very, very slowly pulling out of the parking space.

"You gonna be able to drive this thing?" Charlie asked her.

"Of course," she said. "I'm not very optimistic about parking it, however."

The condo that had been rented was so luxurious Lin Su had to struggle not to gasp. A great room or family room faced a broad patio that fronted the beautiful beach. It was on the ground floor of a large resort and had a full kitchen, dining room, three bedrooms, two of which were masters. In Lin Su's room, there were two queen-size beds so she could share her room with Charlie.

They had a lovely takeout from one of the resort restaurants and ate on the patio. In spite of the time change, it being earlier in Hawaii, Winnie wasn't too tired. She'd also managed to catch a nap on the plane. After having some dinner, Mikhail and Charlie took a walk on the beach while Winnie and Lin Su enjoyed the sunset.

"I think I should take Charlie out to the race start early tomorrow morning. If you think you can miss that part, I'll talk to race officials and find out if we can get you a safe place at the finish where you won't be trampled by spectators."

"That won't be necessary," Winnie said. "Oh, you and Charlie should go for the start. As much as I'd like to see more of the race, I should be satisfied with seeing the finish. If I try to do more, I might be too weak and fatigued to make it to the end. But Virginia sent a VIP seating package for four—she express mailed it last week. She's a genius."

"How did she do that with so little notice?"

"We know people," Winnie said. "Companies I've worked with over the years, bankers and brokers. It's routine for them to procure VIP admission for special events they can offer their clients. I've been to horse races, boat races, golf tournaments. Imagine their surprise when this little crippled lady asked to go to the Kona triathlon. I'm sure there was some scurrying, but we have our condo and our VIP passes. You should go in the morning. I'll save my strength for the finish."

"Wise decision," Lin Su agreed. "Once I figure out parking and where spectators will be allowed, I'll be back for you in plenty of time to watch them come in. Charlie wants to see the start, so we're going to get up at the crack of dawn and head out. Can Mikhail manage to get your breakfast?"

"He does at home," she said. "We'll be fine. Do you realize there will be hundreds of participants?"

Lin Su's mouth fell open. "What?"

"That's right. This is the big one."

"Oh, my God, will we even see him?"

"Yes, darling," she said. "He'll be the one in front." Winnie smiled. "I've been around winners my whole life. Go extra early."

"We will! Thank you, Winnie. This means so much to Charlie. This is so beautiful. So restful. Even without the excitement of the race, I think this is good for you. A lot of flying in just a few days, but still…"

"I'm glad to have this," Winnie said. She reached for Lin Su's hand. "I'm glad to have you and Charlie. And you, young lady, are too stubborn. I want you to fight your instinct to suffer and let yourself enjoy the occasional good fortune. Look at me, darling. Life is too short to waste."

Lin Su knew she was right. Always bracing herself for the next blow was no way to live, no way to raise Charlie. He was such a remarkable kid. In most ways he kept her positive and not the other way around. What did that say about her attitude?

If it wasn't too late, she might try to change that.

★ ★ ★

The race would officially begin at seven but Lin Su and Charlie were at the start site shortly after five and it was already madness. She could only tell by those people who had registered and had their race numbers assigned, wearing them, that they were participants. Had they not had passes to the VIP pavilion, she wasn't sure they would ever figure out where to sit or stand to watch. She wasn't sure she would ever see Blake, at least until he crossed the finish line. As for Winnie—without the passes, she didn't know how she would keep her safe from this teeming throng.

Despite the great crowd of people, the mood seemed serious, or maybe it was hyperfocused. Triathletes stood talking with other athletes or support crew or race support staff. There was some stretching going on, people sorting through their gear, shaking hands with friends and competitors. Lin Su and Charlie had been near the race start for over an hour when an ATV drove up and Blake got out. He wore his skintight racing gear and a T-shirt.

"Look," Charlie said.

"I see," Lin Su said. "Don't bother him. He might not even notice us and that's okay."

Blake smiled and shook hands with a few people who stood around the starting point, from which they would run into the ocean. Gretchen was also out of their ATV, which was loaded with everything from bicycle wheels to coolers. She was laughing, saying hello, handing Blake a plastic bottle of liquid.

"Remember, we don't want to distract him," Lin Su said. But as she watched she could see that he was something of a celebrity in this circle with people approaching, talking, laughing.

Then he began looking around casually, and when his eyes fell on them, he grinned. He seemed to sparkle all over and walked toward them. She couldn't stop herself; she smiled with happiness that he seemed pleased they were there. He shouldn't have been surprised; he knew they'd be there. Shouldn't he be more indifferent? More excited about the race than his spectators?

"You made it." He shook Charlie's hand. "Winnie?"

"We're going to get her a little later so she's not worn-out. Seeing the finish means a lot to her. To all of us."

"Will your team be in the ATV?" Charlie asked.

"Just Gretchen with road repairs and water. If this weren't such a huge event, I'd let Charlie help with the team. But it's a really long day and a lot of people."

"Thousands," Lin Su said.

"I'm going to get ready to go," he said, twisting the cap off his drink and downing it in three swallows. "If I don't see you again until afterward, it's because…"

"Don't look around, Blake," Lin Su said, a begging sound to her voice. "Just know we're around, but don't look. Just concentrate on the race. We'll share highlights tomorrow. Don't…"

"Always telling people what to do," he said, laughing, shaking his head.

"I meant… Oh, you know what I meant! I want to do everything to help and nothing to interfere!"

"I'm happy you're here," he said. "Enjoy the day."

Gretchen was behind him, putting a hand on his shoulder. "Let's get moving," she said. Then looking at them, she smiled. It wasn't the thrilled, excited smile she'd seen Blake wear a few seconds ago. "Hello. Good you could see this. It's an amazing experience." Then to Blake. "Eyes on the start now, okay? Head in the race." And she walked away.

"And don't you look for me," Blake said. "See as much of this circus as you can—there are vendors and services and food everywhere. It's a long day." He ruffled Charlie's black hair. "Have fun today, bud." And then he was gone.

But just that half a minute that he noticed them, noticed her, the pleasure and gratitude on his face, it filled her with joy and ridiculous hope.

The day stretched out forever, and in that hot Hawaiian sun, Lin Su was very grateful for the VIP tent with shade and fans. It was still early when Winnie texted her that she was coming by a hotel car to the triathlon and would call Lin Su if she needed help finding her seating.

As the athletes came in from the swim, Blake was in front and Lin Su almost lost her mind with excitement.

"That's his best event," Charlie said. "Take it easy. The bike kills him."

They watched in fascination as he accomplished the transition, finding his racked bike, his cycling shoes on the bike. He was in the shoes immediately, on the bike and zoom.

There were a couple of spots along the route where they could see the cyclists, but it was approximately four hours before the transition to the marathon. Lin Su and Charlie were ready, witness to another transition. Blake changed shoes, added a belt to which he could strap his water bottle and he stuffed his slim pockets with gel packs that contained carbs, electrolytes, glucose and other ingredients.

"He's behind," Lin Su murmured, biting her lower lip.

"He's good," Charlie said.

"There are at least ten runners ahead of him," she said, sounding worried.

"Only a few, but he's fine. He won't let hotshots screw up his pace. He knows what he's doing. He owns the marathon."

After Blake disappeared from sight, they went to the VIP

tent and had some lunch. It felt to Lin Su as if everyone there was part of a group, that Lin Su and Charlie were alone. She didn't care; this wasn't just about Charlie anymore. While they sat at one of the long tables eating salad and sandwiches, they could see parts of a live video feed of various stages of the race on a screen in the tent. When they were finished eating, Lin Su thought they should try to close their eyes for a little while, but Charlie wasn't having it.

"I'm going to walk part of the route, follow the crowd, see what I see," he said.

"Okay," she said, starting to rise.

"Stay here," he said. "Watch for Winnie and Mikhail. I probably won't see Blake, but I'll see other triathletes here and there. Some of them are just getting on the marathon course. I'll be back."

"Take pictures with your phone," she said. "Text me if you see anything."

After Charlie had left, a few people talked to her, asked her about her interest in the race. She realized some might take her for Hawaiian, but when she explained that Blake Smiley was her neighbor and friend, interest in her immediately grew— with a lot of questions. *Are you dating him? Have you been friends a long time? Is your son in one of his programs?* Programs? She didn't want to admit her ignorance, so didn't answer.

She learned that most spectators came to the race for a couple of hours, maybe a few, but it was rare for people who were not part of a team or club to spend an entire day at the event. And to bear that out, the crowd began to grow again as new spectators arrived. The people in the VIP tent began to crowd in, waiting for the finish.

Winnie and Mikhail appeared and Lin Su rushed to them, surprised. "You found me! Did you have any trouble?"

"They had to fasten Her Majesty into the golf cart," Mikhail said.

"Ack, I can't hang on anymore! But I'm here, that's what matters. How is he doing?"

"I don't know," she said. "He was the first one out of the ocean after the swim, but there were a bunch of runners who started the marathon ahead of him. Charlie said that was normal for him, for his pace, but I know nothing since. They've had some of the race on the screen over there, but I've only seen him a couple of times and I couldn't tell his position. Winnie, have you ever seen so many people in your life?"

"Not so many competing at one event, but, sugar, I've been to the Olympics to watch Grace skate. A lot of people go. The towns are overrun." She looked at her watch. "We want to be at the finish line bleachers an hour before they come in. I'm not missing that!"

"I worry about you in all that sun," Lin Su said.

Mikhail produced an umbrella from the backpack of her wheelchair. "Madam thought perhaps I should fan her with palm fronds, but this works better, I think." Then he went to fetch drinks for them.

For the next two hours, the crowd grew and grew, the noise level intensified, athletes competing in shorter races were coming in, the video screen predicted winners and focused on Blake several times. He had the third best time in the event so far, though he was still behind a lot of runners with six miles to go.

Lin Su was excited, exhausted, exhilarated. She wanted to be present at every race he ran forever and yet never wanted to go to another one. Of all the experiences in her life growing up with the family she landed in, competitive sports like this hadn't existed. She'd been to basketball tournaments, football games, golf tournaments and even horse races, but a race that lasted over eight hours? Never.

Charlie returned; they hurried to the bleachers. Winnie had a handicapped place at the far end of the bleachers, her handlers beside her. Now it was the megaphone reporting on results. Blake was moving up to the front of the pack, one foot at a time.

"He wants this," Charlie said. "He told me. He wants this bad. He thinks he's running out of time to win it—his age, you know. Some of these other guys could do it—there's a guy from Austria who's a favorite, a guy from Germany they think could do it. They're younger."

"Not smarter," Winnie said. "It takes brains and grace under pressure."

"For skating," Mikhail said. "For this, crazy is required."

The last forty minutes were sheer torture. Lin Su nearly wore a hole in her lip, chewing on it. Finally, at a little after three in the afternoon, they came around the curve, the elite men's class. She had to squint to see, but that was Blake, steady as she goes, coming up behind the leader.

She couldn't breathe. He looked fierce yet relaxed. He was wet with sweat; his facial muscles were taut, chiseled. His lean physique showed the hard sinew as he gracefully moved toward the finish, still almost a mile away but yet so close. Then, with more than a half mile to go, he passed the front runner and ran almost elegantly to the finish line.

"Blake Smiley of Thunder Point, Oregon, we have a winner at eight hours, nineteen minutes."

It took hours to get back to Winnie's condo after Blake crossed the finish line. Of course they had to go behind the tape to congratulate him, as did many people. He was gracious despite the fact that he was depleted and maybe a little disoriented. He was coming around thanks to special drinks provided by his trainer; Charlie was beside himself with excitement.

Gretchen was trying to urge him away from the crowd but it took almost an hour before he relented. Before leaving he said, "You're going to be here until Monday, right?"

"Just recover, Blake," Lin Su said. "We'll be around, but we'll see you a lot once we're home. I can't wait to text everyone!"

"I'd like to spend more time with you, but there are sponsors and the team and..."

"We'll be around when you are free of obligations. Right now, make it all about your win! We're so proud of you!" Then she added, "*I'm* so proud of you!"

Getting out of the race area was a challenge. There were going to be runners coming in for hours and hours and the foot traffic was thick. Lin Su and Mikhail took turns pushing Winnie's chair. Then, once they made it to the van, the traffic on the road was heavy; the triathlon had drawn thousands of spectators. If they'd had more energy, they might've gone out to dinner. Winnie was especially worn-out. It was seven before they were back at the condo, eating a light meal on the patio, going over and over every aspect of the race.

Little by little, the condo quieted. Winnie went to bed early. Mikhail found a comfortable chair and ottoman in her room and an extra blanket—even here, he would not relax his vigil. If Winnie awoke in the night, he wanted to be the one to assist her. Charlie sat on the sofa, the TV on and turned low, his laptop on his lap. Within an hour he was slumped on the couch and she closed his laptop and woke him, steering him to bed.

There were people out on the beach, of course, but the patio had a couple of dividing walls separating it from the unit next door and the tiki-lit sidewalk was on the other side of the pool, which was now quiet. She could hear revelers, perhaps celebrating the race, perhaps vacationers. Apparently she was the only one in the house still abuzz with excitement from the astonishing experience of the day. At nine, everyone quiet in the condo, sliding doors ajar so she could hear if Winnie called for her, she fixed herself a rare glass of wine and sat on the chaise, feet up.

Her cell phone rang in the pocket of her capris and it startled her, then shocked her. She was always obsessive about charging it, but it had been in her pocket all day with no worry about that. Other than taking a few pictures of Blake at the finish, she had virtually ignored it. No one ever called her but Winnie or Charlie, on the rare occasion Grace. She pulled it out and looked at the screen. Blake?

"Hi," she said, expecting to find no one there, a butt dial.

"Hi," he said. "I'm just getting to bed but I wanted to call."

"Oh, Blake, did you try Charlie's phone and get no answer? For someone who didn't compete in the race, he sure passed out early."

"I didn't try his phone," Blake said with a slight laugh. "I'm calling you. It was so nice you were there, Lin Su."

"We were all there," she said.

"Yes, and *you* were there. I think I'm growing on you."

"Oh, Blake, you can't still think I don't like you! Not now!"

"I think you're coming around. But you're a hard sell. I've had to pull out and dust off all my old guy skills and charm you to pieces. Before I fell asleep, I wanted to thank you. You were there, you were excited, you were proud. It meant a lot to me."

"Stop," she said, laughing at him. "You were completely mobbed by people! A lot of people were there, excited and proud!"

"I'm not ungrateful," he said. He yawned. "I'm lucky to have sponsors, friends and acquaintances. But I want us to be better friends. To get to know each other."

Her heart started to pound. What was he saying? That he liked her as more than a friend? The way a man likes a girlfriend, someone he has deeper feelings for? What a frightening idea! What if she took that chance and it went badly? Everyone would suffer!

In the end, the only response she could come up with was, "Why?"

Blake laughed. "You are so out of practice," he said. "Worse than I am and I haven't had a woman in my life in quite a while. But at least I remember. Why? Because I think, once we know more about each other, we're going to understand each other. We're going to see we're a lot alike. And I bet we want many of the same things."

"Wait," she said. "You haven't had a woman in your life? What about your trainer? Coach?"

"No," he said. "And I've asked her to stop that proprietary touching and behavior. It gives entirely the wrong impression. I have to sleep, Lin Su. I ate, I had a beer and I'm only awake now because I was too wired to slow down. I have about thirty seconds of consciousness left. That should be enough time for you to tell me you'd like a chance to know me better, too."

"I, ah..."

"Twenty-five seconds. Please, don't jump to negative conclusions. I'm a very polite and considerate guy."

"Well, of course, getting to know you better would be good," she said. "I think. Forgive me, I'm surprised."

"You shouldn't be. And it'll be good." He yawned deeply. "Talk to you later."

"Later," she said. The phone went blank as he signed off and she added, "Sweet dreams..."

Seth said he dreaded his parents' return from their Alaskan cruise, but Iris was more excited than a little kid. She was planning a nice dinner for the whole family for Saturday night so that Seth's two brothers and their wives could help welcome Norm and Gwen home from their first real vacation ever.

"It'll be fun," Iris said. "Your folks get home Friday afternoon and I bet they have pictures and tall tales."

"You do realize Gwen may come home alone," Seth said. "I bet she threw him overboard."

"He seemed to have a very good attitude about the cruise before they left. Gwen said he even packed a couple of the new things she bought for him."

"I can't think of anything that could make him more of a grump than that," Seth said.

"But your mom will be so happy! I'm sure even if Norm was a pain in the butt, she probably had a wonderful time."

"I wouldn't count on that. They push each other's buttons pretty well."

When Iris got home from work on Friday afternoon, her in-laws' car was in the drive. She ran into her house, dropped off her briefcase and some files she brought home and rushed over to the Sileski house. And to her thrilled surprise, Norm answered the door wearing one of his handsome new sweaters and a big smile.

"Welcome home!" Iris said.

"Come in, come in. Gwen is lying down but come in!"

"I hope she's not too tired for a welcome-home dinner at our house tomorrow night," Iris said. "I invited the boys.

Your sons may not be interested but your daughters-in-law definitely are."

"She's not too tired," he said. "It was a great cruise. Look at this boat," he said, pulling out his phone. "There's everything on it. Restaurants, movie theaters, everything. They even have a nursery or something for younger people with smaller kids. They never had anything like that when we were young. Not that we ever went anywhere. We took the boys to Yellowstone, you know. And Mount Rushmore. But no one gave us a hand babysitting so we could go out dancing..."

"You went out dancing?"

"I'm not that much of a dancer. That shouldn't surprise you."

Iris took the phone and began scrolling through the pictures while Norm talked. There was Norm practicing with his life vest, sitting around a fancy dinner table, on the deck of the boat in front of a huge glacier. There was Norm with Gwen and a bunch of other women of a certain age. "Aw, she made friends," Iris said.

"Nice ladies," Norm said. "Have you ever seen food like that in your life?"

Indeed, Norm was infatuated with the food, both the lavish buffets and those formal meals served in the dining room. He also took pictures of the group at their table for ten—he was the only man. He sat in the center of nine women, many dressed to the nines in their formal and semiformal attire. The women, their new friends, looked to be having a wonderful, raucous time.

Gwen looked miserable.

"Gwen doesn't look very happy," Iris observed.

"I think she mighta had a little seasickness. That boat's so big, hardly anybody got seasick. Or maybe she just don't like food made by someone else. Gwen's a good cook, you know."

"I know," Iris said. "Did it ever occur to you to ask her if she was having a good time?"

"I asked her. She said yes. Look at this, Iris—look at this picture. We went on this salmon dinner thing, great place—set up like an outdoor picnic place with picnic tables and fresh-caught salmon cooked on grills right outside. More my speed than the whole fancy dining room part. But there were bears right there, right at the river! I think you have to fight 'em for the fish."

"You had fun," she said, scrolling through picture after picture. There was Norm, grinning like a boy, surrounded by smiling women, frowning wife, picture after picture.

"It was better than I give it credit," he said. "I'm ready to sign up for another one. Maybe Mexico. There's one to Greece, but it might be more than we should spend. I'll have to see. Gwen's not sure. She wants to think about it."

And then Gwen appeared in the doorway, a sour look on her face, pulling her sweater tighter around her.

"Oh, good, you and Iris can talk about the cruise," Norm said. "I want to run over to the station and make sure they're getting by all right. I'll, um, need to take that phone, Iris. But I'll give it back to you next time I see you and you can look at the rest of the pictures. I have to get us a decent camera, a real camera." He pocketed the phone. "You probably don't want to cook after all we ate," he said to Gwen. "Want me to pick up something from the diner? A couple of good old-fashioned hamburgers?"

"I'll cook," she said evenly, arms crossed over her ample chest.

"I'll be back then," he said. "You just about over that little seasickness?"

"I'm over it."

Norm was out the door and Iris sank onto the couch, bewildered.

"You're upset about something," she said. "Wasn't it a nice cruise?"

Gwen went to the chair, Norm's favorite chair. She took a deep breath. "The scenery was very nice. Colder than you think."

"Gwen, what's wrong? You're angry."

"Did you see the pictures?" she asked.

"I saw a lot of his pictures. He was pretty taken with the food."

"The food? He was *taken* with the widows!"

"The widows?"

"That boat was full of widows! They loved Norm! They couldn't shut up, comparing him to their dead husbands, asking him questions about his company. It wasn't a company—it was a gas station! Helping him fill his plate. I thought one of 'em was going to cut his meat! It was disgusting!"

"Those women?" Iris asked.

"Widows," she said.

"You didn't like them?"

"What's to like? They hardly gave me any notice. It was like he was in a damn kissing booth!"

"He kissed them?" Iris asked, aghast.

"Of course he didn't kiss them, but he sure didn't mind all the attention. I'd've been better off if he'd worn his gas station shirt and stood at the rail, pouting. Maybe he coulda slipped and gone..."

"Gwen!"

"It was supposed to be a trip for *us*, not a trip for Norm to play escort to a wife and eight widows. Who never shut up. And thought he was the sweetest man they ever knew."

"Norm? Sweet?"

"That's what I'm telling you," Gwen said. "I never saw him so sweet before. He's been a grumpy pain in my ass for almost fifty years, and all of a sudden with eight widows he's *sweet*." She grunted. "I never."

FOURTEEN

When Lin Su was a senior in high school, a very upscale and expensive Catholic girl's academy, she met Jake at a dance. A mixer. Once every couple of months the boys from Camphill Hall, a prestigious boy's academy, got together with the girls from Sisters of Mercy. Jacob Westermann was a rugby player, handsome and smart. They danced every dance. He called her and said, "We need to get together for a real date. Tell your parents we're going to double, but it'll be just you and me. We need time together to talk. You know?"

She knew what she might be getting herself into. But that was fine with her. She'd only had a couple of brief, boring boyfriends so far and she was ready for a little excitement and romance.

It wasn't yet Christmas when Jake said, "We're going to a party at Todd's and his parents are out of town. Small party. Private party. Wear a skirt." And she had. She went home without her virginity and her panties in her purse.

When she was around Blake, all the lust and irresistible passion of her first, her only, love affair came back to her. All those feelings at least. Given her experience, she had decided that if there was any getting to know each other better with Blake, it would happen in the cool light of day in a place where they weren't too alone. She learned from her mistakes, after all.

But Charlie was fourteen and aching for independence; he had wearied of being her constant companion. She had not had a man in her life since high school. She couldn't deny a certain hunger. This time, however, she wasn't as daring because she was more familiar with the possible consequences.

When Blake got back from Hawaii there was a lot of activity around Winnie's, Cooper's, even Blake's. Everyone wanted to know about the race, about what was next for Blake, how he felt about his win. Their neighbors had learned a lot about triathlons in the past few weeks because of Blake and Charlie; they knew Kona was the big one, the legendary Ironman contest. Just because of circumstances, she saw him often and learned quite a bit, though they weren't alone.

"I can see by the way he looks at you, there's serious interest there," Grace whispered to Lin Su.

"I'm sure you're mistaken about that. He has a vested interest in helping Charlie, that's all. He seems to be a good man."

"Yes to the good man helping Charlie with a training program, but that's not what I see in his eyes when he looks at *you*. Take a chance, Lin Su. I bet you haven't dated in a while."

Hah! A *while*?

Just by keeping her ears sharp, she began to learn things about Blake. He apparently had a poor childhood, raised by a single mother, and even signing up for school- or park-sponsored sports like Little League or soccer were out of the question. "We couldn't have afforded uniforms, much less registration fees. I played a little sandlot soccer and there was a basketball hoop, if we could catch it when the big guys weren't on the court. It was old—a hoop, no net, late at night, outside, only in summer, of course. So a friend of mine, a lawyer who had a similar childhood, and I have been working on a foundation to sponsor underprivileged kids in athletic programs. We have our own corporate sponsors lined up, donors, other foundations and a board of directors setting up the mission statement and governing body. It takes time and will start small. In another five years it will probably be my primary job."

"Because you will have made enough money racing?" Charlie asked.

Blake laughed. "Charlie, I don't make much money racing. Just about enough to pay the expenses. But now that I've won some big ones, I have sponsors and I'm asked to speak. Motivational speaking. It pays the bills and, I admit, it really gets my motor running."

"Speeches encouraging other athletes?" Troy asked.

Blake shook his head. "More generic than that. It's more about being human and survival."

"Of the fittest!" Charlie said.

Again he shook his head. "Survival of the weakest," he said. "It's complicated—but something I'm very familiar with is what it feels like to think you don't stand a chance. It could be poverty, emotional problems, family dysfunction, illness, you name it. It could be asthma," he said, winking at Charlie. "Turning that around isn't easy, but it's possible. You don't have to be in first place to feel like a winner, you just have to beat the thing, whatever it is, that makes you feel failure is inevitable."

"So what kinds of audiences do you have?" Winnie asked.

"All kinds. Schoolkids to executives. Corporate leadership, a group I don't really understand except to know they're competitive in a way only they get. I spoke to a writers' group, a police department, a library district." He looked pointedly at Lin Su. "I did a TED Talk. It hasn't been released yet."

That's when she knew she didn't know enough about him and wanted to understand that mysterious gleam he had in his eyes. Was it for her?

Soon after that, on a rainy afternoon, her phone bleeped with a text.

I lit the fire and made a pot of tea. Want to make a house call while Winnie naps?

She felt panic rise within her. Could this be that moment that would define the next decade of her life? Throw the dice and see if he comes up as honorable and decent as he seems, or find out, in the end, he's got an agenda about getting what he wants?

He helps poor kids, she told herself. He chased thugs with a tire iron to get her swatch back.

"Winnie, while you nap, I'd like to walk next door to Blake's to visit with him for a while. Will you be all right?"

"Of course. You'll have your phone. I can ring you if I need you."

"I am here, of course, not that any of you appreciate me," Mikhail said. "There is no walking in this weather, so I am here."

Lin Su smiled at Winnie. "Don't bother poor Mikhail. Call me. I'll be right next door."

When she settled Winnie for her nap after lunch, Winnie was smiling slyly. "You like him, I think."

Lin Su laughed. "I haven't met a person who doesn't like

Blake Smiley. He might be the most popular man in the world. Seriously, the world."

"I think you like him," Winnie repeated.

"Of course I do, as I just said. I think you'll have a good nap in the rain."

"And I think you'll have a good time in the rain, too."

She threw her jacket over her head and took the front walk that joined all the houses to Cooper's bar straight to Blake's front door. He opened the door with a smile.

"The girl next door has arrived. Come in." He took the rain-drizzled jacket from her and hung it on a peg by the door. "This is a great afternoon. The rain. The fire."

"It's good you like it," she said, slipping out of her clogs and leaving them by the door. "You're going to see a lot of it. Rain, sometimes ice, slush, more rain. And the occasional sunny day. How will that affect your training?"

"Not very much. I have everything I need downstairs— treadmill, bike, weights. Wet suit," he added with a laugh. "I bet that water gets damn cold. But there's a pool at the high school and I have an in with the athletic director."

"You do, don't you. You know, people at the race who knew of you asked if Charlie was in any of your programs. What programs? Your foundation isn't operational yet, is it?"

He shook his head and went to the kitchen to get them tea. "I've sponsored a few training programs for talented but underprivileged kids. Our program isn't up but we already have foundation seed money and give some of it away while we're working and planning. We find them or they find us out of schools, boys' and girls' clubs, neighborhood rec centers, that sort of thing. If the Smiley team sponsors them, they get the equipment and coaching they need to help them on the road to better things, maybe a scholarship. If we can't get 'em early, they might miss the opportunity, and by the time they're twelve or thirteen they're on another course, not always the best course."

"Too bad you can't do the same for academic talent," she said.

"We're working on that. We talk a lot about the whole-kid campaign. They need the whole banana—emotional support, environmental and nutritional support, athletic, academic. The need is too big to imagine but I'm fool enough to imagine it."

I think he's either a fabulous con artist or a genuinely kind man. God knows he can't get money for his cause out of me! she thought.

"Come and sit in here." He picked up a tray with mugs of hot tea and carried it to the living room in front of the fire. "Charlie's thriving," he said.

"Working out is the best idea anyone has suggested."

"It's more than his workouts. I think he likes it here. He likes his school."

"He likes his friends, and not just his fellow students. Friends he's made through my job working for Winnie have been perfect for him, and of course that includes you."

"I got a kick out of him the first day I met him."

"Did you see him as an underprivileged kid?" she asked.

He shook his head. "Not at all. He was a brilliant kid with a laptop."

"But then you saw our trailer park and the mess we were in…"

He shook his head again. "It wasn't that bad, Lin Su. I hope this doesn't sound condescending but it wasn't anything to feel ashamed of. You could've run into those problems in an upper-class neighborhood—break-ins, bullying, drug abuse, et cetera. The last place I lived, I rented a town house. Nice place, gated community. A lot of the kids drove late-model

sports cars or flashy trucks to school. Cortega High School—
the local police called it Cocaine High. The kids were over-
indulged, spoiled, disrespectful vandals. You can only solve so
many problems with money."

"I put too much importance on money sometimes," she
said. "I could have afforded something a little better, but…"

He reached for her hand and held it. "It was sturdy, warm,
had hot water, a working stove and a door that locked. Not a
bad little place, just some bad neighbors. A lot of people would
be grateful for that little trailer."

"You?"

"Oh, I would've been thrilled with it when I was a kid.
My mother and I were in so many rotten flats, shared apartments, tenements… We moved all the time. We even spent
time in shelters."

"Where is your mother now?" she asked.

"Died when I was sixteen."

"Can you talk about her?" she asked.

"She's not easy to understand," he said.

"Neither is my mother. Either of my mothers. Tell me about
yours?"

He sipped some of his tea as he thought. "She was so pretty.
I sometimes wonder if she really was or if that was a little
boy's image. She was pale and blonde and small. When I was
little, under five, she was looking for the right man and went
through a bunch of 'em. And then she found something that
was more satisfying to her than a man. Drugs. She worked as
a waitress in an all-night diner but that wasn't enough money
to keep us as long as she had a habit so she also cleaned office
buildings when she could get the work. I'm not sure when
the habit started—seemed like we lived with it forever. And
I don't know if you'll understand this because I don't under-

stand it—she was an irresponsible mother but she was also devoted. She was whacked-out half the time but I never doubted she loved me. She adored me. She cried a lot because she was such a bad mother.

"By the time I was seven or eight, I was running in the streets. Half the time I got meals at neighbors' houses or scrounged. I didn't go to school regularly, I didn't have discipline or a curfew or boundaries and I'm pretty sure my mother was dealing out of that diner. She might've been selling herself, too, but not around me. Social services took custody of me twice and she worked hard to clean up and get me back both times. But when I was thirteen she'd played all her cards. They took me to foster care again and she was too far gone to make it back. I took the bus to see her on the other side of town a few times, to bring her a can of soup or a sweater, and I saw I was losing her day by day. And a couple of years later she was dead. They said it was an overdose but it was more than that—her body must've given out. She was on a downward spiral my whole life."

"Your father?" she asked hesitantly.

"Never knew one, never heard a name."

"I'm sorry," she said.

"Thanks, but please don't feel sorry for me. It was a rough, poor neighborhood and I wasn't the only kid with those kinds of problems. I was one of the few to get out, however. And it was a genuine miracle. I was in a good foster home and went to a decent school, and even though I was pure trouble, they worked with me, caught me up on the lessons, took extra time with me, introduced me to track. I could've been placed in any other home and gone all the way down to the place my mother lived and died, but I got a second chance because someone gambled on me. I was too mean to care and too angry to appreciate the chance and I fought back hard, but they hung in there with me. I was lucky. Plus, I might've been poor and neglected, but I wasn't unloved or abused or molested, so I had a fighting chance. My foster mother suggested I had a chance to make my mother proud of me. She also made sure I was in counseling with a group of kids more like me. Worked like a charm."

"Is this a story you've told a lot?" she asked.

"It's a story I'm used to now."

"You tell it in your speeches?" she asked.

"About my life, yes. About my mother? Not too much. Telling it to myself was the hard part. I think it was ten years ago or so that I had to figure out what was driving me, what was scaring me and costing me sleep, what extra weight I was carrying. And I didn't do that because I'm sensitive or insightful. I did it because I was angry, screwed up, wanted to win races, and it was like I was just ten pounds too heavy. I got into yoga, started reading more about spiritual freedom, started listening to…" He stopped and laughed. "TED Talks. Not exactly, but stuff like that. As an experiment I just blurted out the unvarnished truth about myself, my roots, and no one died."

He reached for her hand and held it.

"No, I don't talk about her a lot. Only when it's appropriate. It's heavy. I assume you really wanted to know."

She nodded.

"I hope your experience was a lot easier."

She nodded, but she pulled back her hand. Of course her experience was easier! "I was adopted by a white American family. Irish Catholic, as a matter of fact. They were well-to-do. I went to private schools, traveled a lot with my family and classmates. I lived a pretty charmed life."

"Something happened somewhere along the way," he said.

"Why would you say that?" she asked, picking up her mug of tea.

"I don't know," he said. "There's grit in you. You're a survivor, I can see that. It's how I connect with people. I thought we'd have more in common."

"I think we have some things in common," she admitted. "Since I found myself a young single mother, I've gotten tougher."

"No help from those well-to-do Irish Catholic parents?"

She laughed a little ruefully and shook her head. "They were mortified. Furious. Disappointed. I was an honor student. I'd been accepted to Harvard. They'd poured a fortune into my education. They expected better. And...well, they weren't going to help me. Us. I wanted to have my baby and asked for their support and they were adamant—there would be no single mother and fatherless baby in their house. So I left. I made it on my own."

"And Charlie's father?"

"He also wasn't much help, but then he wrecked on a motorcycle in the rain and was completely lost to us so I'll never know if he would have eventually been supportive. Please, I try to paint a more positive picture for Charlie. A person shouldn't grow up thinking the worst of their... Oh, I'm sorry. I didn't mean..."

"I understand what you meant," he said. "But haven't you tried contacting them? Would they have changed their minds once they met Charlie?"

"Leaving was very hard," she said. "It took me quite a while, in fact. In the end I might've done it as much out of spite. Anger. Determined never again to be a part of their grand plan."

The cute little Asian baby, gifted and naturally hard-working, des-

tined for great things… They had two biological daughters who hadn't impressed them, one in the Peace Corps and one majoring in marriage. Lin Su was to be their great achievement. At the very least a physician, at best a great scientist or neurosurgeon. They would proudly take credit for her.

"Adopted," he said.

"I was a happy child," she said, almost defensively. "Until I became a mother, I didn't have problems at home." *See, I'm not really like you.*

He didn't speak for a while. He took another sip of tea. "I figured out something about myself—that I had issues. Not conscious ones. For one, I was afraid of being abandoned. And it wasn't an idle fear—I had been abandoned over and over. For a long time it kept me from healthy relationships with women—I thought they'd eventually leave me. I poured myself into my sport."

"Even your coach?"

He laughed uncomfortably. "She was the exception as a matter of fact. I was in a relationship with Gretchen for a while. After working closely together, we got involved, and by that time I'd resolved some of my issues and wanted a more committed relationship. But she didn't. She's very independent, married to her work, isn't interested in a family, doesn't want to be tied down, doesn't need anyone. Just what I deserved, I guess. I walked away from perfectly great women before even giving them a chance because I was screwed up. Then I chose one who wouldn't commit."

"I think maybe she's reconsidering," Lin Su said.

"Well, I'm not, and I made that clear. It would never work, anyway. We're really not very alike."

"You're everything alike!" she said.

"Doing the same kind of work isn't enough to make a successful relationship. There has to be a lot more than that."

"Well, you'll find the right person," she said, sipping her tea, which had become cool.

"I think I have," he said. "I could be wrong, but I think we have a lot of the same stuff. Even if we come from very different backgrounds, our priorities are similar."

"That's crazy," she said. "Charlie is my priority. Charlie, Winnie, my home life, family life, my work."

He smiled. "Oh, you're right—nothing in common there."

"I don't know what you're looking for, but I bet I'm not it," Lin Su said. "I haven't even been on a date in over fourteen years. Well, not really..."

"Not really?"

She shrugged. "I was in a friend's wedding and I had a partner for that, but it was nothing."

"You're it," he said. "I can tell."

"There's this saying about men and settling down—the most available woman when they're the most ready. They don't even think about it."

"I've thought about it."

"I haven't!"

"All right. I understand completely. You think about it. In the meantime, let's go out to dinner one of these nights."

"I don't know... I don't think that's a great idea. I don't want Charlie thinking..."

"That we're having a date? Trust me, he'd be dating if he could."

Lin Su's phone vibrated in her pocket and she nearly jumped out of her skin. She stood to take it out of her pocket and read the text. She texted back. "Winnie is awake. Time for me to go."

He stood, as well. "We'll just think about that date for a while, then. But not too long. I think we need it."

"We'll see," she said, not looking at him. Out of sheer habit, she picked up the tray of mugs to carry to the kitchen.

"Leave that," he said. "Don't clean up after me. I'll get it."

She left it. Straightening, she went to the door and slipped on her clogs. She grabbed her jacket off the peg. He took it from her hands and put it around her shoulders. Hanging on to it, he pulled her toward him. She looked up at him. He moved toward her mouth slowly, giving her time to shriek or shove him away or kick him in the shins.

She didn't. Instead, when his lips touched hers, so softly, she let out her breath as if she'd been holding it for hours. Her eyes closed. And. Oh. God. He barely kissed her and yet she could feel it zing through her like a current. Her heart nearly exploded out of her chest and her knees melted. But he was holding her up; he was so strong and sure of himself. She felt herself lean into him, her small hands on his waist. His kiss became stronger, more powerful, deftly parting her lips just a little bit, his tongue on the seam of her lips, then inside her mouth.

Oh, damn, this is going to really mess me up, she thought in near despair.

She wanted this. She had wanted this for years. She had so wanted to be held, to be loved, to not be lonely, to have ballast in her life, to have someone who really cared. The wanting made her weak and his arms went around her, holding her. For years she had dreamed of loving a wonderful man. She'd dreamed of him.

He didn't take too much of her. He slowly eased his lips away, giving her a parting lick on her upper lip. Then he kissed her cheek, her eyes and her forehead.

"I wish Winnie hadn't called yet," he said. "But you'd better go see what she needs."

"Uh-huh," she said.

"We'll talk about that date."

"Uh-huh." And she turned away. He opened the door for
her and she pulled the jacket up, over her head, walking briskly
to the house next door.

Blake went back into his living room. He left the tray of
mugs on the coffee table but pushed it aside while he sat in
front of the fire. He kicked off his shoes and put his feet up.
He settled back to relax, a long way from satisfaction. Kissing
her had only made him want more. Much more. As soon as
possible. And he'd better meditate on that because even though
it was evident Lin Su had similar longings, she wasn't ready to
act on them. She was a long way from trusting him.

Blake had a great deal of respect for nature, for human instinct, not that he understood it at all. He was thirty-seven
and had always been drawn to tall, athletic women. They were
usually blonde, which was unsurprising since his mother had
been blonde. But the moment he saw Lin Su he'd been fiercely
attracted to her. She was small, soft, dark, bred of another cul-
ture. She was the most stubborn woman he'd ever known.
She was going to resist him no matter how right it felt to her.

She had responded to him; she wouldn't be able to deny
it. It was probably nothing more complicated than fear. After
all, she'd been without a man in her life. In fact, though he
knew nothing about Charlie's father, he knew he hadn't done
much to protect and care for the little family he'd made. He'd
let her down. She would naturally be afraid of being let down
again. Who wouldn't?

She couldn't open up to him, but that was all right. Someday she would explain things to him, things he already knew. You don't have an ideal childhood in an upscale family only for them to cast you out for something like an accidental pregnancy. There had been much about her years with that adoptive family that had been lacking; he'd bet his right leg on it.

She would be worth the wait. He would have to be more reassuring than he'd ever been before so that she knew she was safe with him, that Charlie would be safe.

Meanwhile, he headed for the gym. The treadmill would help him get through the frustration he was feeling.

FIFTEEN

Grace was standing at the counter, adding up her list of floral orders, when the shop door opened and Ronaldo walked in. He stopped just inside the door and they smiled at each other.

"When you didn't respond to my email, I thought maybe you'd had a change of heart," Grace said. "Or even found something else."

"I wanted to look you straight in the eye and thank you for taking a chance on me."

"I'm assuming you're going to be wearing the nice personality."

"Absolutely. Can I just apologize again?"

"Unnecessary, Ronaldo. And do you understand my plan?" she asked.

"I believe I do, but why don't you just give it to me from the top in case I misunderstood anything."

"Sure. Although I advertised for a manager, I'm offering you a job as a shop employee on a trial basis. Let's say a month. You will probably find yourself taking on manager's duties as well as clerk and shop chores, but I'm not ready to commit to full-time manager with benefits until I'm sure we're compatible."

"I understand. Because I was a little pissy at our first meeting..."

"A *little*?" she asked. "I thought someone peed in your diaper!"

"I've been told I have a moody side," he said contritely. "When I'm stressed, that is. But I promise you, it is something I can control."

"Well, I'll believe it when I see it. And I believe I'll see it within a month."

"I think so," he said, smiling.

"I wasn't expecting you today so I made arrangements to have my mother's nurse babysit the shop for a couple of hours while I keep a doctor's appointment, but if you think you're capable and want to stay awhile, maybe I'll call her and let her have the time for herself. She gets precious little of it."

He took on a pained expression. "Your mother's nurse?"

"Didn't I explain? Winnie has ALS. She's still getting around a little, slowly and very wobbly, but she also uses the wheelchair a lot. She comes across like an indomitable matron, but she's fragile. We're all a little surprised she's doing as well as she is. She's known about the ALS for a few years."

"I'm so sorry to hear this," he said. "You have a lot on your plate."

"Except for the ALS, it's all by choice. But at least we have this time together now. There was a time not very long ago I didn't think we'd ever work things out."

"Of course I'll stay," he said. "You trust me with your shop?"

"Ronaldo, you grew up in the house you now live in with many of the same neighbors you had growing up. The house you recently sold was yours for several years and you're well liked. There are no judgments pending, your credit score is lousy but you don't appear to have much debt. And you haven't been convicted of any crimes."

"There was a speeding ticket a few years ago, but I think he was lying, that cop. I think he had a quota to meet. I never speed. I drive like an old woman."

She laughed at him. "Let me call Lin Su," she said, pulling out her cell. When she was done with that conversation she put her work cell on the counter. "All I need from you is to answer this phone, take orders as best you can or take messages and I'll return the calls. And if there are any purchases, prices for everything in the cooler should be marked."

"What if someone walks in and asks for an arrangement?"

"That's pretty rare, but if it does happen, just do your best. Walk-ins usually just place orders to pick up later or buy what's ready in the cooler. Once in a while one of the guys in the village will ask for a single stem for a wife or girlfriend. I'm sure the prices on a rose or calla lily haven't changed much since you were operational. Vases and other supplies are on the shelves in the back. Think you can handle that?"

"With both hands tied behind my back," he said.

She looked at her watch. "Troy should be here in ten minutes. Anything else you think I should cover for you?"

"Yes, one thing. How have you been feeling?"

"I feel wonderful actually. I get a little heavy by the end of the day, and my ankles have started swelling. Big surprise—I'm on my feet all the time. I've started needing help carrying the heavier stuff—the buckets full of water and fresh stems, big displays, that stuff. But I'm almost to the end. I only have seven weeks to go! We all do!"

"All?" he asked.

"My two girlfriends—Iris and Peyton—are due about the same time. Just before Christmas."

"I hope you're getting a group discount," he said.

"We won't need it," she said. "There's a sizable pool going on in town, proceeds to be split with the winning mother."

Lin Su got the call from Grace just moments before she was to leave Winnie's house to walk into town. She immediately texted Blake.

Are you busy? My afternoon is now free.

The response was immediate. Come!

She peeked into the bedroom to find that Winnie was still awake, holding her book in her lap. She tiptoed in quietly. "Grace just called to say I'm not needed at the shop, but if you're all right, I think I'll step out for an hour or so."

Winnie looked at the time on her cell phone. "I'll see you in a couple of hours, then. Around three-thirty?"

"Perfect," Lin Su said. "I'm not going far. If you're ready to get up sooner, just call or text."

"Mikhail is here, isn't he? He was planning to be here so you could go to the shop."

"In the living room, watching his soaps," she said. "I'll tell him he's in charge for now."

"Don't give him too much authority," Winnie said. "And don't hurry back. I like to think of you enjoying the Ironman."

"I didn't say that's… I don't think Charlie realizes…"

"I'm not going to tell your son where you like to spend afternoons, but there are a lot of loose-lipped creatures around this beach."

"You're right," she said. "I'll think of something."

"It's probably not as complicated as you think. You are two single adults, after all."

She just didn't want him to think anything special was going on. No, that wasn't true. She was trying to keep *herself* from getting carried away.

She walked next door, tapped lightly and the door swung open. She threw herself into his strong arms and he lifted her clear off the floor. Her arms wrapped around his neck, his arms around her waist. Lips came together like lovers long parted; her clogs fell off her feet. After a moment he released her only enough to push the door closed, then went immediately back to devouring her mouth, holding her tightly, running his big hands up and down her back, over her butt.

Way to keep it all in perspective, Lin Su, she thought.

"I needed a little of this," he said, kissing her again.

"You have a little of this every day," she whispered against his mouth. "I was determined not to let this happen."

"I can tell you hate it," he said before covering her mouth again.

Indeed, every day at naptime, unless impossible because of duties, she was at his house and in his arms. And then in the evening he called her when he could. He liked to wait until Charlie was in bed. But fourteen-year-olds didn't go to bed early. Sometimes Charlie stayed up later than Lin Su; sometimes they sneakily texted each other instead of talking.

Blake carried her through his house, navigating with his lips still on hers or on her neck. Then he sat on the couch, holding her on his lap.

"We have to come out now," he whispered.

She made a whining, mewling sound. She dreaded it.

"Everyone probably knows, anyway. Maybe everyone but

Charlie, but if I know Charlie, he's on to us. He doesn't miss a thing."

She left his lips reluctantly. "And what are we supposed to do? Make an announcement?"

He laughed at her. "Things haven't changed that much since high school, Lin Su. I carry your books, walk you to class, we're seen out together Friday night, someone says, 'Are you two seeing each other?' and you say, 'Yes. We connected somehow and now we're dating.'"

"We haven't had a date yet," she said.

"We have to fix that, too. If you want to bring Charlie along, that's fine. Maybe not every time we go out, but sometimes. I like Charlie."

"I don't know why you think everyone knows," she said.

"Well, they're not stupid. They know we're not playing chess when you come over here at naptime. And you get pretty rosy," he added, grinning. "It's a good thing I'm not trying to get ready for a race…"

"Why?"

"I have no schedule! I stay up late hoping to talk to you, get up early. My mind is in a knot thinking about you all the time. Look, I know you're out of practice, if you ever had any, but what's happening here is pretty simple. We're falling in love."

"Lust," she said. "I think it's just lust."

"No," he said. "It's lust, too. But I care about you and I think you care about me. That's more than lust." He grinned. "I like the lust, though. It's very good and one of these days we're going to…"

"Ah!" she said sharply, stopping him.

"Yes, we are," he said. "Everything is just right. We're allowed to kiss and hug and go on dates. We're allowed to fall in love. We can have a physical relationship as long as we both want to."

"I don't want to," she said.

He laughed. "I can hardly peel you off me," he said. "You climb me like a tree and I love it. Take your time, but let's not pretend you don't know what's going on here. And let's not be deceptive. It just never works."

"And then, like high school, do you have what you want and move on to the next cheerleader?"

His expression grew serious. "Is that what happened?" he asked her.

She looked away. He gently grabbed her chin and turned her head back to face him. "Lin Su, is that what happened?"

She shook her head. "Not until I told him I was pregnant," she whispered. "Please, I don't want Charlie to know that. I want him to think his father was a good and faithful man."

"He was just a boy, I think. And you were just a girl. But we're not kids. We're not screwing around in the moment. We both know there's more at stake. We both know there's a fourteen-year-old boy involved and we're not going to risk his feelings. I don't want Charlie to think he can't trust us."

"Does that mean we don't make love until we're serious?" she asked.

"I am serious. But I think you're still a little worried about whether you can trust me. I think the only way I'm going to convince you is by showing you, and if it takes a while, I understand. But you don't have to be afraid I'm fickle."

"You left a lot of perfectly great women because you were afraid to get involved," she reminded him.

"No, I never got involved with a lot of perfectly great women because I was afraid of commitment. I wasn't happy with that, either. I wanted a real relationship, Lin Su. I always

have, since I was a kid. I think underneath it all a lot of people want that."

She had wanted that, she recalled. "I fantasized I would have
that with my first love," she said.

"Yeah, but you were a kid. You're not a kid anymore. You
grew up. Haven't your expectations grown up, too?" He gave
her a kiss. "I think Friday or Saturday night we try a date.
Dinner. We can drive over to Bandon or up to North Bend
if you like. Tell Charlie I asked you out on a date, and if you
feel like inviting him along, that's fine with me. If you don't,
that's fine, too."

"He'll think something is going on with us."

"Something is," he said. "Let's let it. It feels so good. Don't
be afraid—I won't hurt you. And I won't abandon you."

"You can't be sure, Blake. Your feelings could change."

"And so could yours," he said. "But I'm willing to risk it. I
think this works, you and me, and I don't feel like giving it up
just because something might go wrong someday. And I don't
think it's good to be deceptive, to have this secret that we're
seeing each other, that we're romantic, pretending we're not."

"Aren't we just being private?" she said, reaching for a way
out.

"We can be private without pretending we're not involved.
Lin Su, you're sitting on my lap. I just had my tongue down
your throat and we were talking about sex. Like it or not,
we're a couple."

"Ah, jeez. Can't you tell I have a lot to get used to? That
I've never had a man in my life?"

"Well, now you do." He pulled her closer. He kissed her
again. "I think you're afraid of not having all the control. You
like control."

"Survival," she said.

"Oh, I know," he said with a laugh. "That's something I understand."

They spent the next hour making out like teenagers. "I have to get back to Winnie," she finally said. "I promised her I'd be back at three-thirty."

"Think about what we talked about. We don't have to be embarrassed to say we like each other, okay?"

"Okay. I'll practice that."

As she walked back to Winnie's house, she was talking to herself, reminding herself that men and women checked each other out, spent quality time together to see if they were compatible, and people around them knew. Sometimes it was a misstep, and they didn't end up together, but sometimes that was for the best. Yet sometimes… *Yes, we're dating… Blake is such a lovely man…* That didn't sound too scary.

She'd begin by practicing on Winnie. She entered the house quietly. Mikhail was asleep on the sofa in front of the TV, arms crossed over his chest. All those nights in the chair in Winnie's bedroom during the night probably left him tired. She tried not to disturb him as she went to Winnie's bedroom.

She gasped.

Winnie sat on the floor. She looked dazed and her lip was bleeding. She hung on to the leg of her walker with one hand.

"Winnie!" she said, crouching beside her. *"Mikhail!"*

Winnie touched her lip, then her cheek. "Damn," she said.

Mikhail was in the doorway in an instant. "What happens here?" he demanded.

"I guess I fell. It was the damnedest thing—my leg just wasn't there. I was just getting my walker and one leg…"

"Mikhail, call Dr. Grant and tell him Winnie took a fall."

"Help me stand up, Lin Su," she demanded.

"Just wait. Is your leg numb? Tingling?"

"It wasn't asleep," Winnie said. "It just wasn't *there*." She began rubbing her leg through her slacks.

"I'm going to gently move your leg," Lin Su said. "I want to look at it, see if you're injured. Do you feel it now?"

"Barely."

Lin Su slid the pant leg up so she could examine the leg and found the ankle to be slightly swollen.

"It's happening," Winnie said, her voice weak. "I'm losing more function."

"Try not to worry. We're prepared. I think you might have injured your ankle. Let's see what Dr. Grant says."

"He'll be here in half hour, maybe less," Mikhail said.

Lin Su gave Winnie's cheek a soft stroke. "I won't leave you again," she said.

Winnie laughed. "Are you going to give up your entire life for me? We know this is going to get worse."

"I'm going to be here when you need me," Lin Su said. "I won't have you falling because I'm not here."

"I fell because I thought I could stand, not because you were gone. You could have been right beside me when I went down." She touched her rapidly swelling lip. "I hit my face on the damn walker. Now I'll look like the wrath of God!"

"Mikhail, help me lift Winnie to sit on the bed. Then I'll get ice for your lip. The swelling won't last long."

An hour later Scott Grant was examining his handiwork—Winnie's ankle was wrapped in an Ace bandage. By this time Troy and Grace were back from their doctor's appointment and Charlie was home from school. It was a small crowd, gathered around Winnie's bed.

"I don't think we need an X-ray," Scott said. "It's not very swollen, there is no pain…"

"There's also very little feeling," Winnie said.

Scott thumped her calf. "Feel that?"

"I can feel that but I couldn't feel my leg and went down without warning," she said.

"It's not numbness, Winnie. It's muscle failure. You've experienced fatigue of muscles in your extremities—clumsiness and sometimes twitching. Now, with some progression, there is muscle failure. Your leg wouldn't hold you up. Other extremities will follow, hopefully as slowly as your condition has progressed to this stage. You're no longer weight bearing on this leg. I'm afraid your brief freedom with the walker is over. Now it's the wheelchair."

"But if I work on it! Physical therapy. Maybe I can strengthen it!"

He took her hand in his. "Winnie, the prognosis is not good. There are still a lot of mysteries about ALS, but there's one thing we know—it's not reversible. You can no longer depend on this leg. And soon, I'm afraid, it will be both legs. I think we're going to have to make a few adjustments."

"Like what? What more can we do?"

"For starters, you need to buy or rent the appropriate bed, one you can move up and down so you can be transferred to the wheelchair without a major accident. Grace wisely adjusted your bathroom—higher toilet, assistance bars, the right kind of chair to use in the walk-in shower..."

"I'm heading toward the end, then?"

"Winnie, you've experienced very slow progression so far. You've been dealing with this for years when many ALS patients have very little time. I'm counting on the progression remaining slow, but at this point all we can do is adjust to the symptoms and hope for the best."

"What about my physical therapist?"

"If it brings you comfort, it can't hurt anything. But I told you when you hired him—there is no rejuvenation of muscle. You'd get as much comfort from a good masseuse. Maybe more."

She lowered the ice from her lip. Her eyes watered slightly. "I was counting on seeing my granddaughter take her first steps.

"Is that you giving up?" Scott asked. "Your ALS hasn't followed the average progression so far. There's absolutely no way to predict it. And there's no medical evidence to support this but I believe your determination and stubbornness has bought you a good deal of time. It's either that or just plain luck."

"Did too much exertion bring this on?" Grace asked. "Was it the trip to the triathlon?"

"I'm sure that trip caused more than the usual fatigue, but it had nothing to do with her muscles. I'm afraid that's out of our hands."

"I'm glad I went on that trip!" she barked. "It was rejuvenating to my spirit if not my muscles! If I can't be a participant, at least I can be a damn good spectator! Haven't I proven that?"

"You have, Mother," Grace said.

"Can't I try to walk anymore?" she asked.

"Not a chance," Scott said. "We should keep weight off that injured ankle until we see what's up with that. I suspect a minor sprain. And if you decide to try walking, you need a strong person on each side. Let's not break a bone or get a concussion."

Charlie had his phone out and was texting.

"Who are you talking to?" Lin Su quietly demanded.

"I'll skip my workout today," he said. "I'll just tell Blake I'm not coming over."

"No," Winnie said. "You go! It's a commitment. In fact, all of you go! I want a few minutes alone."

"I'll stay, of course," Lin Su said.

"Fine, but stay in another room! I need a few minutes to get my head wrapped around this. I'm not happy about this! I'm not ready for this!"

"Call me for any reason," Scott said, getting ready to leave. "Call even if you only want to talk about it for a while."

"I'll go," Charlie said. "But I won't work out as long..."

Grace kissed her forehead. "I'll check on the shop, close early and be back soon."

"I'll go with. We'll bring dinner home," Troy said.

Lin Su straightened the throw that covered Winnie and drifted silently out of the room.

Mikhail was the last to remain. He looked at her without pity and said, "Ten minutes, then I am back."

Winnie wept for a while, not making a sound until she blew her nose. She would not be pitied! She was too young to die but with some of the risks she'd taken in her life, she should be dead a hundred times. Some of the jumps she'd attempted back in the day were suicidal. When she was competing on the ice, there had not been so many regulations and rules. And of course they'd flown into unfriendly countries from time to time, because the competition was important. Hell, they'd flown and driven through dangerous weather; she'd never missed a competition. She even skated with bronchitis once and landed in the hospital. Then, with a champion daughter in tow, though she'd taken more precautions than with just herself, there had been risks. She'd been in two car accidents and one of her privately rented jets had gone off the runway in a snowstorm.

But she was too young to die. And too proud to die this way. Weak and crippled.

Mikhail walked into the room carrying his newspaper. He might be one of the last people in the state to read an actual paper rather than getting all his news online or on TV. He moved the throw from his chair and sat without saying a word. He shook out his paper, put his reading specs on his nose and looked at the paper.

"I said I wanted to be alone for a while," Winnie said.

"Makes no sense," he returned, not looking at her.

"Go away. I'm having a little cry."

"You do better with audience," he said. "I won't leave you."

"Leave for an hour," she said.

Seemingly exasperated, he put down the paper. He folded and put away his glasses and went to sit on the side of her bed. "I said, I will not leave you."

"You keep saying you're leaving soon," she reminded him with a sniff. She blew her nose again.

"What can I say? I am terrible liar. I will stay."

"Till the end?"

"I don't know if I have that much time," he said. "When is end?"

"That's the problem, Mikhail. We don't know."

"Then I stay," he said. He leaned forward and placed a kiss on her head. "I stay to remind you how lucky you are. To live in house built around you."

"I'll think about that when I'm done here."

"Is possible you could have forced Grace to San Francisco to sit about and wait for you to die. Is possible. But you could not bring all these good people to San Francisco to watch you die. Every day is party here. The little nurse, the boy, the new son, the neighbors, the baby is almost here. We didn't think to see baby! When I go, I hope there is someone."

"If you stay here, I will leave them to you," she said.

"Is generous offer," he admitted. "I will think on it. But today, I will stay with you. You need me. I am the only sense you have some days."

She laughed at him. "And some days you're my only trip to the bathroom."

"I am man of many skills."

"It's not going to get better, you know."

He shrugged. "I won't get better also," he said. "I am old Russian. There is no cure."

She laughed again. She blew her nose. "I wanted to just cry."

"You are lousy at it," he said. He lifted her hand and kissed it. "You are better as queen. Matriarch. Dominatrix."

She roared with laughter. "Dominatrix?" she asked. "Have you been watching cable again?"

"Only when very lonely and tired."

"When you're lonely and tired, you should come to me. While you can."

"I do, Your Majesty. Now, are you going to...what does Grace say? Get it together."

"Just hold me a minute, will you?" she asked.

"Is my best talent," he said, pulling her close. He stroked her back and she rested her head on his shoulder. "See? Everything is okay."

She sighed. It was okay. Some people didn't get this much love in a lifetime. Even after being one of the most impossible mothers in the world, she had her daughter home and she was surrounded by people she loved. In the house that had been built around her.

SIXTEEN

Winnie was not a bit surprised that even Blake showed up for dinner. Charlie had told him she had taken a fall and he wouldn't stay away. And Charlie had, as promised, cut his workout a little short. Grace had closed the shop early and Troy brought home spinach lasagna, garlic bread and pie and ice cream. Grace was putting out plates while Lin Su warmed the dinner and bread.

"I'll set a place for you if you'll stay, Blake," she said.

"Tonight I'd like to stay," he said.

Winnie looked up in surprise. "You don't have to indulge in our blue-collar food just because I twisted my ankle," she said. "We won't be offended if you want to go home to your tree bark, lawn clippings and yak livers."

He grinned at her. "I'll take extra vitamins," he said. "I'm not getting ready for a race right now."

"You won't train?" she asked.

"Of course I will, but I won't follow the rigid protocol—

oh, never mind. You're never going to ease up on my diet. So, I'll have a beer."

"That's what I'm talking about," Troy said, nearly lunging for the refrigerator.

"Tell us what the baby doctor said," Winnie asked.

"We're right on schedule and in perfect health, if a little overweight. I'm going to call Ginger and explain that it wouldn't be a good time for me to come to the Lacoumette farm for her wedding. Peyton can stand up for her."

"Don't be ridiculous," Winnie said to Grace. "Can I please have a glass of wine? I'll want a straw in it, of course, so I'm not wearing it by the end of dinner. Grace, please go to the wedding. You've been looking forward to it. Soon enough you'll have a new baby and a very infirm mother holding you down. This might be one of your last chances to get away."

"I'll be home," Blake said. He automatically got up and went to the wine rack in the kitchen, selecting a bottle. He showed it to Winnie like an experienced waiter.

"Lovely," she approved.

He went to the kitchen to open it and pour. He fixed a glass for Mikhail, as well. "I'll be available if you need help getting around or if you have errands," Blake said.

"That's very kind," Winnie said. "I'd rather you take my nurse on a proper date. Mikhail and I will be fine. We just need a little assist from Lin Su before she leaves for the evening. I'm not going to foolishly try to reach my walker again."

"A movie, maybe," Grace said. "Either a really scary one or a really romantic one."

"Take her to the cliffs up north where the waves are huge. That worked on Grace," Troy said, then he lifted his eyebrows, à la Groucho Marx.

"I want you to go to the wedding, Grace," Winnie said again. "The leaves are turning and it'll be beautiful."

"We even had thoughts of asking if Charlie could go," Grace said. "I think he'd get the biggest kick out of it."

"Charlie is allergic," Lin Su said, bringing the dish of lasagna to the table. "And while I so appreciate all of you planning my social life, I assure you, I'm very capable of taking care of that myself."

"I'm not going to be allergic now," Charlie said. "Nothing's blooming!"

"There are animals," Lin Su said.

"Outdoor animals," Grace said. "Besides, Scott and Peyton are going. You can't ask for a safer trip than that."

"I would prefer he not go."

"I knew it," Charlie said inconsolably.

"I bet you haven't had many trips or nights away from your mother, have you, Charlie?" Winnie asked.

"Oh, sure, I travel like mad."

"I propose a choice," Blake said. "I know it doesn't trump his mother's decision, but Charlie can go with us to a movie or to the farm with Grace and Troy. And his doctor, of course."

"Oh, let me think," Charlie said. "This is a really hard one. I just don't know if I can choose..."

Everyone at the table laughed. Except Lin Su.

"We could always let you choose the movie," Blake said.

"Aw, man," he said, grabbing his head in both hands. "You're killing me!"

Lin Su put the basket of garlic toast on the table.

"Sit down, Lin Su," Winnie said. "No one is going to tell you what to do. You're the mother. Just a little loving interference."

"I can take care of my own social life," she said again.

"Of course you can, darling," Winnie said. "Now, Grace, I want you to plan to go this weekend. After my other leg and my arms follow suit, you might not get away until my granddaughter goes to school."

"I really don't care, Mama. You and the baby are my priorities right now."

"That's really so lovely of you, darling. Now tell us all about this new employee you have..."

Grace began to serve plates of lasagna. "Ronaldo. I think I'm in love, provided he continues to behave himself. He has a very moody side, but he promises to control it."

"I'd have a better shot at Ronaldo than you would," Troy said, grabbing and passing the bread.

There was a lot of laughter, everyone talking at once, teasing one another, no one exempt from the interference at the table. Winnie noticed Lin Su was conspicuously quiet for a while. No wonder—people were interfering in her love life, her mothering decisions, everything but her patient care. She certainly was not singled out—everyone was in everyone else's business. But as Lin Su kept an eye on Winnie's plate, offering assistance to move a wine or water glass, to help her spear a piece of lasagna, she finally came around. The only one who didn't take a lot of ribbing was Blake, probably because he was newest at the table.

Winnie thought about the fact that had she been at home in San Francisco, she would very likely have taken her dinner in her bedroom with the company of the TV. It would have been an expensive and difficult meal prepared for her by a chef, and the housekeeper or nurse who delivered it to her probably wouldn't even stay in the room while she ate unless she needed help.

This is all I need, she thought. *This oddly constructed family.*

★ ★ ★

"Do you really have an interest in going to the farm with Grace and Troy?" Lin Su asked Charlie as they walked across the beach to their loft.

"I think it would be cool," he said.

"Really? A farm? A wedding?" she pushed.

"Not just a farm, Mom. A huge farm. I've heard about Peyton's wedding, people talk about it all the time. These Basque farmers get drunk and dance their butts off."

"Lovely," she said.

"I heard it was fun! I think you could trust me not to get drunk," Charlie said, grinning at her.

"I don't think a responsible parent would send her teenage son to a brawl..."

"You don't think Troy and Scott would make sure I don't get into trouble? You think Grace and Peyton would be a bad influence? You have to look up Basque weddings sometime— the dancing is between the men and it's ceremonial. And there are dogs and horses."

"You're allergic," she reminded him.

"Yeah, but if I start to sneeze or wheeze I can move away from the animals. If their hair is all over the bed I sleep in, I might be in trouble, but..."

"I think you just want to go on a trip without your mother," she said.

"No offense, but it would be cool to go somewhere with Troy and Grace, Peyton and Dr. Grant. But I bet if you wanted to go..."

"I can't leave Winnie, you know that. Especially now."

"Then I think you should just enjoy not worrying about my allergies for a whole weekend, and if I get drunk with the

Basque men and dance my butt off, you can ground me for the rest of the year."

"You think you're funny but I don't," she said.

"Just have a good weekend. Go out with Blake. And try not to get in trouble without me here to look after you."

"I wasn't planning anything like that, you know."

"Not planning it, maybe, but you sure are thinking about it. And whispering into the phone late at night and looking at him with twinkling girl eyes, and when someone says his name, you look down so no one will see you like him." She let out a little gasp. "Listen, I'm okay with it. If that's what you're worried about."

She couldn't help but smile at him. "I was worried about the opposite."

"Huh? What's the opposite of okay?" he asked, pushing his glasses up on his nose.

"I thought you might get too excited. That your expectations would be unrealistic. That I'd go to a movie with a male friend and you'd think it would be serious, lead to marriage or something."

"That *would* be cool," he said. "But you don't have to marry him unless you want to."

"Thank you," she said. "And do you really want to go to that farm?"

"For two nights, Mom. Think you can behave yourself if I'm not here to watch you?" he asked with a devilish grin.

She ruffled his hair. "I'll try."

On Friday morning at nine Lin Su stood outside Winnie's house with Charlie while Troy put a suitcase and Charlie's duffel in the trunk. She did not ask him even once if he had his inhaler and EpiPen. And it was not easy. She also did not say that it was the first time she'd ever be separated from him for over twenty-four hours. Even early in her nursing career when she'd been assigned the graveyard shift, she was only away from him for ten hours. He was probably already more than aware of that fact. But she did say she would miss him.

"I'll miss you, too, Mom," he said sweetly.

"I bet you won't think of me twice," she said.

"Sure I will."

He endured a hug and kiss on the cheek, then he couldn't get on the road fast enough. She just stood there, watching them drive away. She pulled her jacket more tightly around her and the car had long been out of sight when she saw a cyclist come up the road.

Blake rode up to her and stopped. He balanced without putting a foot down, just moving his feet back and forth on the pedals, showing off. He was all sweaty; he'd probably been riding for at least a couple of hours. God, he was gorgeous. She looked at those rock-hard thighs and fought a sigh. His shorts and shirt fit like skin and revealed every muscle; his riding gloves on the handlebars accentuated his strong, sexy forearms.

He finally put his foot on the ground and removed his helmet. "Did you let him go?"

"I told you I said yes."

"I wondered if you'd chicken out at the last minute, come up with a reason he couldn't go."

"Hah. You've obviously never had a teenage boy. I'd never have heard the end of it."

"I've had about a hundred of 'em at one time or another. They're relentless. We have a date tonight, then?"

"Sure. What do you want to do?"

"Well, since I'm devious and just want to be alone with you, I thought I'd cook you a very nice dinner. While I'm finishing that, you can search through the movie guide and pick one. Anything you want."

"Any preferences?" she asked.

"Something that you'll need to be held through, that would be my preference."

"I'll be over after I settle Winnie for the night. Full disclosure—I'm going to tell her we're staying in for dinner and a movie and she should call me for any reason."

"Of course. They're a little shorthanded right now. But you know she won't bother you unless there's an epic disaster."

"I'm going to tell her not to wait that long."

"Everything's going to be fine, you know," he said. "For them. For us." He leaned toward her. "Kiss me."

"Outside? Where anyone can see?"

"Anyone with a telescope, maybe. It's okay, Lin Su. We have permission from the most important guy."

True enough. Charlie had endorsed the idea. "I'm sure he didn't realize all he was agreeing to," she said.

"Oh, trust me, Charlie knows. Charlie is counting the days till he can get it on with a girl."

"Oh, God, please don't even say that."

"Kiss me," he said.

She leaned toward him. She tried giving him a little peck on the lips but he slipped his arm around her and pulled her close for a much deeper kiss. Deep and filled with the promise of greater things to come.

"You're very sneaky," she said. "And you're sweaty."

"It's going to be a very long day," he said. "Get to work. Let me know approximately when you'll be over. Text me."

Time did indeed crawl through the day.

There were a few new routines for Winnie caused by the

progression of her disease. First of all, now that using the
walker alone was out of the question, she had to use the wheelchair to move around. Lin Su would have preferred if Winnie
would settle for the bedpan for those middle of the night bathroom breaks, but she wouldn't have it. Lin Su really couldn't
blame her; that would come soon enough. But she hoped she
had fully convinced Mikhail not to try to just walk her to the
bathroom. Although he was a mighty strong little guy and
Winnie was quite small, it was risky.

She still had some strength in one leg, but it was not dependable. Lin Su taught them how to transfer her in and out of
the chair, over to the commode, back again. A lap robe helped
with modesty, but she assumed that after several months of
spending the night in the same room, Mikhail had taken on
some more personal tasks for Winnie. He had become a very
competent nurse.

Before this was over, there would be many personal duties. Right now Winnie had difficulty with daily living—she
couldn't button her own clothes, couldn't comb her hair, even
brushing her teeth was a challenge. Her hands were trembling
and uncertain and she dropped things easily, so they chose
meals carefully. And the hospital bed was due to be delivered
on Monday—that would allow her to lower the bed so the
transfer to the wheelchair would be safer and it would be easier for her to sit up in bed.

But from this point on, it was only going to be a greater
challenge every day. And although Winnie hated it, she needed
more assistance every day. Soon, even though Mikhail resisted,
she was going to have to consider help for the night. A skilled
nurse's aide would be perfect.

Though it seemed like the day lasted forever, Lin Su was
actually excused from her duties a little early. She took the

time to go back to her loft to freshen up and then knocked on Blake's door.

And walked right into his arms.

She had wondered and worried all day long about what this evening would be like, alone for so many hours. But once in his arms, once his lips touched hers, nothing mattered anymore. Why would she ever be tense or concerned about being with him? He made her feel completely secure.

"This is more than I hoped for," he said. "I was telling myself to be patient, that your day might be extra-long with everyone away."

"It was the opposite. Though she denies it, Winnie put all her energy into getting me out of there early—I think she's matchmaking. I even had time to go home and change. But my car is in your drive. Winnie knows I'm here, of course, but to the rest of the world who passes by your house, well..." She shrugged. "The secret is out."

He took her hand and pulled her inside. "I wasn't keeping it a secret. I don't want to be a secret. I want everyone to know we're together." He pulled out a chair and sat her at the table. It was already appointed with place mats, plates, even a couple of candles, though they weren't lit yet. "I'm going to get you a glass of wine. Then I want you to tell me about your day."

"It's as I knew it would be—the days get a little busier. I've done this before, remember. Winnie isn't my first patient with slowly deteriorating health and mobility. It seems cruelly fast to her, but it's a little bit every day."

He brought her a glass of wine and put one down for himself. Their places were next to each other at the corner of the table. He brought a plate of softened brie, crackers and fruit and sat down beside her.

"She started telling me I could leave early before she even

had her nap. Then when she was up, she asked for an early dinner—something light and easy, something I shouldn't go to any trouble with. Scrambled eggs and toast points. And she wanted her washup and nightgown before dinner. She told me to fold back the bedcovers and leave."

"God bless Winnie," he said, cutting her a slice of brie on a cracker and putting it on her small plate. Then he raised his glass to her. "Now you're all mine."

She took a sip, then a bite. "I'm still trying to figure out how we got here."

He laughed at her. "I got here with a look. I took one look at you and thought, *Her. She's the one.* Then I doubted my own common sense because you were one angry little girl. From that point on I had to work hard for you."

"I wasn't mad," she said.

"Oh, yes, you were. Or maybe self-protective. Proving to you that you didn't have to protect yourself from me wasn't easy. Once you let me kiss you, everything fell into place." He fixed her another cracker and cheese. "I wondered if I'd ever get that close to you."

"Well, I certainly hadn't planned on it," she said with a little laugh. She plucked a slice of apple off the plate. "Are you feeding me crackers and cheese for dinner?"

"Dinner is ready and staying warm," he said.

"I thought I smelled something wonderful."

"Chicken and vegetables with a mushroom rice on the side." Then he leaned toward her for a lovely, slow kiss that tasted of wine and apples.

"Is every day going to be like this?" she asked.

"Better," he said. "Come here." He pulled on her hand until she was sitting on his lap. "Of course we'll make adjustments.

We have Charlie to think about. Why did you let him go? So we could have this time?"

She shook her head. "I don't like it but I have to let him have more freedom or he'll resent me. I don't want that."

"He's a smart kid, Lin Su. He's going to be an easy one to raise." He fed her another apple slice, stole another kiss. "You're delicious," he whispered.

She put her arms around his neck and gave all her attention to the next kiss, moving over his mouth hungrily. Her glass wasn't even half-empty, yet she felt a warmth like wine spread through her, leaving her yearning. "Did you plan this seduction?" she asked a little breathlessly.

"Planned, prayed, hoped… This is all up to you, Lin Su. I know it's been a very long time…"

"Long," she said, kissing him again.

She wanted to tell him things—that this felt right, that he made her want him almost desperately, that she didn't want anything to ever change between them. That he was right: she was falling in love. But she couldn't whisper all these things and kiss him, so she kissed him. The yearning reached all the way into her and drew on her; her nipples felt hard and her pelvis was soft. She wiggled a little on his lap, wanting him, and it was obvious he was aroused.

"Are you starving?" he asked.

A little laugh against his lips escaped her. "Oh, yes," she said. "But I think dinner can wait."

With those words he pressed harder against her, pushing into her, and it felt so good she wanted to cry. But he wasn't giving her any time to think about it. He pushed her off his lap, stood and led her by the hand to his bedroom. She only had time for a glance around before he was on her lips again; that one glance showed her the bed was ready, the comforter folded back and out of the way. The fireplace was lit and a small lamp cast dim shadows around the room.

And Blake put his arms around her, drawing her to him. He slid his warm hands under her sweater and his sure and skilled fingers caressed her, bringing her longing alive. Her sweater was pulled off and tossed away; the lacy bra followed. His shirt disappeared and he held her, chest to chest, skin to skin, hungrily devouring her mouth. He kissed his way down her neck and chest to take a nipple into his mouth and gently tug. With her hands in his hair, she held him there. Her head dropped back and she whispered, "Never stop..."

That brought a lusty chuckle from him and he lifted his head. He pushed her back on the bed and undressed her the rest of the way, boots first, then those tight little jeans. When she was down to a lacy thong, he stopped to just gaze at her a moment. "Good Lord," he whispered. He sat on the bed beside her and ran a curious finger around the front of the thong, following that finger with a soft kiss, a little lick.

And then he quickly stripped and joined her on the bed, pulling her into his arms.

Against his naked body, she gave herself over to him, trusting, thrilled by every touch. She explored him with her hands while he made a slow, luxurious study of her body with his lips and fingers. She was so lost in the moment she wasn't even aware he'd searched in his drawer for a condom until he was rolling it on. And then he was kneeling between her spread legs, finding the way home. Slow and deep, he possessed her.

She let out a low moan and closed her eyes. He was still, filling her. Unmoving, his breath came a little faster. Then he moved, slowly at first, teasing her, bringing the wave of pleasure that was rising and rising in her. She held her breath, her knees bending as she pushed back against him, stroke for stroke, panting, and in no time at all the dam broke and she was sailing away. She grabbed him, holding him tightly inside, the spasms so deliriously, wildly good she felt temporarily blinded, whispering his name over and over.

He was on her lips, kissing her deeply, lovingly, while his body gave back to her what she'd given him. Her arms around him, holding him close, she felt the pulsing pleasure of his climax.

Then they were still. Lovers, breathing fast, clinging to each other, exchanging small kisses, whispering, smiling, laughing a little.

"That was amazing," he said.

"Better than that. I thought it might be awkward."

"Not awkward," he said. "Almost practiced. Perfect."

"Did we make love for hours?" she asked.

He laughed. "Minutes."

"I think I passed out."

"No, you didn't. You were with me all the way. You're beautiful." He ran his hands through her hair, spreading it out on his pillow. "I'm going to want more of you."

"Ooooh, just the mention..." She could feel her insides tighten at the mere suggestion and she was game for more.

And he hummed his agreement.

Dinner was very late and the vegetables had lost their crispness in the warm oven. "I'll have to try to impress you with my cooking another time," Blake said.

"I think I was the one who said dinner could wait, but I admit, I wasn't thinking about the food at all."

"I approve," he said, reaching out and stroking her cheek with a knuckle. He couldn't stop touching her, couldn't allow very much space between them.

He had offered her a robe but she asked for a soft, roomy T-shirt. She sat, quite comfortably, at the table with one slim leg bent up at the knee, her foot on the chair. It gave him enormous pleasure that she was so at ease, both with him and in his house.

They had made love twice and he hoped there would be at least one more time. "Stay with me tonight," he said.

"All night?" she asked.

"Please. There won't be very many nights that's possible."

"What if we don't sleep well together?"

"I'm not worried about that at all. I'm a little worried we won't sleep at all because we're drugged with sex." He felt a shiver run through him. She was amazing. Unexpectedly erotic and free. "I admit, I hadn't expected you to trust me enough to…"

"I completely lost control," she said, briefly glancing away.

He touched her hand. "Don't be shy with me," he said. "You don't have to be embarrassed. You're a dream come true."

"A dream come true in the sack?" she teased.

"There, too."

And soon they were back in bed, making love again, more slowly this time, experimenting a little, trying a little variety, finding the fit always perfect, the satisfaction impossibly great.

And then he held her in his arms and whispered to her, telling her he had never expected to meet someone like her, to find a woman he couldn't imagine ever being parted from at this stage in his life. "Tell me a little more about your life before Charlie."

"Trust is not easy for me," she said. "Like you, I had been abandoned. It makes no sense—my mother didn't throw me away—she was very sick, and I was told she died. Many Vietnamese didn't make it out of the boat lift alive. Many suffered severe illness as refugees. My mother was very, very young when I was born. It was never spoken of but it suggests she wasn't a willing partner when I came along. Somewhere—the refugee camp, here in the US when she was living hand to mouth with other refugees—at some time she became pregnant and was only fifteen when I was born."

It was hard for Blake to imagine. Lin Su was so small. A fifteen-year-old girl, so tiny, giving birth?

"My mother was sent to the US because her father was an American serviceman. I don't know if she ever found him. I think not. But my adoptive parents had very few facts about my family ties. They scooped me up, three years old, dressed me like an American girl doll and raised me in a small mansion. And their friends always said, 'Isn't she cute?' until I was eighteen. I don't believe I was a beloved daughter. By the time I was ten I knew I was their project."

"That would have been lonely," he said.

"It was lonely, but I wasn't sure how to cope. When I was eighteen and pregnant, nowhere to go, I went to a manicure shop owned by a Vietnamese family. They trained me, though I had to take classes and be licensed, but they gave me a way to make money. There were other immigrants who would share space. A little bit of the language came back to me and I was very grateful for them." She turned and looked up at him. "But I didn't belong there, either. If I were ever to look for my people, I wouldn't know where to start.

"So there," she said. "Now you know why I am stubborn and difficult. The only place I feel safe is on my own, with my son."

"Does Charlie know all this? Your personal story? How complicated your life really was?"

"He knows I am adopted, that I was unmarried when he

was born, that I am estranged from my adoptive family. That's more than enough to weigh on a young boy's mind."

"I think he should know all about your journey. So he understands why you are who you are. So he doesn't have questions. So he never feels that he doesn't belong."

"He belongs to me!" she said sternly. "I don't want him to carry my burdens, too."

"As long as you understand that secrets separate people from one another. Not telling important things creates distance."

"I tell all the important things," she said.

"I want you to feel safe with me," he said.

"I've told you more than anyone," she said. "I must feel safe with you or I couldn't be here with you like this."

SEVENTEEN

The leaves continued to color and then quickly fall in the cold rain on the coast of Oregon. Through this brisk and then wet autumn, several couples seemed to be thriving. Blossoming. Lin Su and Blake were spending as much time together as they could wrestle, and it wasn't easy. Many evenings Blake would join Winnie's household for dinner just to be near Lin Su and Charlie. On those nights Lin Su wasn't needed for the dinner and bedtime rituals, he would cook for Lin Su and Charlie. Or he might take them out to dinner. Or, less often, Charlie was content at home in the loft with his laptop, schoolwork and TV while Blake stole Lin Su away for a little time together.

They were the talk of the town. She was glowing in her newfound role as Blake's girlfriend. And Blake seemed to be constantly smiling.

Other couples were also showing great happiness. Grace and Troy, for one. Grace now had dependable help in the flower shop and was slacking off on her workload a little bit, getting ready to have a baby girl. She always knew it would be a girl, and though Troy insisted it would be a son, he was thrilled.

Peyton was seen walking the town's main street or across the beach whenever she could, determined to keep her weight under control so she could regain her figure. Her mother kept shipping fattening Basque food in Styrofoam coolers overnight; it was irresistible. Scott dove in whenever a shipment came, and while Peyton tried to resist, she wasn't doing so well. For the Grants, it would be a boy. Scott was already lobbying for another child after this one to even up the family. The next, he proclaimed, would be a girl.

Iris and Seth Sileski were positively euphoric about the possibilities of their future family—they were having a girl. Sileskis didn't get a lot of girls—there was only the one granddaughter before this one and Seth's parents had brought three sons to the family. Seth and Iris had come together after years of separation—they'd known each other since childhood and now, reunited, in love and marriage, were adding to the local population.

Even some of the more mature couples in town were enjoying bliss just prior to the holidays. Carrie and Rawley were now officially living together in Carrie's house. Ray Anne and Al couldn't be happier or more settled, proud of Al's foster sons and how well they were doing in school and in their home life. Sarah and Cooper were kicking around the idea of squeezing out one more baby before calling it quits on the reproductive front.

But one couple, long married, seemed to be on the skids. Norm Sileski came home from the service station one cold and rainy afternoon just a week before Thanksgiving and his wife, Gwen, said, "I want a divorce."

"Don't be silly," Norm said. "People our age don't get divorced."

"They do now," she said. "I'll keep the house and, since I don't hold an outside job, we'll split the savings and work out alimony. You'll have to move out."

"Is that right?" he said indignantly. "And where exactly am I supposed to go?"

"I'm sure there's a place at the garage, some unused corner you can store a cot. You like it there best, anyway."

"Well, I'm not going to. How about that?"

"I've seen a lawyer," she said. "You'll be served papers and asked to leave."

"Old woman, I think you've finally had one too many hot flashes and fried your brain."

"I haven't had a flash in ten years, that's what you know!" she said.

"All right, I hate like hell to ask this, but what the devil has you asking for a divorce now after all these years?"

"If you have to ask, you don't deserve an answer."

"Is it those widows again? Because they didn't mean no harm."

"Is that what you think?" she shot back. "You'd'a gone home with any one of them!"

"Well, did I?"

"No, but just because you're lazy."

"Lazy! I been working my whole life! Never took a day off! I'm seventy and I'm still bringing home a paycheck! I think you maybe lost your mind!"

"I want you to get dinner at the diner and, on your way, stop at Seth and Iris's house and tell them I'm not having Thanksgiving this year. Because I'm getting divorced. I should be all settled before the baby comes so I can help with the day care."

"I'm not doing that," he said. "That's a damn fool thing to do. I'm ignoring you because of your Alzheimer's, but I'll get dinner at the diner because I'm hungry. And if you want to tell them you're getting a divorce, you go right ahead. Ruin their holiday! See if I get you out of it."

He put his cap on his head and headed out the door.

Gwen called Iris on her cell phone. "Iris, I'm afraid I'm not going to be able to have Thanksgiving for the family this year."

"Oh, I'm sorry to hear that. Aren't you feeling up to it?"

"I'm feeling all right," Gwen said. "But I've decided to get a divorce."

Gwen heard the opening and closing of a door through the phone line and the next thing she knew Iris was waddling into her living room, cell phone in hand.

"You're getting a *what*?" she asked.

Charlie had never seen his mother happier. In fact, though he'd only known Blake for a few months, he'd never seen the Ironman happier, either. By the time Charlie got home from the wedding at the Lacoumette farm, there was an obvious special light shining in both their eyes. They were seen talking softly from time to time, giving each other little fits of secret laughter. And they held hands. Right out in the open.

This was a mother Charlie had never experienced and he liked it. He was having little fantasies about Blake stepping into the role of his stepfather; he couldn't help that. But he kept his mouth shut, crossed his fingers and didn't ask any questions. All that really mattered was that things just stayed nice for everyone concerned. Even if they didn't end up living happily ever after, he'd appreciate it if they'd just remain happy for a while.

When Lin Su had someone other than Charlie to focus on,

to think about all the time, Charlie had a much easier existence. He was progressing in his training, reaching his goals and surpassing them, and he wasn't having asthma attacks. He had started doing some exercising without using his inhaler first and he didn't have to always use it afterward. On a couple of cool, sunny days, Blake loaned him a bike and helmet and they went out for a long ride together. Lin Su hadn't even told him to be careful or asked him if he had his inhaler and EpiPen.

The whole town was getting ready for the long Thanksgiving weekend. Predictably, Lin Su, Charlie and Blake would be sharing Winnie's table. Lin Su and Grace would work on the cooking of a robust turkey and all the trimmings. This might be Grace's last big event—she was having her baby in about three weeks or so and her new employee at the shop, Ronaldo, was delighted to be taking over for the Christmas holidays. She planned to work when she could, helping with arrangements, wreaths and other decorations, but after Thanksgiving she was going to be around the house a lot.

Charlie had a little something going on in his life that no one knew about, and pretty soon, like any second, it was going to come out. He'd been communicating with his aunt Leigh. She'd answered his email, asking about Lin Su, of course. He was cautious. He told her that his mother didn't know Charlie had been searching out his roots and was sure she'd try to talk him out of it if she knew. She might even forbid it. That aside, he had a lot of questions.

So they exchanged emails and she answered what questions she could. Yes, as far as she knew his biological father was alive. He'd been a high school student with Lin Su. When Lin Su left the Simmons family, Jake went to Princeton. He was an attorney like his father, like Leigh and Lin Su's father. Leigh's mother and father divorced almost immediately after Lin Su left, then their mother passed away from cancer soon after at a very young age—fifty-five—and her father, Gordon, had remarried in less than six months to a woman only a few years older than Leigh. A woman her sister Karyn's age. The family relationship was somewhat strained.

After about ten emails, Leigh wanted to speak to Charlie. He warned her that he'd have to find a time when he was alone because he hadn't yet told Lin Su what he'd been doing.

You just tell me when you're available, Charlie, and I'll make the time, Leigh sent back.

When Charlie found a private moment to call his aunt, Leigh said, "You really must tell your mother right away. This is her family. She deserves to know."

"That's why I haven't told her," he said. "Because I asked and asked and she made up stuff, like my biological father was dead, and wouldn't talk about any of it."

"You still have to tell her," Leigh said. "Maybe once it's out, she'll actually be relieved. Pleased. I've wanted to find her for years. It seemed like she was so briefly part of my life."

"But then why didn't you look for us? We weren't hiding."

"Oregon was the last place on earth I expected you to turn up, for one thing. For another, my mother said that when they discouraged her from having a baby while unmarried, she went back to her Vietnamese family on the East Coast. I looked for Huang Chao. I admit, I didn't do an exhaustive search, but I looked. I spoke to a couple of people who had also been immigrants at the same time and they made no connection. But now that I know she's alive and well and that I'm an aunt, I want to see you both. Maybe help you put the pieces back together."

"Why didn't her adoptive father want to know where we were?"

"It's very hard to explain him—he's a selfish man. Unemotional and self-centered and busy with his life. He saw Lin Su as my mother's idea, someone in the past. You have to understand Gordon—he was hardly ever around. When he was around, he was on his phone or in his office. He attended our graduations and Karyn's weddings. He presides over family holidays as if we're all close. But I don't believe he's ever phoned me just to chat. He's just not much of a father."

"I found him first," Charlie said. "But I couldn't find a working email address or anything."

"He's a retired partner now, consulting, traveling, playing a lot of golf. He has an email address—it's one of the ways we communicate, through texts and emails. Very likely he just ignored your emails."

Charlie laughed. "Like me and my mom. That's how she keeps tabs on me. And if I don't text right back, look out."

"Tell me, Charlie—did your mother go back to her people?" Leigh asked.

"In a way. She worked for a Vietnamese family in their shop. We lived with a lot of different people I don't even remember while she worked and went to school to be a nurse. But I had a lot of colds and bronchitis and allergies so she learned the best climates—she couldn't take the East Coast and I couldn't take the winters or allergens, she said. We've been living in Oregon since I was about four."

"And she did all that with no help from her adoptive family," Leigh said, a sadness in her voice. "I want you to tell your mother that I'd like to see you both. Please, Charlie."

"Let me think about it. You don't know her. She gets upset if I even *ask*!"

"Then be brave, but do it. No more living in the shadows. You have family. Your biological grandmother might be alive for all I know. I've read that many immigrating Vietnamese were separated from their families for many years, always searching. Have you ever noticed the number of websites dedicated to finding your Vietnamese family?"

"Where do you think I started?" he asked.

"Lin Su's adoption was sudden and mysterious and my parents said they didn't know much of anything about her, but I find that hard to believe. I really can't see them adopting a child they knew nothing about. They weren't above outrageous stories if it served their purposes. You tell your mother we've been in touch and I'll reach out to my father and ask a few more questions."

"Can't we wait till I'm about thirty and self-supporting?" Charlie asked. "That would be a good time to tell her."

And his aunt Leigh laughed.

Iris tried talking to her mother-in-law about this current divorce insanity, but all she could get out of Gwen was that it was about time she lived her own life. She was tired of being married to a grumpy old man who didn't want to do anything but go to the gas station every day.

"But, Gwen, he took you on a cruise!" Iris said.

"For all the fun that was. He hardly spent a minute with me."

"Is this about those women?" Iris asked.

"He asked the same question. Funny how that comes right to mind, yet no one wants to talk about how terrible it was."

"You two need counseling," Iris said. "I'll find someone for you."

"Well, I'm not going to counseling with him! It's too late for that."

"Then just tell me why? After all these years, after a wonderful family and grandchildren, just tell me why?"

"Oh, darling, it isn't about you!" she insisted. "It's not you or the kids or the new baby! I'll always be your mother-in-law, sweetheart. I'll always be Nana to the baby. And I'll help you with babysitting, of course I will. I might get some kind of job, however."

"Gwen," Iris said sternly. "Why?"

"He doesn't love me, Iris. I think he never has, but my generation… We get married and that's it. Even if we have to live without love in our lives."

"Gwen, Norm is a little grumpy, but he…"

"A *little grumpy*?" she asked, laughing outright. "He didn't talk to his youngest son for how many years? I can't get him to wear a clean shirt to the table! He doesn't care about me! I'm setting him free. I'll be going on my next cruise alone!"

"It's the cruise," Iris told Seth. "This is all about the cruise. Norm was delightful on the cruise. He had a wonderful time. He was very social. There were those widows who flirted with him and he loved it. Gwen's feelings are very hurt. That's all this is."

"He wants to know if he can use our spare room until he finds his own place," Seth said.

"Oh, my God," Iris said. "I think my life just flashed before my eyes."

"Maybe he'll be delightful," Seth said.

"No! No! Tell him to make up with his wife!"

"Iris, when was the last time anyone told Norm anything?"

"Oh, God, you told him yes. You told him he could have the spare room. I'm going to have to kill you!"

"Just for a few days," Seth said. "It won't take him any time at all to hate it. His dinner won't be what he likes, won't be on time. He'll have to do his own laundry. Like I do," he added, lifting one of those handsome, expressive brows. "He can't make it here. And in no time at all there will be a screaming baby keeping him up all night."

"Your days are numbered," Iris said.

"I'll talk to him," Seth promised.

Seth took a slightly different approach than Iris had. He drove his patrol car to the station, wearing his uniform and armed. He parked on the side of the building rather than at the pump, went to find Norm and pulled him away from the other men so they could talk privately. "What in the holy *hell* is going on with you and Mom?"

"If I could explain her, I'd be a millionaire," Norm said.

"She says you don't love her, that you never have," Seth said.

"She has a bug up her ass about that cruise. Worst idea I ever had, that cruise."

"*You* had a good time, but she didn't."

"She worried the whole way up to Seattle that I wasn't going to be nice, that I was going to be cranky and wear my Lucky's shirt to the captain's dinner. She lectured me for days. *Be nice, Norm. Be courteous, Norm.* So I was nice! Sue me."

"Listen to me," Seth said. "I want you to go by the flower shop and buy a great big bouquet. Get a bottle of nice wine— she likes that putrid pink shit. Maybe some chocolates or something. Go home, tell her you love her and work it out!"

"I packed a bag this morning. I'm going to go home and get it, bring it over to your house."

"We're eating out!" Seth said, at the end of his rope.

"Oh? Where? Because I only go to the diner. That Cliffhanger's is too fancy for me."

"We're going to Cliffhanger's," Seth said, though they had no such plans.

"Okay. I'll see you when you get home."

"Dad, you can work this out if you try."

"I dunno about that. She's got a real bug up her ass this time. Might take a medical intervention."

On Wednesday afternoon, the day before Thanksgiving, Charlie went to Blake's as usual. But instead of his workout he asked Blake if they could talk about something.

"Sure," Blake said. "What's on your mind?"

"Well, I did something my mom isn't going to like and I have to tell her. I found her adoptive family. I've been talking to her sister—my aunt Leigh."

Blake was speechless for a moment. "Aw, man…"

"Well, I told you I wanted to know things. And she wouldn't tell me. Plus, she made up shit. My biological father is not dead."

Blake tried to think fast. "Okay, here's the thing I should have thought of first and I didn't. You should have warned her—your mother. You should have said you were going to look for the family if you had the chance, that you were determined. You would've had the argument at the front end of this adventure."

"Too late now," Charlie said. "Aunt Leigh has wanted to know where my mom is for years. She wants to see her, to see me. And that should be a good thing but I know it's not going to be. My mom is going to be mad."

"Why are you so sure of that?"

"Because she told me what she wanted me to believe and I didn't believe it—that's going to piss her off. But hey—I didn't believe it because it wasn't true!"

"There's the part that's going to be awkward," Blake said. "You admitting you didn't believe her."

"But it should be good! She does have family! Maybe my father disappointed her and he'll probably also disappoint me if I ever meet him, but isn't it better to know the truth?"

"Depends on who you ask, Charlie. Some people don't want to know. And some people think there's a time and place to know. Maybe she just wanted you to be old enough to understand."

"I do understand," he said.

"Did she ever tell you not to research this stuff?"

"Nope. I just asked her why she wasn't telling me more details and she said, 'Many reasons.' Like it was not my business. And it is my business."

"You have to tell her," Blake said.

"I know. That's what Aunt Leigh said, too. But I'm not telling her until after Thanksgiving. I think we should have one good holiday before she kills me. Tomorrow we're gonna have a good day, all of us together, and then on the weekend I'll tell her. With you."

"With me?" he asked. "Why me?"

"Don't act like you don't know," Charlie said. "She won't kill me in front of you. And if you act like it's normal, like anyone would want to know and it's okay, then maybe she won't kill me at all."

"She's not going to kill you. She might be upset, though. You might have to grovel a little, ask forgiveness for doing it behind her back, but you're a big boy—you can do that." He took a breath. "Charlie, you're her whole life. She tries to take care of you, protect you. She wouldn't keep important things from you to be mean, you know that."

"I know. But still…"

"You knew she wouldn't want you to do this," Blake said. "You're going to have to take your medicine."

"But I wasn't wrong!"

"It's not about right or wrong. It's about doing something you know would make your mother unhappy and doing it, anyway. That's what you have to own. That's what it means to become a man—you make a decision, you stand by it, you deal with the consequences if there are any. Sometimes fallout that seems all bad is good in the long run. But you won't know that until you walk through the whole flood. You did what you did. Time to step up, man."

"Is that what you did?" he asked.

"You have no idea," Blake said.

EIGHTEEN

Iris Sileski was hosting Thanksgiving dinner at her house. Nine months pregnant, due in three weeks, feeling big as a water buffalo in a tutu, ankles swollen, father-in-law in the spare bedroom, husband working until afternoon, Iris was doing the baking and roasting a turkey. Seth's oldest brother, Boomer, and his wife and kids were going to his wife's family for the holiday, something they seemed to decide after Gwen announced her divorce and moved Norm out of the house.

"Chicken," Iris said to Boomer. "The next time you're in a bad place, call someone who cares!"

Nick, the bachelor brother, was coming. But Nick was not only clueless, he was also unpredictable. If some pretty girl called him with a better offer he might suddenly come down with the flu and miss Iris's dinner. And being the bachelor, he wouldn't be bringing the pies if he did come.

But despite the fact Iris was in a foul mood, she gave the dinner her all. She'd gone to Grace's shop and made herself a beautiful horn of plenty centerpiece, baked three pies, bought a twenty-pound turkey and rigorously cleaned the house.

"Can I help with anything, Iris?" Norm asked her.

"Yes," she said. "You can go next door and do whatever it takes to make up with your wife!"

"Now, Iris," he said. And then he went to the station for a while. God forbid he should vacuum or clean a bathroom. Maybe Gwen had a point…

Seth had volunteered to work most of Thanksgiving Day so other officers could take time with their families. As compensation, he would take an extra-long dinner break, from maybe four till seven, during which time he would have dinner with his family, even though he'd be on call. And as extra compensation, he would have a nice Christmas, working the bare minimum, during which time he expected to have a brand-new baby girl in residence.

When he got home, only Nick and Iris were there. Nick was in front of the TV, watching football, drinking a beer. Iris was in the kitchen, working her tail off. Seth kissed her cheek and asked her how she felt.

"Just great," she said, heavy on the sarcasm.

"I'm sorry, honey," he said. "Can I help?"

"You've got cleanup," she said. "You and any other male Sileskis on the property."

"You bet. Of course. I'm on call, though."

"Ah," she said. "Have you scheduled the call yet?"

"Huh?"

"Never mind," she said. "Just relax. It's almost ready."

"Where's Norm?"

"At the station, of course. I imagine he'll be here the second the dinner bell rings."

And sure enough, he was. Iris said five o'clock and Norm came wandering in at ten minutes to—just enough time to wash his hands. He got a little sidetracked, though. He grabbed a beer and sat down with his boys in the living room, watching the game.

The table was set, the bird was resting, the potatoes mashed, the gravy perfect, the green beans under a pat of butter and the rolls buried in a linen wrap in a wicker basket. Napkins were rolled into holiday rings and the ice water had been poured.

There was a cheer from the living room followed by a lot of male laughter. This was not a sound alien to other Thanksgivings in the Sileski family, but usually there would be Boomer's wife, Sandy, in the kitchen to help Gwen put out the food.

Iris walked right through the living room to the baby's room, and even though she was roughly the size of an RV, she went completely unnoticed. She stood at the end of the crib, looking around at her baby's room—it was so precious. She rubbed her tummy; it was getting hard and solid because there was no more room in there. She really didn't know where she was going to put another three weeks or more. She wanted to hold this baby so dearly.

This was supposed to be the best Thanksgiving of her life—married to the love of her life for eleven months, nine months pregnant, at peace with the family, everyone anxiously awaiting the birth. Instead, what did she have? A day of backbreaking labor that no one really noticed followed by a feast they would all take for granted. And fat ankles.

She went back to the kitchen, again strolling through the living room unnoticed, and put all the food on the table. She began carving the turkey and even the noise from the electric knife only made the men louder. She called them to the table and they all came, slowly, one by one, the TV roaring in the background.

There was laughter and chatter as they loaded up their plates. They talked about the game, the weather, the garage, the sheriff's department, their schedules, and paused every so often when there was a loud report from the TV, from the game. Nick got up from the table, fork still in his hand, and ran to the living room. "Touchdown!" he yelled. "That's my team. Seth owes me two bucks so far but I plan to leave here a rich man!"

Then, remarkably, Nick came back to the dining room and picked up his plate, taking it to the living room, balancing it on his knee to watch the game and report. Within sixty seconds Norm was following his son, leaving Seth alone at the table with Iris.

He looked at her pleadingly. She jerked her head in the direction of the living room and before she could even reconsider Seth packed up his dinner and followed his dad and brother.

No one mentioned the glaring absence of Gwen. Iris had only talked to her a couple of times during the week, passing chitchat, because frankly she was *furious* with them both— Gwen and Norm! She wasn't thrilled with Boomer, Nick or Seth, either.

She sat there picking at her dinner. Seth came in, kissed her on the cheek and asked her if she was okay. "Fine," she said. So he took seconds of dressing, potatoes and gravy.

Right behind him came Nick, reloading. "Outstanding, Iris! Thank you!" She answered that it was a pleasure.

Iris sat there for a while and then she began packing up a hot picnic. If any of the men in the living room bothered to look into the kitchen they would assume she was cleaning up. She had a large pan into which she scooped a generous turkey dinner, enough for two. She poured gravy into a handy glass measuring bowl with a cover. She covered the whole thing with foil, carried the gravy, stuck napkins under her arm and slipped out into the cold night.

Assholes.

She knocked on Gwen's door with her foot. She was actually delighted to see that Gwen was sniffling. "Have you eaten?" Iris asked.

"I'm not very hungry, but please, come in! I might have a little glass of wine. I know you can't, but I think I will." And then she blew her nose.

"Maybe you can stuff down a little because I haven't really had a full dinner yet. I brought enough for both of us. The men are more focused on the ball game and I missed having you at my table."

"But no one else did."

"Get the plates out," Iris said. And she said it sternly.

When Gwen had set the table, Iris served their dinner. The gravy needed a little nuking but everything else had held up just fine. When they were seated before their plates and Gwen had her wine, she dipped her fork into her dinner.

Iris took a few bites before she spoke. "I want you to stop feeling sorry for yourself right now because this was your decision. You sent Norm to our house. And don't expect me to thank you for that, either. If I can't feel sorry for myself, seventeen months pregnant and having slaved over a big holiday meal, then you don't get a pass, either. Besides, not only did no one mention your absence, they didn't notice that I left. You know why? Because they're idiots who can't think past their stomachs, that's why, and they take us for granted. And maybe you're right, maybe we should just divorce the hell out of all of them. But you signed on for this and so did I and if we're a little lonely right now it's because we allowed this to happen and look what it got us. I shouldn't have let Norm move in—I'm too pregnant and touchy for him right now—but instead of saying so, I asked Seth to do it. If Seth had done it, I wouldn't be here and they wouldn't all be sitting in the living room in front of the television with their plates on their laps. I hate them."

Gwen just stared at her while Iris shoveled a few more bites into her mouth. "Iris, you're crying," Gwen finally said.

Iris wiped at her cheeks. "Small wonder," she muttered.

"Honey, you're exhausted," Gwen said. "You're not going back there. When we're done with this beautiful dinner you're going to put your feet up in the living room while I clean up and make you a nice cup of tea. You're not going back to your house until the TV is off and the kitchen is spotless—I'll see to that."

Iris realized something. She should have realized it before. It was a special holiday and she was about to have a baby— without her own mother. For the past several years, since her mother died, Gwen had been her surrogate mother and she'd been counting on Gwen to preside over the dinner and also to be with her when the baby came. Seth would be her coach and partner but Gwen would be her stand-in mother. And what had Gwen done? She drew a line in the sand having finally had enough of Norm's cranky, silent ways. Iris might even sympathize. But did Gwen have to do this *now*?

"I miss my mother," Iris said.

"Of course you do, sweetheart. When we're done and you've had a nice, calming cup of tea, I'll go over to your house and get Norm and bring him home. I don't really want him back but it was so inconsiderate of me to suggest he go to your house. I wasn't thinking. I'm sorry."

"I understand," Iris said with a sniff and a sob. "But wasn't it inconsiderate of him, too? And Seth, for not preventing it?"

"Inbred, I'm afraid," Gwen said.

"Are you really going to divorce him?" Iris asked with a hiccup and another sob.

"Possibly," she said with a shrug. "But now it's more because he doesn't care that I'm divorcing him." She took a sip of her wine. "I might just ignore him for the rest of his life, not that he'd notice."

"Oh, Gwen..."

"I think maybe you're overwrought," Gwen said. "It's not like we haven't bickered for forty-five years." She picked up her fork again. "You did a lovely job on the dinner, Iris."

"Thank you. I have a beautiful centerpiece on the table, too. I wish I'd brought it. We're the only ones who care."

They ate a little more in silence and then Iris pushed her plate away. "I might've overdone it a bit," she said, rubbing her belly. "I might not have eaten a full meal at my house but I sure put a dent in it. I didn't need this much."

The front door opened and Seth, looking frantic, stormed in. "Iris!" He rushed to her, taking into account the remnants of dinner on the table. He dropped to one knee beside her chair. "I thought you were in the bathroom!"

She looked at her watch. "For thirty minutes?" she asked.

"Who am I to judge," he said with a shrug. "Are you all right?"

She was a little flushed and trembling. "Actually, no... I don't feel very well. I think I ate too much. And I have a lot of gas. And I..." She groaned and leaned forward. "Wow," she said through her groan.

Without warning, there was the sound and sensation of dripping. She looked at her husband with wide eyes. "Uh-oh," she said. "My water broke."

He immediately pulled his cell phone out of his pocket. "I guess we're going to the hospital," he said. He called one of the other deputies. "Iris's water broke," he said into the phone. "I'm off call and you're on. I'll be at Pacific Hospital."

Iris had mistakenly believed that since she so efficiently went into labor without even realizing it, since the baby was a little early, the birth would be fast and slick and easy. But it was not. When she did get to the labor and delivery ward, she was four centimeters, which was only one more than necessary to be admitted. And then, thanks to a very tiring day, a lot of stress and a huge double meal, she was sick as a dog. And fretful.

She labored through the night, and even with the assistance of an epidural, she was pretty miserable. Gwen had followed them to the hospital and stayed with Iris and Seth through their very long night and cheered her on when she began to push. Norm had also gone to the hospital and took up his post in the hallway outside Iris's room, getting regular updates from Seth.

Finally little Rose was born. Rose was named after Iris's late mother and, since they had been in the flower business before selling the shop to Grace, naming baby girls for flowers was something of a family tradition.

After Rose made her appearance, after Gwen had taken some pictures and saw that Iris was going to be cleaned up and the delivery room converted into the room where the new little family would spend at least one night, Gwen went to the hospital coffee shop for coffee and whatever breakfast she could find. When she got back to the room a half hour later, Iris was resting, little Rose was in the baby bed beside Iris and Seth was pacing.

"Oh, good, you're back. I want to step out of the room and make my calls."

"You can go to the coffee shop. I had a nice little micro-waved egg sandwich down there. You can stake out a corner, have some coffee and something to eat and use your phone."

"Dad's been here all night," Seth said.

"I noticed," she said.

"Have you talked to him?"

"There isn't much to say. I'm glad he was here for you, Seth. Even if he couldn't be in the room."

"I'm going to send him in to see the baby now."

"Sure," Gwen said. "Of course. We're not going to fight."

Seth gave his mother a kiss on the cheek. "Thank you, Mom. You were wonderful. Thank you."

"I'm glad I was invited."

After Seth left, Gwen gave Iris a soft kiss on the brow. "Sleep, sweetheart. I'll be here watching over the baby for you."

Iris just mumbled and rolled over.

It was only a little while before Rose started snuffling around in the bed and for that Gwen was most grateful. She happily picked up the little bundle and held her close. She hummed very softly, so softly she wouldn't wake Iris.

Then Norm walked in, head down, hands in his pockets. He walked right over to where Gwen sat and looked down at the baby. "She looks like Seth," he said. "But with medi-cal science being advanced like it is these days, that can prob-ably be fixed."

She smiled in spite of herself. "You sure it's advanced enough?"

"Oh, sure," he said. "They pulled my gallbladder out through a straw."

He pulled a chair over right next to Gwen and sat beside her, studying the baby. "Looks like she might have Iris's crazy hair," he said.

"She'll be beautiful like her mama."

They communed in silence for a few minutes.

"You just about all settled down now?" Norm asked her.

"I'm completely calm. What are you getting at?"

"I'm getting at—let's call a truce. We have a new baby in the family. These kids don't need all the ruckus."

"Don't go blaming me," she threatened, but she did so softly. "I wasn't the one flirting with a pack of men on the cruise."

"I *knew* that's what it was. I wasn't flirting. I was pleasant as pie and it just pissed you off."

"No, it didn't. It hurt my feelings. It hurt my feelings very much."

"I thought that's how you wanted me to be," he said. "You worried and harped about it all the way to Seattle! I did just what you wanted."

"I suppose. Except I wanted you to be pleasant for me, not for a bunch of women we barely met. And I don't care what you say—*they* were flirting!"

"That ain't my problem. My problem is the only woman I ever wanted to be nice to me was sour as a rotten peach the whole time. I can't win."

"I am nice to you," she said.

"Gwen," he said in a low whisper. "I just wanted you to be happy for once. I tried hard as I could."

"But you tried to please *them*!"

"They were the only ones nice to me! If you could be half so nice, I'd sure be grateful. You're the only woman I ever wanted to fuss over me."

"I am?" she asked.

"A course you are! Over forty-five years now. Do I have to say it every damn day?"

"Once a year would be a big improvement."

He was quiet for a minute. "I'll mark it down on the calendar," he said. "Now can we please stop this tomfoolery? I'm too old for it."

"Do you want to hold the baby now?" she asked.

"You gonna let me back in my own house?"

"I never did see any lawyer," she confessed, passing him the baby.

"'Course you didn't. We been through too much to get divorced over a bunch of flirty widows. There wasn't a one of 'em I'd have, anyhow. Yap, yap, yap. Pack of yippy poodles woulda been easier on my nerves."

"Norm," she laughed. She leaned toward him and he gave her a little peck on the lips.

"There. That's better," he said.

Gwen glanced at Iris. Her eyes were closed. But she smiled.

Thanksgiving at Winnie's house had been a happy day. Lin Su took care of Winnie and helped Grace prepare the feast. The day was sunny, so a little time throwing the Frisbee on the beach occupied Charlie and Troy. Mikhail enjoyed one of his extra-long walks and had finally traded his board shorts for pants.

After a robust meal, when everyone in the household felt sluggish and lazy, Blake helped Lin Su clean the kitchen. Winnie was napping, Grace and Troy went down to their quarters to rest, Mikhail was on the sunny deck, Charlie was on the couch with his computer on his lap and, feeling almost alone, Blake stole a couple of kisses in the kitchen.

Charlie caught them and smiled with satisfaction. Blake

knew it was not because he was thrilled that his mother was having a nice romance. It was because he was counting on his mother being in love with Blake and therefore would go easy on Charlie when she found out about his family research. Blake had invited Charlie and Lin Su to come next door for lunch the next day, the Friday after Thanksgiving. That's when Charlie was going to tell her.

Blake made a green salad, a bowl of fruit and a bunch of sandwiches, cut in small triangles.

They ate and talked; Blake asked Charlie about what was coming up at school and had he made any plans for his Christmas break. Lin Su had heard that Iris had gone into labor a little early and delivered a baby girl just that morning. And Charlie was clearly nervous, so Blake thought he'd do him a favor and just rip that Band-Aid off.

"Charlie has something he wants to tell you, Lin Su."

"Oh?"

Charlie glared at Blake. Then he took a deep breath and said, "Mom, try to stay calm."

She folded her hands in her lap. "This isn't starting out well," she said.

"Mom, I wanted to know more about where we came from. I started looking up some of the people you talked about, the family that adopted you. I found your sister and we've been in touch with each other. She looked for you but she didn't have the right facts and couldn't find you."

Lin Su froze. Her face had gone pale. "Why would you do that?" she asked.

"I wanted to know things and you wouldn't tell me," he said with a shrug. But he seemed to get smaller in his chair.

There were a few guttural sounds that Blake realized was

Vietnamese spoken softly, lowly, rapidly. He had never witnessed this before but he could see that what Charlie said was
true—anger came out in her native language.

"I told you everything I wanted you to know!" she snapped.
"There is nothing else!"

"There is," Charlie said bravely. "There's a lot more. For one
thing, when you left your adoptive family, they told a story
about it. A lie. They said you went back to your people, like to
your biological family. They said you'd taken back your original name and disappeared. But that wasn't true. You worked
with some Vietnamese—I even sort of remember. It was like
a whole village in a small house or something, but you were
always Lin Su Simmons and we moved away from Boston because of me, because I was sick all the time. And my father
isn't dead."

"*Aeiii,*" she squeaked. "And tell me, Charlie, what good does
knowing that do us now? Does he come and rescue you? Pay
for private schools? Send money? Does it fill you with pride
to know your mother was abandoned?"

"Lin Su, easy does it," Blake said. "Charlie didn't do this *to*
you. He did it for himself. And I don't think he regrets knowing the truth."

"I don't," Charlie said. "Your mother died," he added.

"I know my mother died!" she snapped. "Why do you think
I was adopted?"

"Not that mother. That mother, your Amerasian mother, she
might even be alive. Your adoptive parents had no evidence of
her death. Don't you want to know that if she is? Your adoptive mother died. A couple years after you left. Of cancer, I
think Aunt Leigh said."

"You knew this?" she asked Blake, her eyes flashing.

"Charlie told me he wanted to learn some things about your family if he could. I knew he wanted that."

"And you didn't tell me?"

"I asked him not to, Mom. I didn't know if I'd ever find out anything so why get you all whacked out of shape? But I found your sister Leigh, and she was so happy to hear from me. She wants to see us. She's been trying to figure out some things about your original family. To help. So there don't have to be questions."

"I have no questions," she said with an angry and dismissive wave of her hand.

"Well, you should, because Aunt Leigh thinks your mother might be alive. She's been pressuring her father for more details for you. In case, you know..."

"She's not your aunt!" Lin Su said. "She's just some woman I lived with as a girl. We were never close, we were never family!"

"Yeah, she hates that, but she said when you came to them she was already away at a boarding school and her older sister was in college. It was later, when you were older, that she really took an interest, but she was in her twenties and after college she went to the Peace Corps. She said she saw you about once a year but she loved you."

Lin Su laughed. She blinked a few times. "It was very devoted love, wasn't it? Once a year?"

"She said you'd been gone quite a while before she even knew you'd left. She didn't know you were pregnant until her mother was dying!"

"Very devoted!" Lin Su mocked.

"They lied to you, Mom. You weren't three when you were adopted, you were four—they changed your birthday! Aunt Leigh thinks your mother might be alive, might've given you up for adoption because she couldn't raise you alone. Those people who adopted you—they lied to Aunt Leigh, too. Pretending you were a mystery and that you just left because you didn't want them anymore. It was years before Aunt Leigh knew you were pregnant and your parents wouldn't help you."

"Not. Your. *Aunt!*"

"I'm sorry, Mom. I wanted to know where we came from."

"You came from *me!*"

"Yeah, but not just you," he said meekly.

Lin Su looked into her lap and took a lot of deep calming breaths. Blake watched her carefully. She was so angry. So hurt.

"Are you finished eating?" she asked Charlie.

"Yeah. I guess so."

"I'd like you to excuse yourself. Go home. I'll be there when I'm finished working today. I won't be late. Grace and Troy will be helping."

"Mom, we should talk about this."

"Yes, we'll talk about it. When I get home tonight. Plenty of time for talking then."

Charlie got up from the table and leaned over her, kissing her on the cheek. "I'm sorry I upset you."

NINETEEN

When Charlie had gone, Lin Su slowly and elegantly turned her head to face Blake. "You betrayed me," she said.

He shook his head. "You're upset, but it's going to be all right. I didn't betray you and you know it."

"You involved yourself with Charlie and his secret and kept it from me when I should have known. What other things are you hiding from me?"

"I wasn't hiding anything, Lin Su. All I knew was that Charlie was trying to get information about his family. It is his family, you know. Not just yours."

"And did you tell Charlie the things I told you in confidence?"

"Of course not! And I'll tell you again since you're obviously too angry to listen—I didn't know anything! Until Charlie told me he'd found your adoptive sister, I didn't know what, if anything, he found. When he told me I insisted he tell you right away."

"Did you tell Charlie they took my name away? Those good

people who took me out of my mother's arms and gave me a home? They took the name away because they didn't like the sound of it, but they wanted a cute Asian name!"

"Sweetheart, I think you're completely overwhelmed right now. When you think this through you'll realize he hasn't done anything wrong. He just brought this up before you were ready, that's all. He doesn't want to hurt you."

"So here are two people, a mother and her son, getting along all right, then you decide what's best for us and we have to try to pick up the pieces of the mess."

"No," he said, leaning toward her. He covered her hand but she pulled it away from him. "No, I didn't decide anything, Lin Su. Charlie told me what he was doing. I could have refused to keep his confidence and gone to you but it wouldn't have changed anything. He would have continued his search. He wants to know. And he has a right to know."

A burst of Vietnamese came out of her, shocking Blake again. "Whoa. He said when you get pissed you only speak in Vietnamese…"

"I'm his mother! I know him better than anyone and I decide what is best for him to know, not you!"

"I didn't decide. I was a witness. Nothing more. Please, don't do this to yourself. You can work through this with Charlie. I'll help in any way I can."

"I would prefer you leave my son to me," she said. "I can see I made an error in judgment, confiding in you. That won't happen again."

"You're overreacting," he said. "Let's calm down and have a reasonable conversation. I love you. I would never hurt you."

"And yet you have. You took away my rights as a parent and shamed me as a mother. You let my son do things I forbade. You knew I didn't want Charlie to know things that would only hurt us both. You should have told me at once, but you didn't."

"I think you're out of your mind a little, sweetheart. There's no shame in your history. I didn't shame you and what Charlie found isn't going to hurt him. And as it was not anything you did that was either bad or wrong, there should be no guilt. Can we slow down?" he asked. "Can we be reasonable?"

She stood. "I was afraid I'd regret getting involved with you. This won't work. I'll make other arrangements for Charlie's training. We will be polite when we see each other. And this is goodbye."

"No, it's not, damn it," he said, standing, as well. "You don't get to toss me out of your life and his just because you didn't get your way. It's wrong. It's far more shameful than anything Charlie might've learned."

"You should have thought of that," she said. "You can't come between a mother and her child."a

"I didn't think I was! I was completely loyal to you both! Not an easy task, either. Think about this, Lin Su. You said that with me you had the first stable and healthy relationship since your son was born. Are you really going to throw that away over a small disagreement?"

"In my mind what you've done was not small."

"You're going to throw us away over something like this? A misunderstanding?"

She raised a slim brow. "Are you having trouble understanding this?" she asked. "I would be grateful if we could keep all of this private. I don't want my personal business broadcast to my employer and the town."

He shook his head. "You're going to think about this and realize you've gone completely crazy. Just think it through," he said. "I'm here for you. I'd like to help you pick up the pieces.

I love you and you love me. We have a chance, you and me and Charlie, to make a family out of our crazy pasts. All we have to do is work through it."

"I've had more than enough time to work through my crazy past, thank you."

She walked serenely out of his house and went back to her job.

"God," he said, rubbing a hand around the back of his neck. *Did I think I wouldn't mind helping her untangle her complicated life?*

Lin Su walked across the beach to town around 6:00 p.m. and it was already sunset over the Pacific. If they'd lived farther inland, it would be completely dark. What she saw on the main street was transforming—the entire street had been decorated for Christmas. She had heard something about a town tradition—the stringing of the lights, garlands, electric candles, great boughs of greenery and festive balls. All the shop windows were painted and stenciled and shop owners had put up their Christmas displays. The street was crowded with people still working on the decorations.

Charlie stood between the florist shop and Carrie's deli, leaning a shoulder against the wall. She took in a breath and said, "Hi."

He flinched in surprise. "Hi."

"Do you feel like a hamburger?" she asked.

He shrugged. "I guess. Anything is okay with me. Whatever you want."

"Let's go to the diner," she said. "We can enjoy the Christmas lights."

The diner was busy; a lot of the folks who were decorating decided to stop in for a quick bite rather than going home to cook. Lin Su said hello to about ten people and answered positively when asked how Winnie was getting along. She marveled for at least the hundredth time about how easily she was drawn into the community. This was something she would hate to give up. And yet, when it was time for her to be a friend, she resisted. She didn't like that about herself, but she had her reasons.

Charlie visibly relaxed when they were in the diner. He probably thought there would be no discussion until later, until they were at home alone. But she was of no such mood. As soon as they were seated in a booth and had ordered drinks and hamburgers, she launched her argument.

"Charlie, I'd like it if we could come to an understanding about a couple of things. I think you were wrong to go behind my back and get in touch with members of my family."

He just listened.

"It's going to take me a while to get past that, I'm afraid. You're getting older, I know, and want to make your own decisions about some things, but as long as you're my son, you're going to have to listen to me."

"I always listen."

"I'm very proud of you. You're brilliant and you're wise, but there are still some things I know more about than you do."

"I understand," he said.

"I want you to stop investigating my family. I want you to stop talking to Leigh Simmons. I can't prevent you from doing as you please when you're an adult, but for now, this is what I want."

"I think you're making a mistake," he said. "We've talked. She's awesomely nice and we have a lot to talk about. She knows where we live, and she wants to know us. She feels terrible about the problems you had and hates that you didn't get any help or support. She's not a bad person!"

"Tell her that you've had a conversation with your mother, and if you still feel the same way when you're eighteen, you can get in touch with her then. If she's as awesome as you say, she'll respect my wishes."

He gave his head the slightest shake. He pushed his glasses up on his nose.

"Please," she said.

"If that's what you want," he said.

She could tell she'd reached an impasse with her son, maybe the first one. He had no intention of obeying her. He was going to sneak! Lie to her!

"Charlie, if you defy me, we're going to have trouble on this issue. If it's in your best interest I won't hesitate to quit my job and find us another place to live."

He was stunned. "Because I got in touch with my aunt? Mom, since we've been here, everything good has happened for us. We have good friends, a good place to live. I'm in a good school, no one's chasing me to see if I have money in my pockets. You have a great job and I know you love Winnie. It would be a big mistake to move us away just because you're mad, but if you want to be that stupid…"

"Show respect!" she snapped. "I am your mother!"

"If you mess up this whole thing we've got here just because you're mad at me, just because I did something I've been wanting to do for a long time…"

"If you're still adamant about that, you can pursue it when you're over eighteen. For now, if you want to stay here, you'll do as I say."

"Jesus," he muttered.

"I'll make arrangements with Spencer to continue your training routine at the high school. He offered before but I didn't want to impose and Blake's was more convenient. But under the circumstances, you're going to have to stop spending time at Blake's house. It puts me in a very uncomfortable position."

"What?"

"Apparently I misjudged Blake. Whatever that was, that relationship we began, I've put a stop to it."

"No way. You did what?"

"I can't trust him, Charlie. Not telling me something important about my own son, that's the same as lying."

"No, it's not," he protested. "It just turns out that Blake understood. You don't. You think my history belongs only to you and I think it belongs to both of us! If you don't want to know about it, that's your choice, but I do! And that is not Blake's fault. It wasn't his idea."

She gritted her teeth.

He looked right at her, grim faced, pushed up his glasses again. "No, ma'am," he said. "As long as Blake will let me, I'm going to work out with him. He's an expert and he's my friend. Taking that away from me is not just unfair, it's mean. I'm sorry you're uncomfortable but I'm not doing it. I listen to you all the time but you don't listen to me. I need things, too. I need to know where I came from, who I am. I need my friends. I can show you respect without agreeing with everything you say."

"You're really testing me," she warned.

"Ground me," he said.

"What are you thinking, Charlie?" she said angrily.

"I'm thinking we're having a fight," he said. "If you want me to say yes to everything you tell me to do, I will. But I'm not shunning Blake because you're stubborn and pissed off."

"Charlie!"

"He's been good to us! He helped us! He chased those junkies and got your special things back and he got hurt!" He looked at her earnestly. "What's the matter with you? Are your secrets worth more than a good friend?"

"You have never talked to me this way! The trouble has already started. All because you defy my rules!"

"You were never against me like this before," he said. "You were always my best friend. Now you don't want to be anyone's friend!"

She could tell he was fighting tears.

"You're not the only one who can run away, you know. Is this how it was in your home? Your parents acting like they hate you, like they don't care what you need?"

"You know nothing about it!"

"I'm trying to know about it but you won't let me!"

They stared each other down for a moment.

Their hamburgers arrived and the talking stopped. But Charlie didn't eat. He pushed his plate away. "I'm not hungry," he said. "I'm going home."

He pulled his jacket on and stormed out of the diner, leaving Lin Su to sit alone with two plates of food. Stubbornly, she cut her burger in half and began to eat. When she had finished half her burger she asked for two take-home cartons. She carried them across the street, went through the flower shop to the back stairs and up to her loft. Charlie was sitting on the sofa, laptop open.

"Eat your dinner," she said, putting the carton on the coffee table. Then she went to the bedroom, longing for a door to close.

The days after that confrontation with Charlie were dark for Lin Su. She felt abandoned all over again. Blake called almost every day and she sent him to voice mail where he left messages asking her to please open her mind to the many positive possibilities. He even said, "I know you're listening to my messages because you're stubborn and hardheaded but you're not that stubborn and you know I care about you and Charlie. Please, let's at least talk."

She tried to stop listening to his messages, but since he would never really know, she listened. And she longed for him.

But he was causing her to lose control of Charlie and she couldn't allow it.

Charlie had defied her. He continued to be Blake's friend and student, working out there. They probably talked about what a fool she was behind her back and with a heavy heart she checked around for another job, relieved that none materialized.

"I know there's a problem," Winnie said. "I just don't know what it is."

"There's no problem that I'm aware of."

"Charlie is troubled, you're troubled. Blake doesn't stay for dinner with us anymore."

"Ah, that. Well, that didn't work out for me, Winnie, that's all. I'm afraid I just don't want to date Blake and there's no way to find a happy medium. Charlie is understandably disappointed," she said, trying to back Winnie off the trail. "I was afraid of exactly that, afraid that in seeing Blake, Charlie might have expectations. We'll get through this. Charlie and Blake seem to remain friends at least."

Winnie stared at her for a long moment. "You really underestimate me. My body is deteriorating but my mind is as sharp as it ever was. Remember that when you spin me a tale."

"I have no idea what you mean," Lin Su said.

"And there you go again…"

★ ★ ★

Somewhere in the second week of December, Peyton went
into labor. There was some excitement as her ob-gyn had been
concerned about the baby's position and when labor was well
under way he hadn't yet turned. They didn't wait long before
doing a C-section and bringing a large, healthy baby boy into
the world.

"I'm the last one left," Grace complained. "They all went
early and I'll probably be two weeks late!"

Lin Su was remembering how terrified she was when Charlie was due to be born. Not of giving birth but about how she
would live, how they would survive. She'd even called Marilyn
twice. *Please, don't turn your back on me now! I have a son coming
anytime and I don't know how we'll make it!*

We gave you everything, Marilyn had said. *We gave you a luxurious lifestyle, a fabulous education, everything a child could want.
If you put him up for adoption, I might reconsider. But I won't have
you take further advantage of us.*

In the midst of this traumatic month, Winnie had chosen to
support a fund-raiser. It was a black-tie event in North Bend.
"I bought us a table. We'll all go together. Lin Su, I'll need
you with me. I want you to go. I want Charlie to go."

"Ah, Winnie, I will go to make sure you have all the assistance you need, but I'll go as your nurse, not your guest."

"No, that's not how it will be. I have dresses for you to look
at, dresses I'll probably never wear again. Or, if you prefer,
Grace is going to shop for something in the maternity style and
you can go with her to find your own cocktail dress."

They argued back and forth for a while but the argument was
won by Winnie. Not because she was so eloquent but because
she badgered Lin Su into trying on one of her dresses and Lin

Su fell in love. She hadn't worn a beautiful, fancy dress since high school, since that other life.

Charlie wanted to opt out of the gala and just stay home, but Winnie wouldn't hear of it. "You'll want to go to this one," she said. "Blake is the speaker. It's a fund-raiser for the Neighborhood Club of Coos County. Troy is getting you a shirt and tie."

"Blake?" Lin Su asked, feeling her spirits plummet. "Oh, Winnie…"

"But there's no hard feelings between you," Winnie said, challenging Lin Su's story. "And of course he's a friend of ours. And Charlie's."

Lin Su wasn't fooled. Winnie was matchmaking again. She thought that if Lin Su dressed up and Blake came off well, everything would be fine and go back to the way things were.

She was trapped. But she knew she could be passive and polite and get this event behind her.

The night of the fund-raiser, Lin Su and Charlie put on their fancy clothes at Winnie's house, and right before they were to leave, Troy helped Grace slowly up the stairs from their apartment.

"I'm sorry, Mama, but we're not going to be able to go. I might still be here when you get home later but I'm having contractions. I'm definitely in labor but we've called the midwife and she said to wait until they're a little longer and closer together. It's just that the place for me is definitely not a gala."

"Oh, Grace!" Winnie said. "I should stay here with you!"

"No, you should go. We'll keep you posted on our progress. We might still be waiting for some action at midnight. On the other hand, if we're lucky we'll head for the hospital and let you know."

"Makes sense," Mikhail said. "They don't take attendance at fancy parties. If we leave, we leave." He gave Grace a little kiss on the cheek. "Good luck, *pupsik*. I hope she comes marching out quickly."

The Neighborhood Club gala was held in the ballroom of a large hotel. There was a silent auction of items donated by individuals and businesses. Large round tables were hung with white tablecloths and festive Christmas arrangements. There was a stage and podium with a microphone and some of the Neighborhood Club board members, the director of the club and chair of the event and their spouses were to be seated at the two tables in front of that podium.

Blake was the special guest. His job was to present two awards for special achievements to teens who had been regulars at one of the clubs for a long time and had managed to perform athletically, in community service and academically even though they came from disadvantaged households. The awards would also come with partial scholarships. Then Blake would give a brief keynote before the evening's end.

He had arrived a little early, as he always did. He liked to visit with the gala planners, volunteers, board members or dignitaries who came in support of the nonprofit. He always enjoyed a first look at auction items and would bid on at least a couple. He'd smile, shake a lot of hands, congratulate many and, if there was a God, greet treasured friends.

There would be five hundred guests tonight, a worthy crowd for a town and county this size. He'd spoken at and attended many such events that were far larger in bigger cities. There was one in Phoenix that offered a racehorse and diamond ring as part of their auction items; in New York City the grand item was a Mercedes coupe. His job tonight was to entertain, inspire and motivate.

He chatted with a great many people before he saw who he was looking for. She was not easy to spot because she was so small. Tonight she wore heels, making her almost as tall as Mikhail. Her elegant black dress with a silver wrap clung to that woman's body he had been missing so much. He longed to reach for her and enfold her in his arms. Beside her stood Charlie, as tall as his mother and still growing, wearing a new suit. No one else would realize it but in just a couple of months he'd buffed out a little bit, his shoulders a little broader. And it looked as if someone had not only outfitted him for tonight's event but managed to get him a haircut. He hoped that Lin Su had been the one to make sure Charlie put his best foot forward tonight.

He pushed his way through the crowd of beautifully dressed guests until he reached them. He bent to kiss Winnie's cheek. "Thanks for supporting this fund-raiser, Winnie," he said. He shook Mikhail's hand. Then he reached for Lin Su to give her what could best be described as a social hug. He kissed her on the cheek because she turned her face. "I'm glad you're here. Thanks for coming." He shook Charlie's hand and complimented him on the haircut, making the kid grin. "I saw your place cards on a table up front." He looked around. "I don't see Grace and Troy."

"Well, they are indisposed by early labor," Winnie said. "We had to leave them home. I wanted to stay with Grace but she said she might still be home through the night. They're waiting for the contractions to get stronger and closer."

"So you will understand if we take our leave during your speech," Mikhail said.

"Absolutely!" Blake said. "That's wonderful news! You'll be a grandmother before Christmas!"

"If I'm not, Grace will be very cranky," Winnie said. "I believe you're in demand, Mr. Smiley."

He looked over his shoulder to see that cocktail-toting admirers were lining up behind him, waiting for his conversation to be over so they could meet him.

"Find your table, Winnie. Relax. I think the program will be starting in just fifteen minutes or so."

Then he turned to say hello to other attendees.

As was typical of such evenings, all the salutations and presentations seemed to go on for a very long time. Blake sat at a table right next to Winnie's but all he could really see of Lin Su was her profile. Charlie was one of very few guests under the age of twenty-one and the majority were over forty. Blake couldn't help but notice that a lot of the charity's movers and shakers approached Winnie at her table, introduced themselves and shook her hand. He should have known—Winnie was undoubtedly a well-known donor.

Meals were beginning to be served, decanters of wine were placed on tables and the program began. One by one people stood at the microphone to thank people, introduce hardworking volunteers, say a few words about the positive growth of the organization, give statistics about the number of kids served, special projects completed and future plans for the Neighborhood Club.

Finally, with dinner nearly finished, the recipients of the awards were introduced and Blake stepped up to the stage to hand the plaques to them and shake their hands.

He was introduced to the sound of enthusiastic applause.

"I'm Blake Smiley and I'm a professional athlete and businessman. On your programs tonight you'll see this organization's mission statement. We endeavor to meet the needs of kids from the ages of seven to seventeen who need a place of refuge, encouragement, guidance and companionship. Because of this mission, most Neighborhood Clubs are erected in the poorest neighborhoods. And proceeds from tonight's fund-raiser will, in part, fund the beginning of an internship that will bring students of sociology, psychology and education at the college level to the organization to reduce the ratio of kids to counselors to give better results, so get out your wallets. This is important.

"There were no such clubs or gathering places when I was a kid or where I was a kid. In fact, my presence here tonight is a miracle of great proportions, but it's the kind of miracle I like to talk about because I guess you could say I relate to kids who don't have advantages. A friend of mine asked me if I liked to talk to people about survival of the fittest and I said no. No, I like to talk about survival of the weakest. I was the weakest. I fought rats for food, shared bonfires with transients to stay warm and ate at soup kitchens. And I learned to run.

"I wasn't the only kid who struggled with life. It's a sad but true fact that lots of kids have serious challenges that might make them stronger, but how will they use that strength in the end? What end? When you live in fear, you compensate, find a place where you can be less afraid, and sometimes that place isn't a good place. When you're fourteen, you don't know that what you need is safety, pride and potential. And even if you knew, would you know where to look?

"When I was fourteen, placed in a foster home and forced to attend school, there was a teacher and coach who took one look at me and figured me out. I thought he was an old coot, but it turned out he was thirty-two at the time. He said, 'Where you from, kid?' And I looked him in the eye and said, 'Water Street and Power.' And he grinned at me and said, 'I know that block. I came from right near there. We come outta that block mean as snakes. So, what does a kid like you do for fun?' I think I snarled something like, 'I run for my supper, old man.' And he answered, 'That so?' Then he took me to the track where the track-and-field team were warming up and he said, 'Let's get a time, see what you got.' So I ran for him. He clicked off his stopwatch and said, 'Don't ever lie to me again, boy.' I was so confused. I hadn't lied about my neighborhood. I'd pitched it right in his face so he'd back off and leave me alone. Instead, he said, 'If you came from that street you'd be able to run or you'd look a lot worse than you do. So let's see where you're really from because you look soft to me.'

"So I ran for him, but this time I ran like my life depended on it, like I'd done before, refusing to be afraid of anything, refusing to care about anyone or anything because deep down inside I knew I wasn't good enough for anything but getting away and trying to stay alive. When I was running from guys who wanted to turn me upside down and shake me till a quarter fell out and then kick me for good measure, I knew how to run. Pretty soon they didn't even bother to chase me because I was too fast for them. So I ran for him. And he clicked off the stopwatch and said, 'That's what I'm talking about.'

"That coach or a variation on that coach hangs out at every Neighborhood Club in this county and he's watching for the kid who needs help with homework or learns to open up a little bit while he's shooting pool with counselors and volunteers. He's looking for that kid, like me, who is scared to death, mad as bloody hell, needs to learn some boundaries and has to figure out a better end to his story. He might find it making music or playing team sports or giving back, like going with a group to a pediatrics ward or nursing home. We look at it as just a little molding and reshaping, something that can turn a badass like me into a competitor. You think winner? Oh, you'd be absolutely right, but not the kind of winning you imagine, not the kind that brings gold medals. It's the kind of winning where you finally trade the fear and start working to overcome that thing you're most afraid of. It can be anything. It's not always the stuff that drove someone like me forward. You don't have to live with rats or run from gangbangers to have something to overcome. It could be poverty. It could be loneliness, abuse, a health problem, a struggle with schoolwork. It could even be a weight problem. We all bring baggage with us and it doesn't have a monetary value—it's the weight on our hearts and minds that holds us back.

"At the Neighborhood Club they specialize in fear. They might teach you to run like your life depends on it when no one is chasing you. No matter what it is, they'll dig in and search for some kind of answer.

"When you're lucky enough to find help putting together a satisfying and productive life, as I was, you come away with a few lessons. I'd like to share them with you, if I can, though I'm still learning and growing and nowhere near ready to stop.

"Just because you're poor doesn't mean you have to be poor in spirit.

"Just because you've lost faith doesn't mean you can't learn to trust again.

"Just because you're afraid doesn't mean you're doomed.

"Just because you're angry doesn't mean you have to live in rage.

"Just because you've been wronged doesn't mean you can't forgive, often forgiving yourself first.

"Just because you're hurt doesn't mean you won't heal.

"Just because you fell back a few steps doesn't mean your next step can't move you forward again.

"Just because it's very dark doesn't mean there is no light ahead.

"And just because you've been let down and disappointed doesn't mean you won't find love. The kind of love that is safe, enduring and powerful."

Lin Su listened to Blake's words. She knew she would be impressed; she'd been impressed since the moment they first met. She loved him. While he spoke about the struggle of his life and the powerful forces that seemed to plot against his success, she was examining her own baggage. Every single point he listed applied to her directly. She had resented her adoptive family not caring about her, and now that one did, she resisted. She had been poor and bereft, and now that she lived well, she threatened to throw it all away and move, just to have her way. She had hated Charlie's father for his lack of committed love, so refused to yield to love and trust offered by a better man.

There was a standing ovation for Blake, and Lin Su was the very first to her feet. The only person in the room who didn't stand was Winnie. Blake shook hands with the director, then turned to exit the platform and walk back to his table. His eyes were on Lin Su and her eyes were on him. As he neared his table, she began to walk toward him.

And right into his arms.

He held her close, his big arms enfolding her. She turned her tearing eyes up to his face. "I might be a little stubborn," she said.

"A little?" he asked, smiling.

"I'd like to try to do better. I'd like another chance."

"I love you, Lin Su. As long as you let me, I can be there for you."

"I love you," she said. "I'm a crazy mess. Just so you're warned."

"I'm not afraid," he said. Then he lifted her chin with a finger and kissed her in front of the world.

EPILOGUE

Grace and Troy welcomed their baby girl into the world in the early morning after the fund-raiser. Christmas at Winnie's home was much more populated than anyone expected as Troy's parents and younger brother arrived in Thunder Point to celebrate the arrival of a new granddaughter. Blake offered them bedrooms in his house and joined them all for Christmas dinner.

The new baby was so often in one of her grandmothers' arms she barely needed the sheet changed on her bassinette.

Lin Su and Charlie spent a great deal of time at Blake's house over Christmas Eve and Christmas morning. Blake gave Charlie some athletic gear—bike pants, new running shoes, a jacket, a gym bag. Lin Su gave Blake the hand-monogramed towels, which he found perfect. But the showstopper was a diamond ring for Lin Su. When she opened it and saw what it was, she shot a nervous glance at Charlie.

"Don't sweat it, Mom. He asked my permission."

When Christmas and New Year's had passed, Lin Su made contact with her adoptive sister Leigh. They had several long talks and she could see that what Charlie said was true—she was awesomely nice. She also had a lot of information that helped Lin Su fit together the pieces of her life. According to Leigh, Gordon Simmons had never been an involved father to any of his daughters so in that Lin Su was not alone. It was Marilyn Simmons who had wanted to adopt and to that end Gordon hired a lawyer who dealt in such matters and the lawyer put together a deal with an immigrating Vietnamese woman with a three-year-old child she could not provide for. It was the kind of thing Gordon did—if his wife wanted something, he got it for her and then excused himself from the situation. In speaking to Gordon, Leigh discovered that the story that Lin Su's mother was dying was a lie.

He had information about Lin Su's mother squirreled away in his locked files. "I'm in the process of seeing if I can locate her. I won't do anything without your approval," Leigh said. "Maybe you don't want to have contact with her."

"But I do," Lin Su said. "If only to know she's well. I'm sure if she's alive she has a new life, one that doesn't have room for me. I can live with that but I remember her. Vaguely, but I remember."

It was the middle of February when Leigh Simmons traveled to Thunder Point from the East Coast to reconnect with Lin Su and to meet Charlie. Lin Su asked Blake if the reunion could happen at his house. "You don't have to offer her a guest room—she should be fine in a motel—but I have no space to entertain her."

Nothing, it seemed, could please Blake more. "You've come a long way in a short time," he said.

"Just because my heart was broken doesn't mean it can't be whole again," she said.

When the day came, Lin Su was so jittery and nervous she was forced to take a day off on the promise that, when her sister arrived, Lin Su would take her next door to meet Winnie. When a car door was finally heard in front of Blake's house, Lin Su froze.

Charlie didn't. "She's here!" he said, jumping to his feet and running out the front door.

"It's going to be all right, you know," Blake said. "She's here to make amends. You've already become friends."

Then Charlie shouted from the front door. "Mom! Mom! You are not going to believe this!"

Lin Su stood on shaky legs, ready to accept her estranged sister. When Leigh entered, she let out her breath. She was forty-two and yet had hardly changed. She was tall, slim, blonde and oozed confidence. She had a bright and loving smile that radiated warmth. She didn't wait for Lin Su to make the first move; she rushed to her and embraced her.

"At last, at last," she murmured, holding Lin Su close. Then she withdrew a bit and said, "I found your mama."

Lin Su gasped. "Where?"

"In San Diego. With the rest of your family."

"Family?"

"See for yourself," Leigh said, stepping away.

There stood a grinning Charlie between two women— one Vietnamese and one younger, Amerasian. Her mother; her grandmother.

"Mama?" Lin Su asked weakly, tears streaming.

The younger woman opened her arms. "Huang," she whispered. "You have lived all these years in my heart. Now I have you again in my life."

★ ★ ★ ★ ★